W9-CBA-544

THE
DEVIL
AND
WINNIE
FLYNN

THE
DEVIL
AND
WINNIE
FLYNN

MICOL OSTOW   DAVID OSTOW

Published in the United States by Soho Teen an imprint of
Soho Press, Inc.
853 Broadway
New York, NY 10003

Library of Congress Cataloging-in-Publication Data

Ostow, Micol, author.
The devil and Winnie Flynn / Micol Ostow and David Ostow.

ISBN 978-1-61695-597-7
eISBN 978-1-61695-598-4
1. Supernatural—Fiction. 2. Psychic ability—Fiction. 3. Television
programs—Production and direction—Fiction. 4. Mystery and detective
stories. I. Ostow, David, 1979– author. II. Title.
PZ7.O8475De 2015
[Fic]—dc23   2015009878

Interior illustrations by David Ostow
Interior design by Janine Agro, Soho Press, Inc.

Printed in the United States of America

10 9 8 7 6 5 4 3 2 1

In very loving memory of Marissa Provenza, whose endlessly kind, gentle care of Mazzy made possible the very first words of this book—and so much more. We miss you.
—Micol

For Lily.
—David

DISCLAIMER

The Devil and Winnie Flynn is a work of fiction inspired by the history and lore of the state of New Jersey. As such, while the story incorporates the names of real people, places and events—both historical and contemporary—it places them within a fictional context where historical facts have been manipulated at the authors' discretion for the sake of the story.

Notable among such fictionalizations is the story's inclusion of the name Kallikak. The Kallikak family did in fact exist and their name has relevance within the context of New Jersey history. However, the character of Marie Kallikak is fictitious and her association with the supernatural has no basis in the factual account of the Kallikak family history.

"An unruly demonic darkness, it hangs, waiting for a saving touch."
　　　　　　　—Marissa Provenza, "Legacy of Lunacy"

NOW CASTING—GREATER NJ AREA—*FANTASTIC, FEARSOME NJ*

HAVE YOU/HAS SOMEONE YOU KNOW RECENTLY EXPERIENCED PARA-
NORMAL PHENOMENA? ARE YOU A NEW JERSEY NATIVE LIVING IN
OR AROUND ASBURY PARK, ESSEX COUNTY/TURTLE BACK ROCK, THE
PINE BARRENS, LEEDS POINT, OR TINY TOWN? MAYBE YOU'VE HAD
A "FUNNY FEELING" DRIVING PAST THE DEVIL'S TOWER, OR SEEN
PHANTOM HEADLIGHTS ALONG CLINTON ROAD? MAYBE YOU'VE EVEN
GLIMPSED THE JERSEY DEVIL HIMSELF?

IF SO, WE WANT TO HEAR FROM *YOU*! NOW CASTING FOR THE
FANTASTIC, FEARSOME: NJ EDITION, AND COLLECTING ANY AND
ALL TALES OF HAUNTINGS, PSYCHIC OCCURENCES, OR PARANORMAL
ACTIVITY IN THE GARDEN STATE.

ONLY STRICTLY SERIOUS CANDIDATES NEED APPLY. NO NONBE-
LIEVERS.

Part One:
REALITY

Fantastic, Fearsome: NJ
FULL CAST AND CREW LIST

CREATOR/PRODUCER:
Maggie Leader

ASSISTANT DIRECTOR/PRODUCTION MANAGER:
Jane Levin

SCRIPT SUPERVISOR:
Elena Dempsey

DIRECTOR OF PHOTOGRAPHY/LEAD CAMERA:
Russ Wallace

CAMERA ASSISTANT:
Hillary Brandt
[Just wrapped the new Sex Addicts Matchmaker *pilot, came recommended from LHR.]*

SOUND MIXER:
Wade Clark

GRIP & ELECTRIC:
Lee Joiner and Ernie Tuckerman
[Per Jane: Lee is the redhead!]

PRODUCTION ASSISTANTS:
Winnie Flynn

Amanda Morgan
[peanut allergy. Note to Elena for call sheets re: craft services.]

TALENT (DEVIL HUNTERS):
Seth Jarvis

Casey Whitter
[*POETRY?]

Ivan Fell
[under 18; check with Jane on parental waiver!]

ONE

"The devil hunters are here for wardrobe."

A small, wiry woman with frizzy, loose-cotton hair darts toward me. *Jane*, is what her name is. *Production manager*, which means she's the boss. Right under Aunt Maggie, anyway, who is basically the boss of this whole weirdo world. Jane is wearing a headset, which should communicate no nonsense, but it's hard to take hair like that seriously.

It's hard to take any of this seriously, Lu. Impossible, really. Which is weird, since I'm usually such a serious person.

The Devil Hunters are here for wardrobe.

Hearing that, I expect a pack of goth, *Ghostbuster*-types to stride into our cluster of motel rooms turned makeshift production offices. Powder-white faces, streaky eyeliner, leather, and lace—even in June, in South Jersey—and maybe some backpack-style, strap-on air-ion counter. Something bulky and pseudoscientific, is what I mean, Lu. Something impressive in its commitment to the absurd.

Remember that movie we saw? The one about the ghost hunters, the one that wasn't *Ghostbusters*? I know you do—with those self-proclaimed mediums. Their video cameras, and their overinflated egos.

It takes a lot to assume, Lu. That if there *are* spirits, that if the voices of the undead or whoever, that if they really are out there . . . it's a lot to assume that they'd be hanging out just waiting for you, Mr. and Mrs. Very Special Psychic, to come knocking. That kind of thinking takes real *chutzpah,* you know?

But when the lobby door does open, my assumptions vanish in a cough of wet sea-smell laced with the tang of greasy-delicious boardwalk food.

These people actually look kind of normal. Sort of. As normal as a group of "Devil Hunters" can be, anyway.

There are three of them, a little bit older than we are. Two college students with the world's weirdest summer internship, one high schooler with no discernable reason for being here that I can see. Two guys and a girl, and nary an airion counter or a trace of eyeliner to be found among them. (Maybe they're in a car trunk somewhere nearby.) Okay, so the girl's hair, chin-length and vivid black, is streaked with bold blue stripes that demand attention.

I take an instant dislike to those bold blue stripes. It isn't nice or particularly open-minded, but I do, Lu. You know I don't trust people who demand attention.

The other two are more low-key. Boy-like with a touch of nerd, in that way: faded T-shirts bearing obscure sci-fi references, frayed cargo shorts. All of those pockets make me wonder again about ghost-hunting equipment: minuscule, feather-light flashlights, recording devices, whatever the paranormal equivalent of mace may be. The shorter and squatter of the two wears flip-flops. This is even less appealing to me than blue-streaked hair, though at least his toenails are clipped short and reasonably clean. He's the younger one. His hair is an explosion of curls with no place to grow but out. Maybe *that's* why he's here, with this group. Maybe with hair like that, his options were limited.

The taller of the two—the older guy—has his hair tied back in a ponytail, which . . . you know where I stand on that. He looks nice, though—his shoulders strain against his T-shirt in tight little peaks. This endears me for some reason, so I decide to do my best to reserve judgment on his hairstyle.

We'll see. At least this one's hair grows down, anyway.

Ponytail catches me staring, offers an uncertain smile, then flushes and stares at a point on the floor.

"Winnie," Jane says. I'd forgotten she was there. I almost jump. "Can you take the Devil Hunters to wardrobe?"

I would, I really would. Except:

We don't have *wardrobe.*

I've been a production assistant, or PA, at *Fantastic, Fearsome* for a hot minute, but this I know is true. Maybe there's a rolling garment rack in Aunt Maggie's room, the executive suite (which sounds much fancier than it is). But if so, I haven't seen it.

It's reality TV. People wear their real clothes. Right?

"Maggie," Jane clarifies, accurately interpreting my confounded look. "She wants to meet them in person, check out their style before filming starts. We've only seen the audition tapes." *(Wait—was I supposed to watch the audition tapes?)* She throws an approving side-eye at Blue Hair. "She'll like that dye job. Very punk rock."

Maybe in 1992. I think this as loudly as I can, sending it through the psychic space you and I share, Lu. And I think there's a little *ping* where my ribs knit together that tells me you heard me, you're laughing. Loudly. Even if that's only in my mind, it feels true enough.

But Jane is still waiting on me.

"Right," I say.

Aunt Maggie. My mother's older sister.

We've only just met in person recently, ourselves.

If this were the first act of a horror movie, Maggie would be the boogeyman.

That long-lost relative who steps out of the woodwork after a loved one dies unexpectedly. It barely qualifies as a trope anymore; these days, that's just lazy writing. Second only to the invitation-from-a-reclusive-billionaire-to-spend-a-weekend-in-his-hilltop-mansion premise. So tired. *Don't even do it, kids.* That's what you'd say. *That game never ends well. Ix-nay on the ansion-may.*

But the thing about Maggie is that she's the creator, director, and producer of the *Fantastic, Fearsome US*™ series. Eight seasons and counting, syndicated, spin-offs sold to thirteen different countries. She probably sleeps on a bed of solid gold. She knows the tropes, better than you and I do, I bet—makes her living off of the best of them. She's not the enemy. I don't *think*. And anyway, this isn't a horror movie, it's reality TV. Which is so, so much scarier, Lu.

Maggie's suite, with its sitting area and dinette table, and the giant white board propped against the wall, is just through motel reception and to the right. I'm not sure why the Devil Hunters need a private escort to a room that's maybe twenty feet from where we stand. But I guess when you're the big boss, you can't just have the talent traipsing in and out of your office unaccompanied.

Maggie doesn't seem that big on ceremony thus far, but

maybe it's different if you're family. Even if you're semi-estranged family who've gone seventeen years without any contact.

I rise and nod, slightly nervous but trying to cover, at the Hunters. "I'll take you," I say, mostly in Ponytail's direction. "Follow me."

As I look at Ponytail, I stumble so my hip jostles the corner of a magazine rack. The crumpled, faded pamphlets detailing DINING HIGHLIGHTS OF OCEAN GROVE! (of which, presumably, there are myriad) go flying.

Tomorrow I'll have a weird-shaped bruise on my too-pale skin. I wonder, fleetingly, how any one person could possibly be so incapable of normal human interaction. The look that Blue Hair gives me suggests that she is wondering the very same thing.

But Lu, please don't tell me to *take it easy,* because you know I never do.

I crack the door from reception to the outer breezeway and muster as much dignity as I can (it's not much). When I step outside, onto the pavement, they do follow, so at least that's something.

THE AIR OUTSIDE THE motel is only slightly less suffocating. Though oddly the cigarette smell is stronger. I concentrate on the worn laces of my sneakers. They're not going to be great for off-road running, when we get to the Barrens later. But they're my oldest, most favorite pair of running shoes, *lucky* shoes, you might say, and that has to count for something. Comfort, familiarity—they're important. A girl can only take so much transition at one time, you know?

(Of course you know. You're the one who thought this trip

would be good for me, just the right *kind* of transition, after the past few months.)

"So, you're a PA? You don't seem like someone who'd be *into* this show," Blue Hair observes, making it sound very definitively like an insult. I don't even know what someone who'd be *into Fantastic, Fearsome* would be like, Lu, except I guess maybe there's a presumption of hair dye involved.

"I like horror," I tell her, "movies. *Stories,*" even though that's: 1) an acute understatement, and 2) our dirty little secret, Lu. Yours and mine, kind of our *thing.* The campier, the better. Call it escapism.

"Stories." Blue Hair's word comes out in a hiss. "But you don't, like, *believe* in ghosts." She makes it sound like a veiled threat. Maybe it is. I guess a self-identified Devil Hunter would see it that way, anyway.

"The truth is out there."

This is from the littlest one, the puffy-haired boy with watery eyes and no chin to speak of. He shrugs and turns pink, like he can't believe he actually spoke out loud, and I want to cringe for him because for a moment he seems very worried about how Blue Hair will react to his outburst. *There, there,* I think. *If she's that "punk rock," she's surely overcompensating for something.*

I deflect. "You're a believer. But you get paid to do the series, right?" It comes out a touch more aggressively than intended.

She bristles. "We're very committed to our science," she says, matching my tone. "We believe in the Jersey Devil, and the rich paranormal history of the Garden State."

"Right. But still. You *do* get paid. Right?"

They do. I've faxed, copied, and emailed the budget reports myself. The show pays for the on-air "experts," not that this girl could possibly be a legitimate expert in anything other than Being the Worst. I don't even know what I'm trying to prove by pushing the point.

Ponytail laughs, then covers his mouth like he's surprised by his own reaction. He doesn't look up when Blue Hair and I both whirl toward him in perfect synchronicity.

The door to Maggie's suite swings open.

"Is that the Devil Hunters, Winnie?" Maggie's voice is low and smoky, commanding and disembodied, like Dorothy's Wizard, ensconced firmly behind his curtain.

"It is," I reply. I'm embarrassed by the catch in my voice, a high-pitched squeak so unlike Maggie's sultry tenor. Did my mother have a voice like Maggie's, or like mine? Suddenly, I can't remember. I guess the little details are the easiest to lose hold of.

"Well, send them in," she continues as though I'd actually need to issue a separate directive to them. Like they aren't standing right exactly next to me. "I want to have a look at them." She makes it sound as though they aren't people at all, but artifacts, non-sentient beings. Lab rats. *Talent.*

Blue Hair shoves past me. It doesn't bother me as much as I think she wants it to, though it *does* bother me a little, if we're going to be perfectly honest here, Lu. And then the other guy goes in behind her, and then it's just Ponytail and me, not-looking at each other in the most active, most intense way two people can *not-do* anything. For a moment I think he's going to say something to me, but then there's a shout—*"Seth!"* from inside the trailer, and I guess Seth is him, that's who he is, and in he goes, to "wardrobe."

And suddenly, I can't remember what those people wore in that movie. The one we watched that time.

How is a ghost hunter *supposed* to dress, Lu?

Fantastic, Fearsome: NJ application form

Please include two recent COLOR photos, one head shot and one full body, along with your application form and a short video (up to three minutes) explaining why you're interested in our show.

Name: Casey Whitter

Age: 19

Occupation: student/paranormal researcher

Please give us a short bio about yourself. Include talents, hobbies, skills, etc.

I'm originally from Wayne, NJ, finishing up my freshman year at Montclair State University, so I'm a true "Jersey Girl." Next year I have to declare my major and I want to design my own course in paranormal studies. Being on "Fantastic, Fearsome" should help convince the anthro department to let me!

Actually, I'm a little bit psychic and I take everything about the paranormal, occult, etc., very seriously. Maggie Leader is basically my hero. She's such a role model. Last semester I led a pagan chanting circle, and some of those girls said I reminded them of Maggie. So many of the occult "experts" you guys get are such clichés (no offense). I mean those kooky white-haired fortune-teller-y mediums all blend together after a while if you watch the show as much as I do. It would be cool to have young, cute talent for this season. And the other two Hunters I work with, of course. Seth and Ivan (fun fact: I used to tutor him when I was in high school and he was in junior high. Now he's a Hunter. I guess I just have that kind of influence on people).

My talents: I'm very outspoken. When I'm in a group, like with the Devil Hunters, I always end up being the one in charge. My mom calls it a "strong personality." It isn't for everyone, but that's the way I like it! Besides, unlike the others, I can sense when a place has any paranormal energy going on, even without all the gear and the instruments.

I know I would really add another layer to your show.

If you asked the guys, they'd probably say I'm like the mother hen of our group, like the glue. Seth is probably the most serious of us, but I'm the most organized. I keep us proactive about our mission. We ARE going to find the Jersey Devil! So why not let us find it for you?

Also I write poetry. I was thinking I could post it, maybe on the show's Tumblr or something. It's really intense and private, but I think it's good to show viewers my spiritual side. So they see what it's like, being so tuned in to the supernatural.

Everyone thinks it would be so much fun to be psychic, like it's all reading minds or guessing lottery numbers. But really, it's a total mixed blessing. Viewers should know the truth. It can be really overwhelming. It's just . . . it's hard, being a Hunter. And it can be lonely, too. People don't really "get" us, or what we're doing. So that's hard.

But it's really important, too. We're doing really important work.

Shattered Glass

Your eye
A mirror held to the world,
Reflecting wholeness
A seamless tapestry by Minerva's
steady hand,
A picture to be framed and hung,
Complete.

But mine,
Shattered by the blow of Turenn's fury,
A tray of jagged shards,
Reflects at all angles the light of before
and beyond,
A film shot out of sequence but somehow
truer for its
Brokenness   —CM Whitter mmxiv

"Ocean is more ancient than
the mountains, and freighted
with the memories and
dreams of time"
                    —HP Lovecraft

Possible sighting?
Tracey 973   -11-2034

Seth—veggie lomein
Ivan—wonton zp, egg roll,
gen tsao chix, dr pepper—coke if needs

SETH:
Okay, um, hi. Is this on?

Fuzzy HAND comes close into the frame, camera
TILTS, then steadies. PULL BACK to REVEAL **SETH**,
early twenties, shaggy brown ponytail and
kind hazel eyes. His audition clip is being
filmed on his home computer, clearly set up in
his CHILDHOOD BEDROOM. An AUTOGRAPHED COPY of
the original movie poster for *Blade Runner* is
visible just behind his head, and his T-shirt
shows a reproduction of the Grady twins from
Kubrik's *The Shining*.

SETH
Okay. Yeah. Sorry about that. This is . . .
weird. I'm not a camera guy. Or a computer guy.
Not really a tech guy at all. That's Ivan's
thing. Kid's still in high school, it's amazing,
he takes the whole ghost-hunting thing more
seriously than—well, maybe more seriously than
Maggie Leader, actually. Just barely.

(beat)

Sorry if that sounded, I don't know, obnoxious.
So, like I'm sure she said on her application,
it was Casey's idea to try out for this show. I,

uh, don't really love the spotlight, you know?
I'm the kind of person who mostly sticks to
small groups of people I already know.

(flushes, laughs)

But when we—The Hunters, I mean—when we heard
you guys were coming to Jersey, that you were
looking for the Devil, we just . . . Well, that
was it. I mean, we had to do it. I can get used
to the cameras, you know, if you like us. If you
want us. Because we're going to find the Devil.
That's not even a question.

(pauses, straightens)

SETH:
I guess you could say my family has a long
history of being, um . . . interested in the
occult. And especially the Jersey Devil. We're
from Jersey, for, like, generations now, and
my father is obsessed with all the folklore. I
mean, you should see his library.

(blinks, swallows)

And my mom is . . . not around, these days.

(recovering)

So, you know, what family there is, I have their
support with all of this. And it would be cool

to get school credit. Casey said she's trying to
get a "paranormal studies" major approved at
Montclair. But really . . . We're pretty expert,
the group. Found each other through a New Jersey
Devils meet-up last spring and we've been on the
hunt ever since.

(deep breath)

And you know, don't be fooled by Ivan, just
because he's still in high school. I feel like
. . . there's a chance he might've joined up
with us because he's got a little thing for
Casey, or he used to. But he's in it now. And
I think Casey's right about getting younger
people on the show. We could open up a whole
new demographic for you. And Ivan's kind of a
genius. Like the Jason Bourne of the paranormal
investigators world. Or Doogie Howser. You know,
that old show with the young doctor from before
he was Barney? Or Doctor Horrible.

(shakes his head and smiles)

Sorry, geek moment. But, anyway. Devil Hunters.
Yeah.You should cast us. Seriously.
We could rock that for you.

The FUZZY, OUT-OF-FOCUS ARM comes back in on a
CLOSE-UP. There is a CLICKING SOUND, and the
screen FADES TO GRAY.

TWO

But—wait, Lucia. Let's back up for a minute, here. We're walking into this program *in media res*. And as with any great tragicomic melodrama, there's a juicy backstory looming just below the surface, waiting to be peeled back, to be worked into the plot. So let's lay the groundwork now, if you will.

You will, Lu, right? Of course. You always do. That's why we're friends, you and I.

Let's start with a game. An "oldie but a goodie," carried over from the car rides of our early childhood. We loved this one. Remember?

I Spy. Our favorite.

Not a game you can play with only one person, I know. But you're not here—you have a bike tour of the Pacific Coast Highway, while I have a family-tragedy-turned-last-minute internship in television—in *reality television*!—smack-dab dead center in America's armpit. You're here inside my head, inside my thoughts, Lucia. You know me well enough that you can probably predict those thoughts before they even form.

It's you and me in my brain right now, Lu. So, all right, then:

I spy with my little eye . . . something . . .

Broken.

Yeah. Something broken. Something battered, deflated, defeated. Something sad.

Asbury Park.

You're shaking your head with disapproval. *"Winnie Flynn. That is certainly a glass-half-empty sort of view of things."*

You use my full name when you're being judgmental. I usually let it go because, usually, it's funny. Well, fine. Maybe so. But it's this place, not me. Never mind the horrible aching sadness of the last three months; this is not about me. This is I Spy, and I can't help the bleak view from the motel parking lot. I don't make up the rules here. I'm not the boss of any of this. If I were, I'd still be in Portland, with you. If I were, Mom would still be alive.

But I'm not. And she's not.

I spy a vista collapsing in upon itself, cloudy streaks of gray and choking loneliness: a dusty, abandoned soundstage. I spy a swollen, murky shoreline that makes me want to curl my knees into my chest and tuck my forehead down. I spy despair, decay. Gloom. Doom.

"Is it possible you're being dramatic, Winnie?"

Well, yes. Anything is possible, Lu. It's only the beach. Or, "the Shore," as they say down here.

But hey, I'm just calling it like I see it.

Besides, Lu, it's barely been three months since my mother killed herself.

Her death—her *suicide*—it's fresh. And it leaves an impression. Even though Dad swears it had nothing to do with me, with us. How can he know? I mean, how can he *really*, for-real-for-sure, *know*? He can't. No one can. If we knew anything, we would have seen this coming. We could have stopped it. We could have helped her. We *would* have.

At the funeral, you were standing next to me when Aunt Maggie appeared through the Oregon mist, floating across the cemetery path like some kind of tanned, tooth-veneered Angel of Mercy, Hollywood-style. *Mom's* eyes were peering out of this stranger's face. She was going back to her home state, *Mom's* home state. Back, to film *Fantastic, Fearsome: New Jersey*. She'd rented a chain of motel rooms, *these* rooms, a block from the salt-logged boardwalk down in Asbury Park. She was going to film all through July, all around the state.

She wanted me to come. She wanted us, finally, to get to know each other.

Dad wanted me to go, too.

We had a little disagreement, as you may recall. I wasn't sure about his judgment; he was grief-crazed, after all. But *you* agreed with him. You thought I needed a change of scenery, a distraction. And anyway, he was going to spend all summer on that journal piece he's been angsting over, burying himself in work like he always does when real life gets too icky. The Absent-Minded Professor. He's straight from central casting, himself.

Besides, real life *did* get too icky. Not just for him. For me.

So yes, it was necessary: leaving Portland, leaving home, leaving all the familiarities. Like her bathrobe. The blue flannel with the ugly floral print. It's still hanging on the hook inside her closet door. It still smells—faintly—like her face lotion. Ginger and citrus.

Or, it still did the day I left, anyway.

Part of me couldn't imagine being all by myself this summer. Couldn't imagine that being with Maggie wouldn't just dredge up a litany of *new* painful questions about Mom. But you get used to it. (That was the grief counselor's theory. You get used to almost anything. He wore a very shiny watch, the counselor, so I have to assume he was good at his job. Shiny watches have a reassuring quality.) And that means that I'll get used to Asbury Park and this motel's particular odor: a queasy mix of sea air, motor oil, and something like old tuna salad.

I can only expect I'll get used to Aunt Maggie, too.

No, she didn't explain why she and Mom had fallen out of touch. Bygones were better off bygone. But Life Is Too Short, she realized (the cliché her exact words, sounding as if they were all capitalized), and she wanted to Be There for Me Now, and maybe I needed a Change of Pace, In Light of Everything? Dad was easy to convince, even without your help. Maggie's show—her whole empire—is so well known, after all. She's famous, allegedly stable . . . ergo: not a kidnapping psychopath. Family Is Important, you *should* Get Back to Your Roots, yada yada, blah blah blah. You guys were on the same page.

I brought the journal you gave me this past birthday with me, because, as you say, "the Internet isn't *real*, Winn." I'm the only one who knows you well enough to know that your story isn't bullshit: You don't even have an email address. *No email?* People like that don't exist, right? Except in the case of my best friend. And anyway, even if you won't see these pages, at least, if I keep writing, I won't be completely alone. At least then, I won't be playing I Spy entirely on my own. Even when I'm the only one here.

Maybe by the end of the summer it will be a sort of scrapbook of this experience.

Maybe I'll even show it to you. You being the only one

who's ever known the real, true truth of me. Maybe by then you'll have joined Gmail, if only to get into college.

Have I mentioned you're a good best friend, Lucia? If you were here, that's what I'd tell you. But you're not, so instead, I'm writing it down.

Instead, it's I Spy all by my lonesome. Only my personal demons to keep me company. A closet full of skeletons.

"Winnie." You wag a finger. *"That's not what you're here for."*

And you're right, really. Right now, it's about the fantastic. The fearsome. The haunted, haunting myths and mysteries of what could, in truth, be thought of as my once-upon-a-homeland. My *motherland,* oh, ha-ha, no pun intended, of course.

Aunt Maggie makes her living trading on strange tales. I'm just her unlikely protégé for the next few weeks. Right now, my own skeletons have nothing to do with the story.

Right now, I'm just here for the ghosts.

You and I, duh—of course we knew *Fantastic, Fearsome,* had even caught a few episodes online at your place, where Mom wasn't around to make her I'm-totally-not-disapproving disapproving face. But we didn't know New Jersey, even though Mom and Maggie grew up here. Step one in Embracing My Legacy (my legacy! Which somehow includes *Fantastic: Fearsome!*), you said, was reading up on my history.

And Asbury Park has some history.

A HUNDRED-PLUS YEARS AGO, this place was a destination. Palace Amusements was building up piece by piece, starting with a candy-swirled colorful carousel; tourists flocked majestic hotels overlooking the ocean. Bruce Springsteen grew up around here. A whole bunch of his songs are basically about this place. *Greetings from Asbury Park, NJ,* is one of those iconic, pop-culture touchstones that locals like to wave in your face like a bright flag of victory.

Pride is so weird.

Of course, lately, whatever interest in the Jersey Shore lingers has gravitated south, toward Seaside—where beefy, orange-skinned aliens sell screen-printed T-shirts to the greasy-haired, hungover masses. Aunt Maggie's not the first TV producer to take an interest in Jersey. Obviously. But she's got the vibe down. Self-tanning. Gym memberships. Hot tubs fetid as a petri dish. So-called "reality," constructed from cheap Swedish furnishings, recycled tabloid rumors, and silicone wheeled into the jaundiced spotlight like a shiny sideshow attraction. *Shudder.*

But we were talking about history.

When the SS *Morro Castle* crashed against the coastline here in 1934, it coincided with the Great Depression. Locally, it ushered in an aura of malaise and overall *meh* that I'm not sure was ever totally shaken off.

"Winnie." A note of warning creeps into your tone. *"No. Don't."*

Because you know me too well, Lu. You know what leap of linguistics and logic my brain is going to take at the mention of the word . . .

Depression.

There's that ache again. Old Reliable. At least Asbury Park looks the way the inside of my brain feels. In movie terms that's called *pathetic fallacy*, I think. But Lu, it's crushing, this feeling of *sad* knotted around me, draped like one of those lead X-ray dentist's bibs, weighing me down. You're one of the only people I trust with that truth. You're one of the few who knows how hard I struggle to be solid, to be stony and contained. While inside, every thought, every feeling, all of

those tiny shattered pieces are jagged and sharp and ampli-
fied, bubbling in the back of my throat like tar.

And if Aunt Maggie has her way, it's going to get "fearsome" here over the course of the next few weeks. Don't say
you weren't warned.

On the other hand, it's going to be fantastic, too.

Or so I'm told.

EXT. ASBURY PARK BOARDWALK—DAY

WIDE SHOT

CAMERA PANS across the bleak, gray landscape.
We linger on bits of fast-food litter, scrawled
graffiti, places in the boardwalk that are
splintered and rotting.

CLOSE-UP on various "for rent" signs displayed
prominently in ocean-facing shop windows,
iron grates long rusted. Everything conveys
hopelessness, surrender.

> HOST/MAGGIE (VOICE OVER):
> Asbury Park. The name alone conjures
> images of a long-ago era in New Jersey's
> pop cultural history.

FLASH CUTS:

Convention Hall

Madam Marie's Fortunes

The Stone Pony

CLOSE-UP:

Vintage aerial view of landscape

                    MAGGIE (CONT'D):
Beginning with the infamous *Morro Castle*
shipwreck of 1934, the "City by the Sea"
has known its fair share of disasters—

                    (beat)

Both natural and unnatural alike.

              (more upbeat, perky)

Now, join *Fearsome, Fantastic New Jersey*
as we peer into the haunting history of
the Garden State's most notorious piers.
And remember, viewers, as we always say—

              (beat—ominous again)

There's nothing to fear . . . but the
fantastic!

                                    CUT TO:

Opening credits sequence.

                                    FADE OUT

In the Garden State
the most fearsome flowers grow in the shade...

FANTASTIC FEARSOME

new jersey

Wednesdays 10/9C
After So You Think You Can Commune With The Dead

ParaNormal Channel
MILES FROM NORMAL

www.fantasticfearsome.com

THREE

"It's not going to work."

Morning. The motor oil/tuna smell is especially strong today.

It's so humid my hair hangs in wet clumps, even though it's been over an hour since I showered. The sun is a blurry blaze through the streaked picture window, and the AC coughs in a way that doesn't inspire confidence.

I woke at six. Our call time wasn't until eight, but a pack of rabid seagulls decided to engage in passionate debate outside my room—until a supersized garbage truck choked its way into the parking lot. New Jersey has supersized garbage, I guess. But by then I was halfway into my running shorts and out the door for a quick two or three miler.

It's been a long day, Lu. And I haven't even had breakfast yet.

"It will be fine, sweet pea," Maggie says. Her raspy voice is extra sultry right now, all honey and gravel at this hour.

"It's too tight."

That's Jane, hunched over the long plastic folding table

we set up in Maggie's suite. I say *we,* meaning Amanda and me. Yesterday, Amanda—the other PA, I told you about her, with the blonde hair, and those expensive-looking cropped jeans that were cuffed *just so*—and I were dispatched to Costco in search of the various furnishings required to set up a temporary office.

Can you picture the Jersey Costco, Lu? Our cashier had plastic glitter starfish dangling from her ears. It was amazing. I will have to bring a pair back for you as a souvenir.

Now the table is smothered in scripts and Sharpies and battered coffee mugs, with binder-clip sculptures and crumpled, lip gloss–stained napkins. Maybe thirteen minutes, max, since we set it up; but it already looks like the crew has been here for weeks. They are an efficient bunch. I start to wonder if I'll get in the way. Jane and Maggie huddle over the day's shot list, bickering like old neighbors before we head to the Asbury Park Paranormal Odditorium.

The *Asbury Park Paranormal Odditorium,* Lucia. Squeal with me, now. How did we *not* know this place existed? Tragic circumstances notwithstanding, there are way worse places to spend an afternoon.

Jane frowns. "It's too tight, Meg," she says again. *Meg.* That's how you know they're practically sisters, that they've been working together basically since their respective embryonic states. "We have too much to shoot at the museum." She ticks off the list on her hand. "The tour, the interview, the séance . . ."

"We'll split the cameras. Hillary will go with you to the museum; Russ will come with me to take care of pickup. I want to have more than enough." Maggie pauses. "I'm sure you think that's excessive."

"*More than enough* is inherently excessive. *More. Than.* It literally means, 'an excessive amount.' It conflicts with our schedule." Jane jabs a finger at the shot list for emphasis. "Which is tight."

"Our schedule is padded, jelly bean—thanks to *your* genius planning skills. I don't give you nearly enough credit, Janie." Maggie's voice is very measured now, overly sweet. She picks up a mug that's been resting at her elbow, sips, and makes a sour face.

From the corner of the room, Amanda leaps to pluck the cup from her. I watch as she rinses it and refills it from our tiny machine ("—black, two Splendas, never stevia because it has that aftertaste, you know what I mean, lovely—") without missing a beat.

Amanda's jeans are cuffed again today. She seems nice enough, and I have to admire her ability to read my aunt, but I think she's one of Those Girls. (She has *bangs*, Lu. Perky cuffed jeans and bangs. The sartorial intersection of too-much-time-on-your-hands and trying-too-hard. I'm wearing nylon running shorts. Mostly I was just proud of myself that they were clean-ish.)

Maggie, fortified by her fresh cup of coffee, flicks a hand in the general direction of Amanda and me. "Hillary will go in the van. Russ and I will go in my car. You girls will take the SUV to get the food."

Amanda whips out her iPhone. She furtively taps a new note: COSTCO—FRUIT PLATTER?

It occurs to me: What if she *stitches* those cuffs in place?

Jane looks doubtful. "You need *lead* camera for pickup?"

"Russ has an eye for the extraneous," Maggie says. "He goes rogue, freestyle. We get great material. Hillary only needs to do the formal segments. She's seen the show. She's worked on her own. She knows what we need. It's paint by numbers. Buttercup, it's *fine*."

From outside, I hear a short, low rumble, like a momentary roll of thunder. I lean to Amanda.

"Is it supposed to . . . to . . ." There's a tickle in my throat and I cough right into Amanda's ear. It's not graceful. "Sorry. Rain?" Humiliation washes over me. Those Girls do not cough in other people's ears.

"I don't think so," she stage-whispers, gracious enough, but edging way from me.

Jane sighs. "You make a compelling argument, Meg." She rises, shuffling some papers together and tucking them under her arm. "Fine. I guess we'll make it work."

"Yes, cookie," Maggie says, and I marvel at her limitless array of sweets-related endearments. She's making me hungry. "That's just what I'm thinking."

She peeks up, looks directly at me, and locks in.

Mom's eyes.

"Are you okay, Winnie?"

I clear my throat. Mostly I'm relieved she calls me Winnie and not, I don't know, cinnamon twist or donut butt because frankly, either of those seem like real possibilities, Lu, and I'm just not ready. She couldn't possibly know that Mom always called me lemon drop. She couldn't possibly know that.

"I'm fine," I say.

(I'm not fine. *Mom's eyes. Lemon drop.*)

She winks at me. "Great," she says. "And when you're shopping, don't forget to pick up more—"

"—Splenda," Amanda cuts in, iPhone back out, tapping furiously.

"Exactly, *pumpkin.*"

Maggie disappears into her bedroom. Jane slides her prescription sunglasses down her nose. I glance at my watch.

"We're supposed to be at the museum in forty minutes. Is there going to be time for the food?"

Amanda smiles, her teeth a row of gleaming pearls.

"No, you don't get it, Winnie." Her tone is not unkind. *Understatement of the summer.* I'm silent. I couldn't even begin to explain. She sort-of shoulders against me in a slight, on-purpose, friendly way. "We're the PAs, Winnie."

"That part, I know."

"What I'm saying is—whatever the crew needs, we *make* the time." She grabs my wrist. "Just come. I'll show you."

And I go with her, I go along, because it's my job and because . . . I mean, she's saying she'll show me, and you know, *someone* has to.

"You've got jeans, right?"

I follow her gaze to my shorts. The clean ones. The only things I could imagine wearing, in this cotton-candy-sticky humidity. "I have jeans. In my room."

"Change," she says. "I know it's gross out. But you're going to want pockets."

Pockets. Sensible. Maybe she gets a temporary pass on the cuffs.

"Trust me," she says. And I know you'd tell me that I should, but it won't surprise you that I can't, not really. Not just yet.

AMANDA'S BEHIND THE WHEEL of the SUV. While I *can* drive, I haven't had my license for very long, and seriously, just even getting up into the SUV involved a Herculean *step-hop-leap-launch* kind of move that accentuated what you lovingly call my "diesel quads." (And while we're on the subject, Lu? *Diesel:* not a compliment. Not to me, anyway.)

"My mother touched the Jersey Devil, you know?"

She says this casually, the way you'd tell someone that you were thinking of, oh, I don't know, maybe having pizza for lunch.

My mother touched the Jersey Devil.

And suddenly, those cuffed pants seem less like a deliberate (if misguided) stylistic tic and more like evidence of a repressed psychopath. As you and I *well know*, Lu, the whole point—the whole *fun*, I mean—of all of that paranormal ghost-y woo-woo stuff, is that it's completely and totally *fake*.

I was hoping we'd all be in on this same joke.

Amanda throws me a side-eye, waiting. We turn a corner. The garbage bag–sized quantity of bagels we've procured collapses across the backseat like a giant, lumpy slug.

"I . . . oh." I have no idea how to respond. *How interesting, I think you might be insane?* Or, *and does your mother hear voices, too?* Or I could go the jokey route. *Was it a good touch or a bad touch? Fingers crossed she's not carrying Rosemary's baby, ha-ha!*

It doesn't matter. I've waited too long and she's off again.

"I know, I know," Amanda says. "You must have, like, tons of those kinds of stories yourself. I mean, growing up with Maggie for an aunt, and stuff. Obviously, I don't have, like, a *legacy* the way *you* do." Her voice is earnest. She turns to me. This causes the car to swerve and me to flinch.

I nod toward the windshield and try to communicate *eyes on the road* without actually saying as much.

"Sorry," she continues, cutting the wheel. We straighten so quickly my neck snaps back. "Sorry. Again. Jeez." She glances at the GPS and flips her long blonde ponytail over one shoulder. "So, yeah. I mean, I don't have a legacy or, um, my own experience with the paranormal. But my mother, she was an aspiring actress. She did a few B movies, slashers, I mean, really low-rent stuff, back when *she* was in college. And in the end she gave up acting, and the funny thing is, she used to say she never believed in the supernatural, ever, *especially* from being on-set and seeing, you know—"

"—how the sausage is made," I cut in. Because what she's saying, it makes total sense to me and I just can't help myself.

"Right, exactly!" We swerve again. A passing blue sedan honks at us. Amanda makes a rude gesture out the window. "So she didn't believe in it, you know. And then one summer, after she was married but before my brother was born— my older brother, Thad, he's, um, a lawyer now—that one summer, she went camping with my dad in the Barrens."

She starts to turn toward me and I panic, reach out, and grab the steering wheel. She rolls her eyes, but we both smile a little. I let go, shaky.

"I know you're not from here, but you know the Barrens?" she asks.

The Pine Barrens. "I know Wikipedia says it's where the Jersey Devil was born?" My voice turns up, making it a question.

"Yeah. And that's where he's still, um, sighted sometimes. The Jersey Devil. By, like, people."

"People like your mother." I try to keep my voice from catching on the word. *Mother.* Amanda doesn't notice.

"Right. She was—well, honestly?" She pauses, hesitant, then giggles. "She was *peeing*, late at night, how embarrassing is *that*? She'd snuck out of the tent and gone off by herself. And the way she tells it, she was just, uh, getting herself back together when she felt a scratchy, you know, hand—like a paw, really—on the back of her neck."

"The Devil." I wouldn't have thought that the Devil had paws. Would you, Lu?

"Right!" She's excited, as if I guessed this from context and not from her actual words. As if I'm a true believer. "So, anyway, she likes to say that there's never been a really good movie about the Jersey Devil."

"*The Last Broadcast?*"

Amanda raises an eyebrow, surprised in a good way that I've heard of it. Yes, I'm a little bit proud of myself for making her eyebrow fly up like that.

"Well, okay, yeah, *seminal.* But still. There's room for a story that focuses more on the creature itself. In my opinion. He's—it's—I mean, it's a big deal. Phenomenal Week? January sixteenth through the twenty-third, 1903, the Devil was sighted *daily* in New Jersey."

She means this, Lu. I can hear in her voice how much she means this. She used the word "seminal" in conversation. But people see Sasquatch daily, too. Don't they? I hold my tongue.

"So now I'm at UCLA, studying communications. Not exactly what my mom was doing, back when she was doing anything. Not the same as being in front of the camera, I know. But still, film. And so, getting this internship! It's amazing."

All of her scattered little phrases, her strung-together-like-Christmas-lights sentence fragments, they connect to create a glow that explodes across her face. She beams. "I swear, it's like the only time in my whole life that something I'm doing is more exciting to my parents—my mom, anyway—than my stupid lawyer brother."

(You're thinking, *she sure does hate lawyers*, and I'm sorry about that. I'm sure if she met your dad she'd feel differently, Lu.)

"Wow," I say.

"I know, I *know*," she insists. "To you, this is nothing."

"I didn't grow up with Maggie," I say, almost apologetic.

"She and my mom, they . . . I'm not sure, actually," I admit. "I guess they grew apart at some point." *I guess.*

"Huh," Amanda says.

Relief washes over me as she slows to a stop. We've arrived at the back end of a small parking lot. The van is here, cords snaking from its open rear doors, crates and boxes and over-stuffed plastic bins scattered across the asphalt like an obstacle course. None of the crew is in sight. Maggie's car isn't here yet. Does that mean she's still shooting pickup? And if so, does *that* mean Jane was right when she complained that the timing was too tight? I know I'm new to this, but it's very hard to believe that anything of substance will get done without Maggie around. That's just the effect she has, what she *projects.*

Amanda kills the ignition. "So if she's not into the para-normal stuff, like Maggie, what does your mom do? What's she like?"

The question hangs between us as the engine gives a final cough.

"She's . . ." The air is thick, pressing against my chest. "She . . ." *Just say it. Just say it.* The words tumble out. "She's dead."

Amanda's face crumples into fifteen different expressions at the same time.

I feel like I'm drowning, Lu, but at least it's out there. At least I won't have to say that particular string of horrible words to Amanda ever again. But this silence is just too much. I scramble to open the passenger-side door, and I can't even say anything else, can't explain or apologize, because all of my other words were devoured by that one intractable, impossible truth.

And then, mercifully, I'm out of the car.

We've got work to do, Lu.

FOUR

"Did we cut? We cut, right? I can take a quick five?" The Odd-itorium curator, the on-air talent for this segment, is eager to clarify. She's also having a coughing fit.

Genie Lockwood is a bizarre new age incarnation of a mob wife, her curvy-but-lithe physique recalling one of the lesser female players in *Goodfellas*. Spray-tanned limbs (and no stranger to real-deal sun worship), frosted waves of cascading hair, dark lip liner edging a hard-set smirk. She dares you not to take her professional title seriously: *Paranormal Expert & Psychic Medium* (Lu, I saw her business card). Her accent could cut glass.

It's fantastic.

So she's *that* kind of Jersey. But she's also got three different silver chains dangling around her neck, and I'm guessing each one has some kind of special spiritual mojo to it.

She coughs again, thick and rattling: the reason we did, in fact, cut. "I *need* a smoke," she gasps. The death wheeze tells me otherwise, but it's really none of my business. "I'm sorry." She sounds very matter-of-fact, not sorry at all, if you ask me.

Instantly, I adore her.

Coughs happen. It's musty in here. Cluttered, lined with overflowing bookshelves from ceiling to floor, wall to wall, and scattered with table displays of paranormal curios and artifacts. Ernie and Lee, the grip and electrician, had to rearrange some of it when they draped their boom mics and lights in the corners.

There's also a murky bell jar on a stool just left of Genie's ankle. I mention it because whatever creature's skeleton sits inside has two skulls, Lu. What *has* Genie been up to with a hot-glue gun?

Elena, (the script supervisor, remember?) tries for cheerful, but her words are clipped. "Fine, then. Sure. Someone will come outside and grab you when we're ready."

Genie shakes her head. "Outside? In that humidity? No, thanks. I'll be in the back room. Gotta set it up for tomorrow's séance, anyway." Off of Elena's reaction she adds, "Relax. The smoke adds ambiance. Trust me." She waves at the three Devil Hunters. "Come on. We need to run through the program, anyway."

It turns out they've worked together before, which shouldn't be a surprise. Now, they want to be at the top of their game for the show. Genie's been primping. And the Hunters are clad today in matching army-green tees and khaki cargo shorts—and yes, finally, those special ghost-hunt-y tool belts slung around their waists. Jersey Devil or no Jersey Devil. I have to admit their official presentation is very impressive.

Hillary, the assistant camera operator, leans in and peers at something on the small monitor, then fiddles with a dial or a knob or something I can't really see.

"It's okay," she soothes, as though Elena is a wild animal who must be approached gently. "We've definitely got what we need here. The coughing only came at the very end of the last take. The important part was the opening line: 'The Asbury Park Paranormal Odditorium is the nexus of occult information in the Garden State, which makes me the region's foremost expert.'" Her cadence is flat, rushed as she quotes.

Jane chimes in. "We can cut everything after that, use voice-over later if we need to. We've got seven takes of her intro. I like the drama of number one—her intonation was good—but there was that ambulance in the window that had its flashers on. So we'll dub the audio from that one over the footage of something later." The two share a glance, then look imploringly at Elena. "Come see. We'll pick one now. You'll feel better."

Elena turns to Wade, the sound mixer. "What do you think?"

Wade is small and wiry, with an enormous chestnut Afro that bobs as he offers a noncommittal shrug. "I'm not sure about the thing with the ambulance, but we can have a look."

"Fab. You know where to find us." Genie runs an acrylic French tip through her hair. She steps with deliberate care past the two-headed monster jar and disappears through the door at the back of the room marked the door marked PRIVATE: PLEASE KNOCK. SÉANCE MAY BE IN SESSION. The Hunters follow behind at a respectful distance.

Amanda grabs me by the elbow. "I'll stay out here to go through the footage with them, just in case they need a gopher. You should go with Genie and the Hunters."

"I thought they were taking five." I definitely do not need to be involved in their five. Although . . . the main museum space has mutants in glass jars and life-sized voodoo effigies crafted from bundles of twig. It makes a girl wonder what's going on in the private office, séance or not. I want to see a brain marked ABBY NORMAL, Lucia. If there is one, I promise to take a picture of it for you. A real picture on actual film that you can hold in your hands. How much would that rule?

Amanda shakes her head. "No such thing as taking five, even when the cameras are off. Stick with them, pay attention to what they talk about, what comes up. You never know how a story line is going to develop. Even when we're not actually rolling, we're kind of always rolling." She bites her lip. "Does that make sense?"

"Sort of."

Even without the cameras, we're always rolling.

Sure. Okay. Whatever. *Abby Normal. Chucky dolls. A videotape that kills you seven days after you watch it.* Yes, please. All of the above.

I head to the back room.

AS SOON AS I push through the door, I'm enveloped in cigar smoke. It's so thick my eyes water. I flash back to long-ago Portland Thanksgivings, when Poppy Flynn was still alive. After the turkey, he'd escape to his ancient leather recliner and spark up. He called it his "annual Bacchanal." Dad didn't approve, and Nana would squawk for at least a minute or two, but Mom always insisted that an old man was entitled to his one vice.

Mom was so much more patient than the rest of us. Do you remember that, Lu?

The familiar stench is potent in a way that's surreal; I almost expect to find Poppy behind the hazy smoke screen, feet propped up and grinning. But it's Genie, of course, behind a sturdy wooden desk. Her teeth are clenched around the cigar, the sharp hollows under her eyes more pronounced in the shadows of the back room.

She is smoking a cigar.

I am enthralled. Even though my clothes are going to stink later.

"Hey," I say.

"Amanda sent you back here." Genie manages to smile

while still keeping her teeth clamped around the stogie. "She's a smarty-pants, that one. Keeps you busy while she gets to sidle up to the big bosses."

"I mean, she's doing this for college credit," I reply.

Is that an apology? Self-defense? I don't even care, really. Let Amanda sort through footage; I just want my fifteen minutes with a monkey's paw as long as I'm here.

While the museum storefront resembles a macabre thrift shop, this room could be the set of a classic horror movie or noir detective series. It's smaller, with only one narrow window at the very back—it would overlook the parking lot if it weren't shaded by a heavy, earth-toned drape. The floor is linoleum, not exactly grand, but the black-and-white-checkered tiles scream "old school" in a way that makes the possibility of being haunted or otherwise otherworldly seem . . . well, possible.

Ghosts = *possible* right now, Lu.

I am actually saying that to you. I am even meaning it, a little bit. How crazy is that?

Really, it's the walls that do it: genuine seventies-rec-room-style wood paneling, which, like Genie's accent, is terrible and amazing all at once. There are floor-to-ceiling shelves crammed with aging leather books. Cracked spines, yellowing pages, documents that have been highlighted, scribbled on, marked up . . . they jut in kooky angles like the jagged teeth of some ancient mythical creature. Against one wall is nothing but a stack of boxes—organized according to *some* system I can see but not fathom, possibly hieroglyphics.

The Hunters are here, too.

They're hunched around a dark wooden table in the center of the room. On its scratched and pockmarked surface sits a flurry of dog-eared file folders with block-letter printing in bold Sharpie strokes:

Devil sightings: 1990–2005, PHENOMENAL WEEK 190, Exorcism: Jensen, L. Age 28. 6/19/88, CLINTON ROAD DISAPPEARANCES.

"You do . . . exorcisms?" I hadn't meant to speak out loud, Lu, I swear.

Casey shoots me a withering look. Without answering, she scoots her chair toward Seth's and leans in, like she's curious. She's so close to him right now, she can probably feel his breath on her neck. And if there's one thing we've all learned from the ongoing vampire trend, it's that the right kind of breath on your neck can be pretty hot.

Seth looks like he might have the right kind of neck-breath.

"Exorcisms, disenchantments, protection spells, ghost tours, séances," Genie says. "We're pretty much a one-stop paranormal shop." *Puff, puff, smile.* "The best of our kind, I assure you."

Her desk is as cluttered as anything else in the museum. On it sits a framed photograph of Genie and seven other people tricked out like *Ghostbusters*, beaming away at the camera. One of those people is a slightly younger Seth. In the picture, his hair is shorter. His jury-rigged Spengler jumpsuit makes me smile. It looks so . . . earnest.

"So people are, um, *possessed* by the Jersey Devil?"

"*God,*" Casey cuts in, "You *said* you did your homework." She shakes her head. "This is why horror fans make the worst paranormal investigators."

"I'm *not* a paranormal investigator," I remind her.

"No, *you're* just the boss's niece."

Seth clears his throat. "People are possessed by demons, spirits, or entities from the beyond. Creatures that have been cast from their physical form."

"But the Devil still has his form. Like the Loch Ness Monster, or, uh, Sasquatch," I venture.

Seth grimaces slightly at the mention of Sasquatch, though to his credit, his contempt for me is more tempered than Casey's. "Except the Jersey Devil is real."

"Because people *saw* it during 'Phenomenal Week'?" I point to a wicked-looking daguerreotype hanging on the wall. In it, the Devil looms on one leg, his long, sharp beak angled down, wings spanned wide, talons extended. "This . . . bird-man-devil . . . thingy . . ." I trail off, at a momentary loss.

See, what you have to understand about the Jersey Devil, Lu, is that it's this weird kind of dinosaur-ish creature. At least in all the imagery I've seen (because believe it or not, *Casey,* I *did* do my homework before coming here). And while, yeah, I definitely would not want this creepy, raptor-like thing springing out at me on a dark and lonely night, it still doesn't really hold its own. It pales in comparison to something like, you know, a zombie or a werewolf or even the ghost of someone you once knew and loved.

Bottom line: he's kind of goofy, the Devil.

"People *did* see him during Phenomenal Week," Seth says. "It was the highest number of recorded sightings in history. But people still see him today. And unlike, you know, imaginary beings like *Sasquatch*"—he fixes me with a steady gaze—"the Jersey Devil is the only paranormal entity with enough potential corporeal force to cause real harm to the living."

He is *dead serious*, Lu. He 100 percent means the words that are coming out of his mouth right now.

"That's why we hunt him. Whenever there are reported sightings, we're on the scene. Because unlike an undead creature, the Devil can do some major damage."

Of course. "Of course."

"And the Devil is our specialty," Seth adds. "But, like Genie says, we're experts. So whatever your paranormal issue is, we've probably got it covered."

Of course. "Of *course.*"

"You think this is all ridiculous." Genie breaks in, grinning. "You don't buy any of it, not for a second." She takes a long, languid drag on her cigar. "Hell, you probably think I glued together that poor creature in the bell jar you saw in the front room."

I flush. If nothing else, maybe she *is* a mind-reader. "Like Casey said, I *do* love horror movies." I mean it as an apology to Casey but it probably comes across as an insult.

"So do I," Genie says. "But the real deal is *so* much more interesting."

It's the word *real* that trips me. I don't know how to pretend to believe. I don't especially want to. "I just . . ." I shrug. "I can't."

It's the first time I've confessed the truth out loud. I wonder if I'll be fired and sent back to Portland.

Genie stubs her cigar against a chipped ceramic GREET-INGS FROM ASBURY PARK souvenir ashtray. She moves from the desk to the round table. Seth shuffles closer to Casey to make space for Genie. She nods at me.

"Take off your shirt."

"Pardon?"

This is . . . unexpected, Lu. Not to mention, it's been a

while since anyone has made that type of request of me. (I know, I know, Todd Walker, last winter break. Can we not, please? He kissed like a porcupine. And you know exactly what I mean by that.)

"You've got a tank top on under that sweatshirt," Genie says. "Which is understandable, because that monster"—she points to an air conditioner–shaped lump protruding from beneath the window shade—"does not have a *medium* setting. But, hon, the thing is: if we're going to read your stones, you want to get your skin, your vital energy, closer to the surface. Otherwise there's just no point in throwing the bones at all. So take off that hoodie"—she waves again at the chairs scattered around the séance table—"and have a seat."

"I . . . ?" My mouth drops open. "Pardon?" I repeat.

Seth rises, reaches for a rickety library ladder. He turns to make his way to a gray cardboard box at the top of one of the highest shelves. From over his shoulder he calls to me. "We're going to do a reading."

"For you, hon," Genie clarifies. "We'll make you a believer yet. It's called divination." She regards me with calm precision. "Are you ready?"

Of course I'm not ready. But what have I really got to lose? Because divination isn't real, there's nothing to fear, there's no such thing as contacting the Great Beyond. It's all just parlor tricks. Parlor tricks, death, and the stories we tell ourselves—the stories we surround ourselves in—late at night.

I swallow. "Sure."

FIVE

Ivan rubs his hands together. "Roll them bones."

I shiver, having removed my hoodie as instructed. That monstrous window unit is working overtime to prove itself.

Cleromancy. In ancient Rome it was consecrated to the god Mercury, the patron saint of fortune-telling. Nice work if you can get it, right? Although, it's like—what did he really need with a job, anyway, Lu? Seeing as how he was already a god and all. *A god and all.* Just one more thing I don't believe in.

"Are you ready, hon?" Genie asks.

That question, again. Still valid. Her stubbed-out cigar rests in an ashtray, ringed at its frayed tip with a waxy lipstick smear. She has lowered the lights and lit some candles.

"It's nothing to be afraid of, you know," Seth says. He flicks his eyes at me from beside Genie. "The bones themselves don't have *power*, like to curse you, or anything. It's just . . . an interpretation. Prediction, you know? Based on an old practice called sortition."

"It's gonna be cool," Ivan insists, eyes gleaming. His hair's taken on a life of its own, snaking in electric coils.

"I mean, it's not like a *power*, or a *curse*," Casey agrees. "It's just the *truth*." She's next to Seth, that shock of blue hair escaping from behind one ear and swinging toward his shoulder before she tucks it back again. Somehow, she manages to brush her fingers over his forearm in the process. "It's just uncovering the truth. *That* shouldn't be too scary."

And even though she's joking—she's mocking me, she's pretty much laughing at me *right in front of my face*—she's right. It *shouldn't* be too scary. It really shouldn't.

And yet . . . there's something. In my head, I mean. There's still that lingering question of whether belief is necessary in order to fuel the paranormal.

That's just philosophy 101, right? *If the bones are cast in a forest, and no one is there to read them, do they still prophesize?* And while they surely, certainly, almost-completely-and-definitely *don't* . . . Well. We've all seen *Evil Dead.* Whether you believe in these things or not, it's never the best idea to go around reading from the ancient journal you dug up in the cabin cellar. That's just good common sense.

Don't dig, I think. *Literally, or otherwise. Don't. Because Mom's not there.*

But what if she is?

And what if she isn't?

Across the table, Casey sighs. "Well, it probably won't reveal anything for you, anyway. Too much of a skeptic."

It's *such* an immature challenge, Lu. I wish it didn't get under my skin.

"Shh," Genie says, sharp. "She's a Leader. Whatever she's got, it's a little bit stronger, and a little bit closer to the surface, than it is in the rest of us."

And I sit up extra-straight on that wobbly, splintering, smoke-stinky chair because really, I'm not a Leader, I'm a

Flynn. And really, Mom felt the same way. I figure that's why she kept Dad and me as far from Aunt Maggie as possible. If Mom *did* have access to some strong, powerful energy, stirring just beneath the surface of her skin, she had to have a reason not to want it, I'm saying. The power. A reason not to use it. Not to *be using it*, right now, to reach me.

I lean forward, ignoring the gooseflesh on my arms. "All right," I say. "Roll 'em."

Of course, they're not *actually* bones, just misshapen pebbles rattling around in a dusty fake-velvet drawstring bag. Some have little scribbles on them, like the most obvious prop from the cheesiest low-budget hoodoo thriller. *They're not actually bones.* Smoke and mirrors, Lu.

Genie reaches for a small square of faded cloth: a scrap you'd use for quilting, or a memento. "The divination surface." She spreads it out on the table in front of her, smooths it with her hand. Seth hands her a glass bottle filled with sand the color of a stormy sky, which she uncorks, pouring the sand in a circle on the cloth. When she's done, she places the bottle down and clears her raspy throat. "Join hands, please."

We do. I have to stretch a bit to reach Genie. The tips of her fingernails scrape my palm as we twine our fingers together.

On my other side is Ivan. His hand is sweaty—odd, given the arctic climate.

"I should have meditated on these stones before you got here, hon," Genie tells me, sounding apologetic. "But I have a feeling it won't matter, with you."

On the table next to me, one of the candles flickers, sputters out. And I can't lie, Lucia—it's eerie. *It won't matter with you.* Because I'm a Leader, right?

"Go ahead," Genie urges.

"I-I'm not sure what I'm supposed to do." I have a brief mental flash of that movie, that spiritual medium. You know who I mean, Lu—the one with the squeaky voice. *There is no death. There is only a transition to a different sphere of consciousness.* But in the movie, her name is Tangina, Lu, and then I almost giggle. Nervous laughter. One of my things. I bite my lip.

Ivan's hand twitches in my own. "Questions. You have to ask questions."

I don't know where to begin. All the movie marathons, all the make-believe séances I've watched—everything, even *Tangina*—they vanish from my brain like a trapdoor has been pulled. I'm a blank, a black hole.

"Start with a yes or no," Genie suggests gently.

A yes or no.

"Did my mother love Aunt Maggie?" The question flies out of my mouth. I'm suddenly a ventriloquist's dummy, apparently. (Oh God, Lu—that episode of *Twilight Zone.* *"The Dummy." I'm the dummy!*) I hadn't known I was going to ask it, hadn't realized it was something I was so truly curious about. But of course, it makes sense. As much sense as anything else around here, anyway.

Genie bypasses the velvet bag, frees my hand, and dips her own into a bowl of gemstones: smooth and translucent, in glinting purples and reds. She scoops up a palm full, twists her wrist like a magician, and scatters the pieces across the circle. Quick as lightning, she counts them up: four purple, three red. She looks at me. "Yes. She did."

Well, then.

"You can tell that just from those little . . . rocks?"

"Purple is positive, red is negative," Seth explains. "More purple than red means the answer is yes."

"But that's just . . ." *Ridiculous* is the obvious answer,

obviously what I want to say, but I manage to course-correct.
". . . so arbitrary."

Isn't it, Mom? And also: Are you there? And of course there's
no answer, because buying into this whole charade is just
a tiny leap from being one of those presumably grown-ass
people who actually read their daily horoscopes. Who follow
those things to the letter. Mom never bothered with horoscopes. (She was a Capricorn.)

Seth shrugs: *suit yourself.* "Try again."

"Um. Would Mom want me to be here this summer? Would
she be happy, I mean?" Because I do wonder about that.

Shake. Toss. Rattle. Scatter.

Three purples. Three reds. A tie.

"So what does *that* mean? How can it be tied?"

Casey rolls her eyes. "It just can. Why not?"

Seth fiddles with the edge of the divining cloth. "It just
means yes *and* no," he says. "She would and she wouldn't."
He tilts his head at me, eyes boring into mine. "I mean, can
you think of why? Like why it would be tied?"

But Lu, when it comes to my mother, I *can't* think. I
can't possibly fathom *any* of the whys. Why did she leave
us, after all?

"I . . . don't know anything about her relationship to
Maggie." It feels like I'm forcing the words past a throat
full of wet cotton, churning them through a cement mixer,
choking them out. My eyes fill and the surface of the table
blurs for a moment. The room is so, so quiet. The only sound
is the uneven hum of the air conditioner.

Another candle sputters out, and a splotchy tear falls from
my cheek. It leaves a trace of wetness on the table. I rub it
with the tip of my index finger, and it is *so awkward* in that
room, Lu, that I wish I *did* have a magic power, that I could

shape-shift or dissolve into thin air. My skin feels prickly, but almost like from the inside, somehow. All I can think is *don't, don't, don't,* and it means at least twelve different things, in that moment.

Genie reaches for my hand again.

I flinch, almost pull away, but realize there's no point. And besides, her skin is softer than you might think (given the perma-tan and what it suggests about her beauty regimen). Honestly: her hand holding mine feels kind of nice. Mom wasn't a big hand-holder. It's probably why I'm not, as you know, so warm-and-fuzzy. She nods toward the candle, its wick still smoking. *Power,* she mouths, but so subtly that maybe I'm the only one at the table who sees her. Or is supposed to.

I shrug, because of course, I don't really believe her, but just at this moment, I also don't totally not.

"Maybe we should switch to the runes," she says.

Runes are an alternative to crystals. They're the sort of markings you'd find carved into a tree trunk, for instance, if you were trapped in a forest in search of the Blair Witch. In that case, I can't say runes worked out so well for the people involved.

Genie works her hand into the velvet bag, forcing the drawstring open. When she withdraws, her fist is closed, tight enough that her knuckles are pale.

"Roll them bones," Ivan whispers again.

And this time, he's right; the tiny shapes in Genie's hands are yellowed and uneven, so that they *could,* in fact, be bones or teeth or some other form of unidentifiable organic matter. *Best not to dwell.*

The bones/stones/whatever are marked, too, etched à la *Blair Witch* with little scrawls and scribbles. Again, there's a chill, and I have a moment of wondering, *again*, what *exactly* it is that I do or don't believe in.

Genie flicks her wrist casually, splays her palm. *Shake. Toss. Rattle. Scatter.* The stones—animal bones? enamel? fossilized pieces kidnapped by a robber baron of the occult?—tumble across the surface of the divination cloth. Two come to rest squarely in the center of the circle. She picks up the one closest to the circle's center, examines it. "Uruz." She nods. "That makes sense. You've recently lost someone."

Which is the truth. *But.* She could have said anything, could have made up any particular reading or interpretation that she wanted to. The Hunters would have gone along with it, I think. And the dead-mom thing? Well, that's just a gimme. And I am *not* going to cry in this room anymore.

Seth scoops up a stone that's traveled just outside of the sand.

"This one's Uruz, too."

I wave my hand at him. "Well, I only have just the one mother, and she's gone. So." I smirk. *See? Your little supernatural game of marbles is basically all just crap.*

"If it falls outside the circle, its meaning is inverted," Seth says. His tone is even, almost gentle—a rebuttal of my shaky, teary smirk. He leans all the way across the table. All at once he's so close I catch a brief whiff of his shampoo, which is woodsy like patchouli oil and Christmastime. He hands the stone to me.

I take it and look down, so as not to meet his eyes. I trace the symbol, a jagged, squared-off, upside-down *U* with my finger. "Inverted like how?"

"Technically, it means you'll, uh, rise from the remains of what was lost. Old values will be reborn. Um, in you."

I fix my gaze on the second candle to go out, on the

still-smoldering wick. *Reborn*. What would that even mean? Are we being literal, here? "Well, that sounds kind of unpleasant," I say.

Genie coughs. "A Leader." Her voice, still gravelly, is softer now. "Isn't that what I said?"

But what would that mean, what would that mean? The irony, too, is not lost on me, because as I'm sure you remember, Lu, the last thing I *led* was the eighth-grade track team. That didn't end so well. (Issues with delegation.) Still, I don't dare breathe . . .

And then: a crashing cacophony. A bang followed by a slam followed by a thud. We all shoot about three inches straight up in our seats before we realize what happened.

The hulking AC unit has full-on plummeted out of the window.

Ivan stands. "Yikes!" The bones in his spine poke through the back of his T-shirt as he cranes his neck.

The door to the back room opens. Elena pokes her head in. "Was that the AC?" she asks. And before anyone can answer, she adds, "Glad I moved the equipment that was piled back there." She glances at the table: the sand, the bones, the colored gems. She has no reaction. But then again, she's a regular on *Fantastic, Fearless*. She's seen this stuff before. "Are you guys done in here?"

"I think we're fine for now," Genie says, patting my hand covertly.

"Good." Elena's eyes are hard; she's in all-business mode. "Did you get any of it on film?" She looks at me.

Right. Amanda did say we're never really off-duty. "Uh, no. Sorry." But not *really* sorry, you know, that there isn't footage of me crying during a bone-casting session.

Elena looks weary, like she expected no less from me. It's

fair but still not the best feeling. "Okay, well. Whatever. We're moving on. Genie, we need to film you doing a tour of the shop. And we want some of the backstory on your work with the Hunters. Seth, Casey—come on."

"Come on," Casey repeats, wrapping a hand around Seth's forearm, looking mighty pleased with herself.

"What about me?" Ivan asks, nonplussed. His whiny-little-brother vibe makes him easy to overlook. He doesn't seem so into that.

"Relax, Baby Jane, there's plenty of camera time to go around," Elena reassures him. "But for now, we're splitting you up. Russ and Maggie are meeting us here. You're going with Hillary and Winnie to Convention Hall."

SIX

Convention Hall creeps toward the shoreline. It's a behe-
moth, Convention Hall. It spans the boardwalk, connected
to the iconic Palace Theater by the Grand Arcade. On this
humid day, through the haze of sunshine, I have a momentary sense of what this place used to be. Because this place
has ghosts, Lu. Asbury Park does. If I blink, they reveal
themselves against the inside of my eyelids, photo negatives,
sepia-toned images torn from a history book. They brush
past me, beside me, through me, clinging like tattered fabric
to the molecules in the atmosphere.

At least, that's what Ivan says.

Ions, he uses the word *ions*, not molecules (so I was right
about the air-ion counter after all!), and he says you can
recognize the presence of spirits in the air based on the
movement of ionic particles. Or something.

"That science seems . . . inconclusive," I say. Never mind
the overwhelming heaviness of the air here, the weight and
feel of all the individual histories, all the individual *people*
who once walked this stretch of sand, now gone.

"I mean, I can see where it's hard to accept," Ivan concedes. "Maybe you'll, like, get it more, once you see us in action. Seeing is believing, et cetera, et cetera."

Seeing.

My mother's wrist, freshly slashed, vertical lines red and wet. Her body, dead long enough that the blood had ceased to flow. Her vacant, glassy eyes. Her arm, slim and impossibly stone white—it was the arm of a statue, a figurine. It couldn't possibly be the arm of a human who was, once upon a time, my mother. *Dangling from the edge of our claw-foot tub. Et cetera, et cetera.*

So, yes. Seeing is believing.

(She didn't leave a note.)

I take a deep breath. "What the hell. I'm going to be here all summer, right? Prove me wrong, dude."

Prove me wrong, Mom. Talk to me.

"I mean, no offense, but we're not interested in proving anything to you. It's Maggie we're trying to impress."

"No shit," I say, pointing to his T-shirt. It reads TAKE ME TO YOUR LEADER beneath a retro version of the *Fantastic, Fearsome* logo. "And no offense taken." But: offense is *sort of* taken, although with Ivan, I feel like it's some actual clinical thing he does, with the antisocial outbursts. I doubt he can help himself.

"But you *like horror*," he says, insistent. As it's the thousand-and-tenth time I've heard that since I got here, it's getting old. "So why not take it one step further?"

I snort. "Well, that's the dumbest argument I've heard so far. *No offense.*" I nod at the water, foam, and seaweed drifting back and forth. "I liked the little mermaid fairy tale, too. I don't *actually* believe in underwater sirens luring sailors to their"—I stumble on the phrase—"untimely deaths."

Ivan's sunglasses are wire-rimmed, John Lennon–style, and they're slipping a little in the heat. He pushes them back up the bridge of his nose. "So, what's the alternative, then? Where do *you* think we go after we die?"

I have nothing to say to that. Because: *Where are you, Mom?* And I wish I didn't mean it, but I really believe the answer is: nowhere.

"We used to come on weekends, believe it or not," Ivan says, changing the subject. "To the Arcade I mean."

I look at him. "Why wouldn't I believe it?"

"Oh." He reddens. "It's just . . . a little, uh, lame, I guess. Touristy." He waves a hand, as if I haven't noticed the throngs in clumps of two, three, five; backward baseball caps, DIY muscle tees, bejeweled flip-flops—worn in, rubbed down. Bumpy, mosquito-bitten ankles. Smeared cheeks bearing the remains of frozen custard—and what is that even, Lucia? How is it different from frozen yogurt? Please tell me.

"Touristy can be fun," I say, trying to reboot. "As long as you weren't wearing"—I jerk my head toward a beefy, barrel-chested man in a neon-green mesh tank top—*"that."*

Ivan laughs. "I don't even know where you'd *buy* that. Except maybe in 1983."

I look to where Hillary is setting up her camera, tripod adjusted to specifically frame the ocean behind Ivan as he sits on a boardwalk bench for his interview. She's fiddling with something that raises the camera higher. We've been lingering alongside the wooden rail of the boardwalk's edge. "Should we help her?"

"Maybe *you* should. I'm the talent," Ivan says.

"Fair enough." But I don't. I'm not ready to move just yet. There's a breeze rolling off of the ocean in rhythm with the waves, and I have the slightest sense of release. It's a nice change of pace. I'm gonna go with it, Lu, for just a few more minutes, I think.

"The SS *Morro Castle* washed up *right there*," Ivan says. "It came cruising in toward Convention Hall literally burning up. Beached, or was anchored or something, like straight up against the hall."

I nod. "I've seen some of the pictures." A wake of foam and smoke, the ship listing side to side. "New Jersey's own *Titanic*."

"I should have brought my EMF meter. Left it in the kit with Casey and Seth," Ivan says. "All those bodies. This place must read off the charts."

"Remind me to bring my tin-foil hat tomorrow," I say.

"Haven't you looked at tomorrow's call sheet?" Hillary cuts in, without moving from her post by the benches. "Maggie's bringing the three of you back here tomorrow with your equipment to do an energy read. Right now, we just want the full deets on the Devil."

Ivan starts, looks left and right with suspicion. "How did she hear that?"

"You're miked," I remind him. We both are. Tiny boxes are taped to our backs and tucked into our waistbands. How could he possibly have forgotten? Mine's been making me super-sweaty, and its edges are very pointy.

"We're almost ready, guys," Hillary adds. "Probably five more minutes. You might want to go over the questions you're going to ask, Winnie, so that Ivan can have his answers at least a little bit prepped. We need to sound candid, not unfocused."

"Right." *Right.* "But, um, just to confirm—*I'm* not going to be on camera, right?"

"Nope. Not today, anyway. Maggie was pissed you wouldn't let her get your bangs trimmed before filming."

She was? No one told me. It didn't seem important, when she mentioned it. Is there something wrong with my hair?

"For now it's just going to be audio of your questions, and we'll edit Ivan's answers. We may even do subtitles or voice-over later on in post."

"Cool." I nod like I have any idea what this means. But really: as long as I'm not on camera, we're good. Even if it means there's something fundamentally wrong with my hair that I wasn't aware of.

"So, okay." I reach into my back pocket. (Lu: Amanda was really onto something re: jeans and pockets, so I humbly rescind all of that previous snark.) I fish out a crumpled printout: my "notes" on the subject of the Jersey Devil. "According to Wikipedia, the Jersey Devil is a legendary creature—meaning, like, a creature from an actual legend, *not* legendary like Bruce Springsteen's set at The Stone Pony."

"Whoa, *knowledge*. Look who's a quick-change Jersey Girl," Ivan says.

"Quick-change? You're thinking of my mother, who couldn't get out of this state fast enough." I clear my throat, not sure why I volunteered that tidbit. "The Devil. *A legendary figure* hailing from the Pine Barrens."

Ivan grins, and for a split second he goes from "baby brother" to "eager little boy." It kind of makes me want to hug him, almost. "Oh, yeah. The Barrens. Very woodsy-creepy–*Cabin Fever*. Can't wait till we get down there."

PHENOMENAL WEEK 1909
Notable Sightings of the Leeds Devil

TRENTON

BRISTOL PA: POLICE FIRE ON MYSTERIOUS RAMPAGING BEAST TO NO APPARENT AVAIL

BURLINGTON NJ: LOCAL RESIDENT DESCRIBES ENCOUNTER WITH "A JABBERWOCK WITH NO TEETH, EYES LIKE BLAZING COALS AND OTHER TERRIFYING ATTRIBUTES"

PHILADELPHIA

DELAWARE RIVER

CAMDEN NJ: DEVIL TERRORIZES OCCUPANTS AT LOCAL SOCIAL CLUB

HADDON HEIGHTS NJ: DEVIL ATTACKS TROLLEY CAR

INTERVIEW FOOTAGE—IVAN FELL—TAPE 1.4—DEVIL LORE

INTERVIEWER (W.F., OFFSCREEN):
So, what is the Jersey Devil?

IVAN:
(smiles)

Google it, you'll get millions of different hits.
The physical description, I mean. Anything from
goofy-cartoon to, like, a really menacing
old-school thing, like a gargoyle or something.
"A flying biped with hooves." That's the one
detail everyone agrees on.

(OFFSCREEN):
So, like a dinosaur, then?

IVAN:
(grimaces)

Sure. A dinosaur. Like a freaking velociraptor
that could rip your head off before you ever saw
it coming, maybe.

(leans toward the camera)

What? Yeah, okay, I'm glad you're

(air quotes)

familiar with Jurassic Park.

(OFFSCREEN):
Jeez. Touchy.

IVAN:
(folds arms)

I can't do the interview if you're going to,
like, laugh in my face. The Devil, so, she
looks like a really fierce, winged thing. Some
people say a kangaroo, but I'd say, like,
angrier than a kangaroo.

(beat)

Don't laugh about that. Thank you. Anyway, the
Jersey Devil has been haunting the Garden State
for almost three hundred years. In 1735, they say,
Mother Leeds gave birth to her thirteenth child.

(beat)

Leeds. One of the founding families of New
Jersey. You know, Casey told me you didn't
really bother with the research, but I didn't
think . . . well, anyway. So Mother Leeds was
one of them, and I guess she wasn't so psyched
about having thirteen kids—can't really blame
her, right? And so as she was, um, giving birth,
she freaked out, and said, *"Let this one be a
devil!"* And so, it was.

(OFFSCREEN):
Meaning, an angry kangaroo came out, and the
Jersey Devil was born?

IVAN:
Pretty much, yeah. That's what they say.
That's what *we* say. The Devil Hunters. The baby
was born normal, but right away it started to
change. It grew wings and horns and all of that
shit. And then flew up the chimney out into the
Barrens, where it haunts people to this very
day. Supposedly it killed some of the midwives
before it flew away.

(OFFSCREEN):
And you believe all this?

IVAN:
Yeah, of course. The Leeds family, all their
descendants, they were persecuted for
generations.

(in response to offscreen coughing)

Hey—are you okay?
(REACHES for a water bottle, HANDS IT
out of frame)

Here. Don't die. At first they called it a living
dragon. Sightings were recorded throughout the
eighteenth and nineteenth centuries. We've got
all of them documented in Genie's library.

(STEPS out of frame briefly, the sound of
clapping on a back can be heard)

Seriously, are you sure you're not choking
or something?

(OFFSCREEN):
(through coughing)
I just want to get through this segment.
It's fine.

(cough)

Phenomenal Week. Tell me about that.

IVAN:
Right. Phenomenal Week. January sixteenth
through the twenty-third, 1909. Most Jersey
Devil sightings in a seven-day period, ever.
Mysterious footprints appeared across fields,
household pets and farm animals went missing,
or worse—were found later, torn apart. By the
end of the week, people wouldn't leave their
houses to go to work. Widespread panic. Eye-
witness accounts placed it in Camden, New
Jersey; and Bristol, Pennsylvania. In both
cases, police opened fire on the Devil, but
obviously, didn't bring it down.

(OFFSCREEN):
Obviously.

IVAN:

Look, you can joke all you want, but this thing
is real, and if anyone's going to get it on
camera for your aunt, it's our team.

(OFFSCREEN):

It's pretty hard not to joke about an
angry kangaroo.

IVAN:

Unless it's terrorizing your friends or your
family.

(pauses, thoughtful)

You know, my mother touched it. Once.

(alarmed)

Hey! Wait—seriously, let's get you, like, some
lozenges or tea. Maybe you've got allergies or
something. It's really humid down the shore.
Out-of-towners can't always take it.

(OFFSCREEN):

(uncontrollable COUGHING and THROAT CLEARING)

CUT

SEVEN

t is not not-embarrassing. Listening to myself hack up a lung on auto-playback, Lucia. I will tell you that. And I am not *not-*thankful that my weird old-man phlegm attack happened in front of Ivan, instead of anyone else. Small favors, etc. Thank the unnamed deity of your choice, to which I do not sub-scribe.

Logging the day's interview tapes involves rewinding my Devil Q&A with Ivan at least thirty times, to the point where I've memorized the individual sounds of my intermittent coughing fits. But I'm almost done, down to TAPE 1.4: DEVIL LORE—PHENOMENAL WEEK in my labeling.

Then Amanda appears in the doorway of the office.

She's more frazzled than I've seen her yet, a hunk of blonde hair escaping from the knot at the top of her head and her cheeks flushed. But her eyes are bright, so it seems like a good, exhilarated sort of frazzled. I glance at my phone. 5:14. I hadn't realized how late it was getting.

"It's late," Amanda says, echoing my thoughts. "We're gonna have to do a dinner run soon."

"Great." I stand and stretch my arms overhead. "I'm ready when you are." My back's starting to cramp up from too many hours on the crappy folding chair, and now that the subject of food's come up, my stomach gives a rumble.

"Where are Maggie and Jane? Inner Sanctum?" Amanda nods over my shoulder, toward the closed door leading to Maggie's bedroom proper.

"Um, yeah." Now that I think about it, they've been cooped up in there for ages, going over the dailies (at least, the stuff I wasn't logging), and putting together tomorrow's call sheet. "We've barely been shooting a day. What could they possibly be going over for this long?"

"Are you kidding?" Amanda laughs. "It takes a lot of obsessing to tease out the potential story line threads. And then once you've got an idea you want to run with, you've got to go back through everything again trying to find complementary footage. And put together scripts for the next shoot so that you can be sure to get new material to go along with that story."

"Scripts. For reality TV. Who knew?" I mean, obviously, I knew it was heavily edited, Lu, but *scripts*? For a *reality show*? Shouldn't that be an oxymoron?

"Yeah. And since we're just at the beginning of the shoot, like you say, they want to keep an eye out for *any* potential drama to follow."

"Or to instigate," I mumble.

"For sure!" Amanda agrees cheerily. "I mean, even that Seth–Casey romance angle—completely unbelievable, he's way too cute for her. If they want to really sell that, they're going to have to build it up themselves. Hence, sending them off on their own today while you were interviewing Xander Harris's imaginary younger brother."

I blink. "You watch *Buffy*?" Then again, the titular vampire slayer was meant to be fashionable, at least for fictional Sunnydale, in the all-too-real nineties. Maybe this information *does* jibe with Amanda's style sense. They kind of look alike.

She shrugs. "I watched what Maggie watches when I found out I got this internship. Also, I love it when the blonde girl kicks ass."

"You should try . . ." *Kill Bill*, I'm thinking. But I'm distracted, trail off. I shake my head. *Something else she said . . . possibly nagging at me more than the Joss Whedon reference . . .* My stomach turns over again, and this time, not out of hunger.

"Wait. A Seth–Casey romance angle?" I accidentally do a little up-talk and wince.

"I know, it's ridiculous. I mean, Seth's adorable if you're into that stealth-nerd thing—"

(I am. As you know, Lu.)

"—so it's not, like, crazy that Casey would be crushing on him."

"You think she is?" The words are out before I can think them through. *Shut up shut up, shut up, Winnie.* I have to get this sudden-onset, honesty Tourette's syndrome under control before I let loose with something that *really* can't be shoved back into Pandora's box.

Amanda makes a face at me like I'm a mental patient or worse. "Duh, that's why she's so weird around you. Come on."

Wait—*what?* So much *what* to follow up on . . .

"But he's clearly not into her at all, just totally focused on his ghost-hunting stuff, which is either weird or adorable, depending on your preference, I guess. But *anyway* . . . I'm sure they'll be able to drag it out for at least a *few* episodes if they can scrape together enough reaction shots from other scenes. I'm telling you, don't believe what you see on TV,

Winnie. *Especially* reality TV. You'll see. Take it from a semi-insider. If it weren't for my family's *personal* experience with the supernatural, I'd never even be able to look at Maggie with a straight face. I mean, you can make *anything* seem true if you just tweak the camera angles the right way, you know?"

"Sure." But I *don't* know. Isn't that obvious? I'm learning, though, and fast, I guess. "Smoke and mirrors."

"More than that," Amanda counters. "*Smoke and mirrors* makes it sound like magic. But really, it's more like your beloved aunt Maggie playing God. That's the skill of the all-powerful director."

"She's not . . ." I begin, because she *isn't*, as in: neither beloved (at least, not yet, though we're edging into be-liked territory slowly), nor God (that I can tell). But my stomach, my mind, my brain, they turn over again like the clank of a boardwalk Ferris wheel completing one rotation.

If it weren't for my family's personal *experience.*

Her family's. *Amanda's.*

"My mother touched the Jersey Devil."

I heard that today, from Ivan. But I heard it from *Amanda* first. Was Ivan lying, then? Co-opting Amanda's Devil-sighting for himself?

I think he was.

But *why*?

Hmm. I can't press Amanda, couldn't investigate further even if I wanted to, because she's on a mission now that we've got all the small talk out of the way. She has a job to do (and technically, so do I). Dinner. We're the PAs, and we're on dinner duty right now. Amanda raises a closed fist and raps lightly on Maggie's bedroom door. "Food run!" she calls brightly. From behind the door, there's a scurry of activity, and then the door swings open and Jane peeks out.

"Perfect timing," she says.

"Buttercups!" Aunt Maggie's throaty voice, from beyond the doorway. "I had the *most fantastic* idea about dinner!"

"No pun intended?" Amanda chirps, and the three of them collapse into a level of amusement that is completely unwarranted, if you want my unbiased opinion, Lu. But I am not even really paying attention.

Ivan. Lying. Would he? About such a small, stupid, insignificant thing? Why?

NARRATION—MAGGIE LEADER—TAPE 3.5—SETH & CASEY

EXT. ASBURY PARK BOARDWALK—DAY
WIDE SHOT

CAMERA PANS

FLASH CUTS:
TILLIE/WONDER BAR BEACH/BRICKWALL TAVERN

CUT TO:
MAGGIE, set up for her interview in front of a
replica "Greetings from Asbury Park" backdrop.

MAGGIE:
Why did I pair Casey up with Seth for the
Paranormal Odditorium shoot?

(beat)

Oh, brownie bite, did you *see* the way she's been
looking at him? Honestly, I have no idea whether
he has any feelings for her, but why not give
the little Tootsie Roll a boost?

(CUPS HANDS into HEART SHAPE.)

MAGGIE:
We're at the shore, a little summer love
among the young 'uns makes sense.

> (wags finger)

And it makes for good TV, too.

> (smiles)

It's the same reason I decided to send the
Devil Hunters and the PAs to the boardwalk
together to get dinner. The crew and I are
grown adults. We can order our own food for
one night. My little sugarplums work so hard,
they deserve some downtime. A chance to be kids
together. To have some fun. Who knows what it
could lead to with Seth and Casey—with any of
them, really? Besides . . . Any psychic connection that two investigators have is only gonna
enhance their work. At the end of the day, it's
all about the work, really. What can I say?
Anything for my show.

CUT.

INTERVIEW FOOTAGE—CASEY WHITTER—TAPE 1.8—SETH CRUSH

> CASEY:
> (giggles, twirls a strand of blue hair around a
> finger)

Um, I'm not sure why Maggie decided to pair
me up with Seth at the Paranormal Odditorium.
I don't know, maybe *he* even suggested it? We've
been working together since the summer before

freshman year. And I guess, sometimes feelings just develop when you're involved so closely in something so intense.

(beat)

Seth and I are both really intense people. But who knows? I mean, maybe Maggie just saw some-thing that even Seth and I haven't fully realized yet. Like, even if I'm *slightly* psychic,it would make sense that Maggie's powers could pick up some little spark that I missed.

CUT

INTERVIEW FOOTAGE—SETH JARVIS—TAPE 2.2—CASEY ROMANCE?

SETH:
(squinting at the camera)

Why did Maggie split Casey and me up from the rest of the group?

(frowning)

Wait—you seriously think that was on purpose?

(laughs and shakes his head)

Come on. That's dumb. No comment.

CUT

EIGHT

"Um, so?" *What happened to dinner?* It feels pesty, like a bratty baby brother, to ask the question, but I'm starving, Lu. The noises coming from my stomach have gone from "curious" to "aggressive" to "subhuman." Which is appropriate enough, given the company, but it's still embarrassing. Not to mention how cranky I get when my blood sugar is low. And I ran this morning, too.

From over her shoulder, Casey flashes me a cold look, then locks step with Seth as our not-so-merry band makes its way down the North Beach boardwalk. She's been next to Seth since we left the motel. This is a fact, I am quickly discovering, that I am incapable of not-noticing.

It's a horrible thing to learn about oneself, Lu.

I fervently wish Amanda hadn't said anything to me about a possible story line, a possible romance between them. My involuntary interest is starting to verge on CW-drama levels of stalk-age. And *that's* almost more embarrassing than the sea-monster noises coming from my stomach. (But not quite.)

"Is anyone hungry?" I press. "Maggie told us to go get something to eat, that we were off for dinner."

"Exactly," Amanda says. Her pert blonde ponytail bobs in agreement. "She said we're *off* for *dinner.*"

I give her a quizzical face. What am I missing here?

"Meaning, we can try to squeeze a little fun in before the séance tomorrow, which is going to be another grueling shoot," she says. "Did you see we have a seven A.M. call time? That means getting up *before seven.* It's going to be a long day. Can't we just, like, chill for a little bit? We'll get some pizza soon."

"What's *with* that call time, by the way?" Ivan whines, reminding me (thankfully) that there's one person in our group who's way better than I am at filling the bratty kid-brother role. His white-boy Afro is particularly voluminous tonight. He's doing his best to keep stride with Casey and Seth, although Casey veers away from him—and all the closer to Seth—anytime he manages to close the gap at all. "Séances are usually held at *night.*"

"Do the ghosts wear watches? How . . . civilized." I can't help myself.

In front of me, Seth lowers his head and picks up his pace. Somehow, the gesture speaks of tacit approval, and somehow I like the way that makes me feel. (You have permission to gag the next time you see me, Lu. That was revolting. Chalk it up to the blood-sugar situation.)

"It's a good question," he says.

Casey widens her eyes, like this is the last thing she expected him to say.

You and me both, sister.

"It's not that the ghosts can or can't tell time," he continues. "And it's not even that we're trying to create atmo-sphere. Though, *of course*, the atmosphere doesn't hurt. It's important to be in the right mind frame, the zone, you know, in order to do what we do."

The sarcasm bubbles up like a physical sensation inside me, like an impulse as strong and undeniable as a sneeze. But another glance at those cheekbones, at the sincerity in those glittering, flinty eyes of his (What color are they? Gray? Brown? I've never seen anything like them on a human being, Lucia) and I bite back the words. My ears and eyes may be open ever so slightly wider. Maybe my mind does, too.

"But atmosphere aside, the reason we do these things at night is because in the darkness, our senses are heightened. It's harder to see, naturally, so we're listening, we're thinking, we're *feeling* much more deeply, much more acutely than we do when the lights are on."

He stops short, closes his eyes, takes a breath. With anyone else, the earnestness might be too extreme, too pure to tolerate. But with Seth, it feels true. And I'm not the only one who feels it; glancing around, almost everyone is either looking out to the sea or staring at Seth, soaking in the salty air, *feeling* the evening. Believe it or not, it's nice. To have our senses heightened. To be aware. It's the opposite of how I usually go about things these days.

Ivan ruins the moment. "But we have to be there tomorrow at *nine*! It's just not right. Come *on.*"

Amanda snorts. "You're lucky. Winnie and I have to be there at seven to set up. That means being awake *before seven.*" She shoots me a vaguely accusatory look. "We aren't all up with the crack of the garbage trucks to be all physically fit. *Some* of us are not naturally morning people."

"I'm . . . sorry?" I couldn't care less about fitness, of course. The running has nothing to do with that. No, it's that there's something indefinable that I'm desperate to outrun.

Probably my own demons. Though genetics suggest that may be impossible.

Amanda's over it. She makes another *pfft* sound. "We have to cover up the windows of the museum from the outside and stuff to make it *seem* like the shoot takes place at night."

"*What?*" That's just lunacy. "Why not just *shoot it at night?*"

She gives me a *beats me* look. "Talk to Jane. I am not the schedule guru. I guess there are other things we need to do at night?"

"But not *this* night," Casey says.

Yes, another unfortunate aspect of our current reality, much like the early call times: invented story lines involving boys who could probably do better in the (please, let it be) faux-mance department. "I mean, we could stand around complaining about the schedule, or we could actually try and enjoy this time off. *Right?*" Casey flashes what she probably thinks is a coquettish glance at Seth, all spidery eyelashes and facial twitching.

Ohhh, I do not like her, Lu.

She leans over a bit awkwardly, punches Seth in the arm. "We can help with that." Another not-quite-age-appropriate giggle. I notice it makes Ivan wince, too.

Seth gives an easy smile, like he's basically okay with being awkward-crush-punched by Casey. He un-shoulders a comically oversized backpack that somehow I hadn't even noticed he'd been lugging all along. "I have a few ideas," he says.

"Oh my God, I, like, did not even realize you brought that!" Amanda cries.

Her reaction feels over the top. "It's just a backpack," I point out.

Amanda gives me an *I-can't-even-believe-you* look. "It's his ghost-busting kit."

Of course it is. And I can't believe me, either. I should have known. So far, he really has lugged that thing along like an external vital organ. And in that moment, I also know I need to be quicker on the draw. I'm here; I'm in this, regardless of how I arrived in the first place. I need to be more like Amanda. More like *Maggie*. More like a Leader, maybe. Also: I need to know what that means—being a Leader—in the first place.

Seth's backpack is olive green and weathered, frayed at the straps, but sturdy enough that it stands straight up on its own on the ground. In addition to a cavernous main compartment, it's got side pockets and front pouches, and three separate mesh sling areas that, for now, at least, house dog-eared cards, memos, and notes to self.

He turns to Amanda. "You carry a camera with you everywhere, right?"

"Well, just my phone, but yeah."

Seth smirks. "Like you would *ever* be caught dead without a phone that didn't have decent video built in."

"Fine, fine." She giggles, sounding awfully like Casey, and raises those tanned, slender arms: *You got me.* "Yes. I am a slave to the moving pictures."

"You're obsessed," he says. "We have that in common. We also both know that the boardwalk is teeming with spirits."

My gaze shifts between the two. The air is thick with an acrid, salty-sweet, fried-gumbo smell. Funnel cake, corn dogs, fatty hunks of meat on a spit. Carnival food. Imaginary food. Ephemera. Strangely, though, I'm actually not that hungry anymore. Curiosity has won out for the time being.

"Wait." Amanda's eyes sparkle. "You're going to do an investigation. Right now, for us. Just off the cuff." She beams in approval. "That. Is. *Amazing.*"

"It's what we do best," Casey cuts in, clearly glad to have an excuse. The *duh* is implied in her tone.

Amanda slides her hand into her back jeans pocket, whips out her trusty phone. "I'll film it. Who knows, maybe it'll end up on the show. Or even just, like, bonus content on the blog. Or it'll just be something awesome for us, like for a keepsake."

"Shit, yeah, you'll film it," Ivan says, voice rising. "*Verite* is where it's at. *Especially* with paranormal investigations."

Verite: the art of filming so as to convey candid realism. It's a funny term to apply to ghost-hunting, don't you think, Lu? And I guess it could be both funny and fun, getting to see the Hunters do what it is they do best, you know? But it's so much safer not to press, to assume that the *normal* trumps the *para* in everyday life. Wasn't it enough temptation of fate with the runes?

Roll them bones.

I take a breath. "I'm sorry, it's just . . . So, for our night out—our night *off,* mind you, that everyone was all super-psyched about? What we're going to do tonight is exactly what we're being paid to do every day for our jobs? But just for fun?" It's the best argument I can think of on the spot.

"You're an intern," Casey says. "You don't get paid."

I imagine punching her in the face. "That's not the point."

"The *point,*" Seth interjects, before this can turn ugly, a sad cliché of a reality TV girl fight, "is that this *is* what we do. In our downtime. For 'fun.' I know you don't believe in us, Winnie. In, um, what we do. But we're Hunters. We have a cause, and it's real. It's not a hobby, Winn. It's a skill. It's a *gift.*"

"It's, like, a *duty,*" Ivan says, so solemn I have to cough back a laugh.

I keep coughing for a second. That warm tickle builds in the back of my throat and I swallow it down. Who would have thought humidity levels would be worse at the Jersey Shore than the Pacific Northwest?

"Fine," I say finally. "Okay, then."

Seth's face lights up. He kneels and begins unpacking things from his terrifying bag: lenses and lights, rectangular devices that look like walkie-talkies or remote controls, crackling with energy even in resting mode. He carries these things with him *all of the time*, Lu. All that baggage. It must be so heavy. How does a normal-looking guy like Seth get into something like Hunting in the first place?

"The shoreline is *lousy* with psychic residue," Ivan comments, breaking my mini-trance. "It's because of what I was saying before, you know, about the SS *Morro*."

I clear my throat. "You guys are going to come back yourselves later to take readings. Isn't that what you told me during our interview?"

"But now we're going to show you how the Devil Hunters do paranormal investigation," Seth answers. "You're a Leader. We *will* bring you over to our side. It's in your blood."

"And since the cleromancy was so persuasive . . ." The comment is still somehow tinged with foreboding that I push away, out of my mind: *blood*.

"Be patient. Genie's readings are never wrong," Seth insists. "We're used to the skepticism, Winnie." (Again, again—there's that tiny sizzle, that *frisson* at hearing my name roll off of his tongue.) "We can wait you out."

There's a snap. A small flash sparkles in the air. "Just testing the filter," Amanda explains. She peeps out from behind her tiny phone lens. "We're rolling. I bought tons of extra data, just for this summer. Who's your favorite Hollywood scout?" She flashes a gleaming white, movie-star smile. "Mom says it's a write-off. Say cheese, Winnie. You love horror movies? Now's your chance to star in one."

NINE

I've seen EMF detectors in movies, obviously. But I can't say I ever thought I'd be holding one in my hand—with the intention of using it, no less.

"The cornerstone of any good ghost hunt," Seth says. He switches a toggle on the side of the machine so it comes alive, humming in my palm.

"What do they use for the bad ghost hunts?" I murmur.

Seth smiles. I look up so I don't have to look at him. The night sky is nothing like the one I see back home. It's black, misted over like stretched-thin cotton wool, a veil, not quite smothering us.

"Pay attention," Casey says to me. "Quit joking around, or give the EMF reader to someone else."

Believe it or not, her words hold little malice, Lu. In fact, she makes a pretty good point. "Sorry. I don't want to screw up your investigation." I actually find myself meaning it, to the extent that I *can* mean something like this, something in this context. I'm a skeptic, but why should I ruin the fun for everyone else?

Seth reaches out, curls my fingers around the meter and I freeze. "Just be open-minded," he whispers.

"Okay," I whisper back. It stands against my best judgment, against every single thing that makes me who I am. Then again, that judgment, good or bad—all of my so-called *me* . . . it brought me to this place. That's what this summer boils down to: Me. Who I am. Who I should be.

"Okay." It bears repeating.

"You're measuring the electromagnetic charge of the atmosphere," Seth explains. "Here"—he points to the screen, which blinks *0.0* with assured insistence—"is your base level. When the numbers go up . . ."

"There's something in the air?"

He flicks his gaze from the screen to my eyes. "Yes. 'Something.'"

"And Ivan's infrared camera *sees* it?" (I actually asked this question, Lu, with a straight face, wanting to know.)

"More or less." Ivan waves a clunky device that resembles an old-fashioned telescope. "Picks up auras."

"So you just, uh, hit record with that thing, and let it go through the investigation?"

Possibly sensing my genuine curiosity, Casey is gentler than I'd expect in her reply. "Yeah. During the investigation, I mostly just leave it running. I mean, I'm watching the sound waves on the recorder screen to catch any real blips in the radar, but generally, the EVP—electronic voice phenomena—only comes out in the playback. That's the whole point—it picks up things you don't hear *during* the investigation. You have to be really patient, receptive, sift through a lot of white noise on the recording. But it's worth it."

"Winnie *is* receptive," Seth says.

I glance down at my EMF meter. *0.0, 0.0, 0.0.* Flashing like a screaming red pulse.

"Being receptive is what leaves a person open to being taken for a ride," I hear myself say. I'm trying Lu, I promise I am, but I have to be real. *Being receptive* is what leads a person to wonder if the runes are going to contain a message from her dead mother. *Being receptive* is what leads a person to crushing disappointment, again and again and again.

The meter sizzles and pops in my palm, as if in response to my thoughts. The reading doesn't change, even though my heart thumps. *Ghosts. Don't. Exist.*

"No one's trying to trick you, Winnie," Seth says. "This isn't a game."

I don't know how to reply to that. *Deflect, deflect.* "So, um, what are we thinking? SS *Morro Castle* survivors?"

"Uh, sure," Seth says. "Maybe. But that's not who we're looking for. This area is more haunted than that."

"Wait!" Amanda cries. She fiddles with something on her phone. "Say that part again. But, like, more dramatically, if you can." She holds the phone up to Seth's face, so close he shifts back slightly. *"This area is more haunted than just the SS Morro crash,"* she prompts. "What does that mean?"

Seth faces the camera head-on. "Have you heard the term, 'wreckers'?"

I shake my head. *Wreckers.* It sounds so violent, so literal. Nothing ghostly about that word at all. The EMF meter pops, gives a jiggle, and a jolt travels from my fingertips through the length of my spine.

TEN

"Rolling," Amanda says. "No—wait." She taps at her phone, lifts it back up and focuses on Casey, who's adopted an appropriately somber demeanor. "*Now* we're rolling." She nods at Casey. "I mean: *Action.*"

Casey smoothes her hair out of her eyes. "I'm Casey Whitter, here with Seth Jarvis and Ivan Fell. The three of us, in affiliation with the Asbury Park Paranormal Odditorium, are official paranormal investigators, and Hunters of the New Jersey Devil." She pauses, looking uncertain. "Was that okay?"

Amanda nods. "Great. Don't worry about multiple takes or anything. The whole point of this is to be totally DIY about it. So when you're going, just keep going. Like, unless you actually hear me yell *cut.*"

"Right, okay," Casey says. Her eyes dart back and forth in some kind of silent evaluation. "Where was I?" Then she readjusts, as if remembering that ghost hunting is serious business with a capital Biz, and her mouth resets to sullen.

"We're here with Winnie Flynn, niece of *Fantastic, Fearsome* franchise creator, Maggie Leader"—this part, somewhat reluctantly—"at Convention Hall in Asbury Park."

Amanda sweeps the camera in a wide panorama. I flinch involuntarily and Ivan rushes beside me, props my EMF reader-holding hand up into range. He waves my hand back and forth like a puppet, joking. I shrug him off with a mini-glare.

"As you can see," Casey says, acknowledging our little moment of theatricality, "Winnie is monitoring our EMF reader tonight, and Ivan is behind the infrared lens, and I've got our EVP recorder going, as usual. As our paranormal expert, Seth is going to be conducting the investigation. He'll tell you a little more about why we're here, and what we're looking for."

Seth shuffles forward, clearly not 100 percent comfortable with his roll as spokesperson. He shoves his hands into the pockets of his cargo shorts.

"Yeah." He coughs and clears his throat self-consciously. "Yes," he says with more authority now. "This area retains a *lot* of psychic residue." He gazes directly into the camera, directly into the soul of our imaginary audience. And even though he's not looking at me, Lu, I feel his gaze. "Honestly, I always say you can feel it, just standing here. The energy." He pulls his hands from his pockets and holds them palms up, as if to say, *Well? Can you?*

On cue, Ivan and Casey share a meaningful look with Seth. *We can*, they communicate to each other, wordlessly. *We can*. I want to laugh. Or scream. *Really?*

Because even though I'm creeped out, the reader still says 0.0—that's a big, honking *nada* to you and me, Lu—so am I the one who should feel embarrassed here?

Amanda swivels the camera my way. "Winnie, you totally deny the existence of psychic phenomenon, even though

Maggie Leader is your aunt. So, are you saying you don't feel *any* energy in the air?"

Yes. Yes, Amanda. I'm saying *exactly* that, of course—but I don't appreciate being called out. On tape, no less. "I . . ." I falter. The EMF reader feels heavy in my palm. Like a Halloween costume accessory, a toy. "I just want proof. Evidence," I say finally. "Isn't that what most people are looking for?"

Isn't it?

"Fair enough," Seth says easily. "That makes total sense. And that's easy. Seriously. We can get you that." It's a promise: thoughtful, close, intimate.

"So, let's talk about the SS *Morro Castle,*" Amanda says, eager.

"Well, I think Ivan and Casey covered a lot of that in their interviews already," Seth says smoothly. "So let's not, uh, bother repeating ourselves."

"Good call," Amanda replies.

I wonder if I'm the only one of our group that can tell she's irked by Seth's dismissal. I wonder, Lu, if I'm slowly edging toward that point where I understand her in that intimate way that girls—that *friends*—understand each other, the way you and I do.

Couldn't be.

Besides, her annoyance fades when she opens her mouth again. She's a pro, that one. "You mentioned the word *wreckers.*"

That word. Mysterious, romantic, gothic, and ripe.

Seth grins. "I did."

He climbs up onto the boardwalk railing, legs dangling against the metal bars, arms balanced across the top posts on either side of him. He turns first toward the WELCOME TO ASBURY PARK sign that spans the archway from Convention Hall to the Paramount Theater.

Some of the shuffling tourists are mildly curious about the

cluster of us here on the railing, but most are indifferent, on their way to somewhere else, some other place in time. There is an energy here, yes. And while it may not be humming with enthusiasm or strength, it is, nonetheless, the energy of life.

So I'm still waiting on Seth's proof.

"The *Morro Castle* crashed in 1934," Seth says. "But almost a hundred years earlier, this beach saw the destruction of a different ship. The *New Era.*" He takes a beat, plays for the camera. It surprises me that he knows to do this, knows *how* to do this. "Ironic name. Hopeful. It was an immigrant ship. You see . . . *wrecking* is the practice of looting from a ship-wrecked vessel foundering near the shore. Once upon a time, it was how some ancient kingdoms built their wealth."

"Ancient kingdoms," I echo flatly. I have to say something because we're entering *crock-of-shit* territory, now, Lu.

Seth and Amanda both turn to me.

"Come on," I say.

"Yeah, why are we talking about ancient kingdoms? Can't we get to the *ghost* stuff?" Ivan agrees, which annoys me more than if no one agreed with me at all. I roll my eyes. But just as I do, the EMF reader crackles in my hand. I look down.

0.5.

Ivan raises an eyebrow, points at the readout. I shrug, gesture toward a harried young mother on a cell phone dashing past us. *Life, you see?* Because Lu, I keep telling them all—I *did* my homework: a 0.5 reading could easily be the result of small electronic appliances in the vicinity. Larger surges in activity could come from brewing storm systems. EMF detectors are famously unreliable tools. Electric blankets, hair dryers, television sets—they all produce electromagnetic pulses. *Things* do. And people do, too. We all pulse. We all radiate.

0.5.

I shake my head. *It's not proof,* is the unspoken commentary. Seth seems to understand, picks up where he left off.

"So wreckers," he goes on, "were worse than the typical plunderers. They would lure ships to the shoreline. Like sirens, in the old legends, I mean. They'd hang lanterns along the shore, create the appearance of a moored ship or a lighthouse. Approaching vessels would see the lights and misjudge how shallow the waters were . . ."

A hissing sounds from the machine in my hand. *0.7.*

It's nothing. I insist upon it: *It's nothing. We all pulse. We all radiate.*

Seth leaves the sentence hanging. He glides from the railing back down onto the boardwalk. Ivan and Casey scramble after him, grabbing at equipment and making space for him as he leads us forward. Amanda taps at her phone a few times, then raises it again, keeping Seth in frame, stark against the monochrome night sky.

I bring up the rear, EMF detector in hand. *0.7. 0.5. 0.7. 0.2. 0.0.*

It's energy. It's life.

People give us a wide berth. Soon, we're alone at the edge of the deck, flush against the waterfront, feeling its spray on our skin.

"Disease caused the *New Era* to crash," Seth says, apparently picking up his monologue. "It was pretty common on ships back then. Close quarters. One person has some illness and soon it's spread through the group. Factor in the hygiene issues, and it's amazing any ships ever made it to shore with any live bodies at all."

"So gross," Casey comments, but she's grinning.

"Wreckers had lured the ship to shore, of course. Once it crashed, they killed everyone on board who was still alive."

I peer over the edge of the deck, down toward the sand. It's mucky in this light, like quicksand or mud. I shiver.

Seth is staring down there, too. "The wreckers dragged the bodies to shore and spread them out. Then they cut off all their clothes."

"Why?" I ask in a choked breath.

"Immigrants traveling to a new country usually sewed their valuables into their clothing," Ivan says, pragmatic.

The thought, the mental image of all of those sick, ravaged bodies, naked on the sand . . . "Oh," I manage, hoarse. "So you're saying those passengers . . . they're haunting this building?"

"Well, duh. But *we're* not the only ones saying it," Casey corrects me. "That's not the end of the story."

0.5. 0.0. The reader buzzes in my hand.

"Turns out, tides are kind of an unreliable method for disposing of bodies," Seth says. "It only took a few days before the naked corpses from the *New Era* started turning up on nearby beaches. Also, bits of ship wreckage, caught in the drift. The authorities pieced together what happened, and collected the bodies as they washed up."

"A very tidy ending to a gruesome story?" I ask, hopeful.

Seth shakes his head and points behind us. "They had to store the bodies someplace, so they took them to this building. The building that's now Convention Hall."

My stomach roils. The meter buzzes. *0.8.*

"For whatever reason, it became a grotesque sort of attraction," he continues. "People would come to see the bodies, not to identify them, but just for their own amusement. They'd pay money for admittance."

My palm is electric. But I'm frozen. I can't breathe. *1.0. 1.2. 1.7.*

"The numbers don't lie," Ivan observes, peeking at the counter.

My throat tickles and I swallow down a cough, thinking: *But the numbers do lie! They definitely, completely do.*

Although I'm the one lying now.

There's something here, Lu. There's an energy that is or isn't what's being picked up on the reader, and it's skimming the surface of my skin, splitting me into fragments because: *I feel it.* But I keep my face neutral, as best as I can. Whatever I'm feeling? The numbers aren't proof. Of anything.

I look to Seth. He's staring at Convention Hall.

"Genie's got all the investigations filed and documented," Casey chimes in. "But there's more. Performers. At the Paramount. Lots of them talk about how they, um, *feel* something when they're onstage. Like they can sense a presence."

"Oh, they *feel something*?" I snip. "And I'm sure they're all completely sober when they take the stage, right?"

This has somehow become personal. Possibly, it's related to the vibrations in my palm, that ones that snake down my spine, setting my toes and fingertips on fire.

Casey sighs. "Look, we can't *make* you believe. But what does that thing say now?"

"There are tons of people wandering around," I mutter. *"Emitting energy."* I can't even bring myself to tell her: *2.5.*

She lets out a disappointed sigh. Then she takes a deep breath. She lets a calm wash over her. She closes her eyes for a beat. When she opens them, she speaks again.

"We are here to contact the spirits who perished on the *New Era*." She enunciates, the words loud and clear and slow, without a trace of self-consciousness or hesitation. She *projects.* "If you are the energy we sense, please give us a sign."

The EMF detector hisses like a cobra. I flinch. *3.3.*

"We know you likely linger on our plane out of anger, out of fear. Perhaps you're seeking revenge." She holds her hands out facedown, at arm's length, like she's grounding herself, like she's releasing her words into the atmosphere in some physical way.

"But those who have brought you harm are long gone. We implore you to move on, to find peace."

4.1. 4.9. 5.6.

"There is no solace for you here."

6.8. 7.0. I'm a jagged fork of lightning, poised to slash the sky in two.

9.9. The reader has become a live thing in my hand, jittering and pricking at me like a wild animal. *10.6.* I bite back a gasp. *11.2.* I wiggle my fingers around the device, wanting to be rid of it, winding up, preparing to throw it at one of the Hunters—anything to get it *out of my hand,* away from my body, out of contact with my smoking, boiling skin—when Amanda shrieks and drops her phone.

"What? What happened?" Casey drops to her knees, scrambles to retrieve the phone. "It's fine. No damage," she proclaims, straightening again.

Amanda offers her a grateful look, one hand still clapped in shock over her mouth.

"What did you see?" Seth asks, brusque. He reaches out, pulls the phone away from Casey. He taps at the screen a few times, presumably rewinding the footage. "Did you get any . . ." He smiles. "Yup. Jackpot."

My skin explodes in gooseflesh.

I don't want this jackpot; *STOPSTOPSTOP!* my brain screams. Still, Seth is moving toward me, close and closer, holding out the phone.

My eyes find the screen. I can't help myself.

At first, I can't make sense of what I'm seeing. Then my vision adjusts. It's us—mostly Seth and Casey, but there's Ivan eyeing the EVP recorder. And there I am, gazing with dread at the EMF detector in my hand like it's a phantom limb, returned. All of our toys, all of the machines—they're all beeping and spiking and flaring the way you might expect. Even if you were a skeptic. *Especially* if you were a skeptic. But there's something else in the shot, too.

More than something. Some-*things*. They appear in the last few seconds of the last few frames. Glowing spheres, floating in the air, reflected in the glassy sheen of the ocean's surface. Hundreds of them.

If I believed in such things, I'd say I was looking at footage of ghosts, Lucia. That's what such luminous orbs are believed to be, among paranormal investigating circles. *Ghosts.* On tape. Right before my eyes.

I say, "It can all be explained away." Which is something, of course, that we all already knew. Except, of course, for that tiny sliver of hope I have. That godforsaken *hope* that still, somehow, remains. That part, I don't get at all. And so for now, it remains my own little secret.

"Explain, *schmexplain.* That's some golden footage right there. We got it. We *did* it! We *rock!* And now, we celebrate!" Amanda says. Her eyes have the shine of a recently indoctrinated Scientologist.

"Food?" I ask. Although my appetite is now fully MIA.

Casey grunts dismissively. "Come on. We're *celebrating.* Screw food. We can do better than that."

Well, we'll see about that, Lu. As usual, I'm the skeptic. I'm sure you'd expect nothing less.

INTERVIEW FOOTAGE—GENIE LOCKWOOD—TAPE
1.2—MUSEUM HISTORY

GENIE sits behind her desk at the Paranormal
Odditorium. DIRECTLY BEHIND HER HEAD a replica
antique WANTED POSTER for the JERSEY DEVIL is
visible. Beside that is a large MAP of DEVIL
SIGHTINGS throughout NJ HISTORY. A small plastic
BOBBLEHEAD DEVIL dances at the edge of her desk.

GENIE:
Mind if I smoke?

She produces a TILLIE-HEADED ZIPPO LIGHTER from a
desk drawer, flicks it open and lights a FAT CIGAR.

INTERVIEWER (W.F., OFFSCREEN):
Oh, well . . . I'm not really—okay, um. But
maybe—well, it *is* your place. So . . .

GENIE:
(laughs, takes a deep, full puff)

That it is, hon. That it is. So why don't you
just relax, and we can have a little chat?
I doubt you were sent to lecture me on the dangers of smoking.

(OFFSCREEN):
Good point. Right.

(small whisper)

Smoking kills.

GENIE:
Is that so? Yeah, maybe I heard something
like that, once. But, I've got *much* bigger
things to worry about down here.

(OFFSCREEN):
So you're a Hunter, too, in a way? And all of
these things are, um . . . this is your
collection of spoils?

GENIE:
(leans forward, ashes cigar)

Listen, Winnie—I'm not a Hunter the way that
little girl, that Casey, or even Ivan is—

(OFFSCREEN):
Even though you work with them.

GENIE:
Yeah, I work with them. And they're good at what
they do, you know. *Seth* is, anyway. He's the
real deal.

(pauses, smiles)

Cute, too, right?

(OFFSCREEN):

I—um . . .

GENIE:

Calm down, your face is going to catch fire,
Winnie Flynn. You're adorable. So, Flynn . . .
that's your father's name, huh?

(OFFSCREEN):

Yeah, but this interview is really about you—

GENIE:

It's your mother, isn't it? Who's Maggie's
sister?

(beat)

(OFFSCREEN):

Was. She's not . . . I mean, my mother's not
anything anymore. She died. Three months ago.

GENIE:
(softens)

Oh, sweetie. I'm sorry to hear that. Was it
sudden?

(OFFSCREEN):

For me, yeah. Probably not so much for her.

(beat)

It was suicide.

Genie LEANS FORWARD, EXTENDS HER ARM, putting a
HAND on WINNIE'S KNEE just out of camera frame.

> GENIE:
> That's gotta be hard, hon. I *am* sorry.
> Were they close, your mother and Maggie, then?

> (OFFSCREEN):
> The first time I met Maggie was at my mother's
> funeral. As far as I know, they never talked.
> But what do I know? I mean, as far as I *know*, my
> mother was happy. And then she killed herself.

> GENIE:
> (sympathetic)

Yeah, I got the impression there was some . . .
family backstory, after we did your reading.

> (sighs)

Family is hard. It's always complicated. Lots of
history. It's the same with me and my sisters.

> (OFFSCREEN):
> Do you have a big family? Are they in the . . .
> ghost business, too?

> GENIE:
> Too big. Not big enough. Anyway, none of them

stuck around here. And yeah, they have the gift,
like me. But I haven't seen them in decades.

(shrugs)

Sometimes that's just the way life goes.

(OFFSCREEN):
But they had psychic—er, paranormal—or, whatever
you call them—They had that, too? You guys are
all . . . certain? You're *convinced* of this?

GENIE:
(grins, blinks rapidly, tearing up)

Of course I am. Winnie, I do know a little bit
about what you're going through. I'm not gonna
say it's the exact same thing. We both know
that's a lie, but I've been there. I have my own
demons.

(OFFSCREEN):
I'm sorry.

GENIE:
Of course you are, hon.

(sniffs, tries to brighten)

But the good news is, I got the *real, literal*
demons here, too. Although I know you don't buy
it. You're still holding out.

(OFFSCREEN):
I don't. I . . . *can't.* So prove me wrong. I
mean . . . that's what I keep telling Seth:
Prove me wrong. *Show me.*

GENIE:
Oh, honey, I'm pretty sure by the time you're
done filming, you won't need any proof from me.

(OFFSCREEN):
(snorts)

That's what they all say.

GENIE:
Yeah, but I'm that one who *knows* these things.
It's in my blood. Hell, it's in *your* blood.
You'll see.

CUT

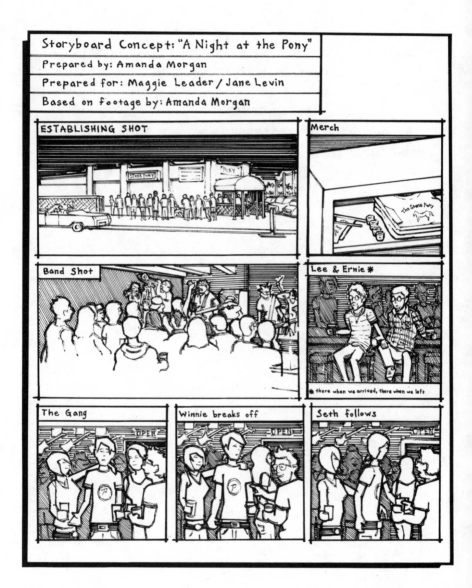

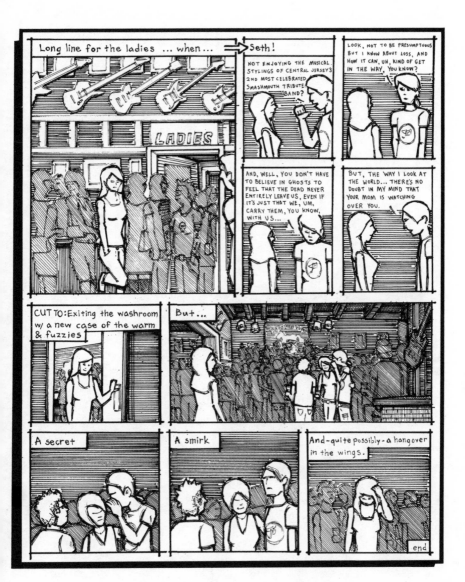

ELEVEN

My motel room is tilted. It's the first thing I notice when I get back from The Stone Pony: the room is tilted, shifted at an odd angle not generally encountered in structurally sound buildings.

Huh. What do you know about that, *Lu?*

I hiccup.

Then I giggle. Then I wobble just the littlest bit. I reach out and grab the corner of the cheap dresser against the wall and think about the EMF reader, about gravity and energy and magnetic pull, and I wonder, just for a knife's edge of a moment, if I'm not currently experiencing some sort of proof, as Seth might call it, right here, right now, in room 24 of the Sea Breeze Lodge. Some sort of magical energy.

Wait, no. I'm just drunk.

I mean, it's not like I've never snuck a shot or two from my parents' liquor cabinet, or sipped tentatively at a watery beer at one of the parties you dragged me to. I'm a person, a relatively *normal* person—we can both agree on that, yes? Up until three months ago, I was reasonably socially adjusted.

The girls on the track team, Morgan from my photography elective . . . you, of course . . . and even—well, there were a *few* fumbling, date-ish kinds of things here and there.

No, I'm not Amanda, with the silky-smooth perma-blowout and game-show hostess smile, and those magical jeans of the constantly perfect fit. But I'm normal enough. Or I was. Like, a basically normal teenage girl. And so, I've had a drink or two before.

But this is different. This is *drunk.* This is room-tilting, hiccuping, suddenly-and-against-all-odds-questioning-my-belief-in-the-paranormal *drunk.* And while I'm feeling pretty mellow about it in the moment—*here comes another giggle, look at that, Lu*—I have a feeling tomorrow morning is going to be a different story.

Tomorrow morning. Early call time. *Just like every other morning, Winnie.*

The floor sways beneath me and I grip the dresser edge like my life depends on it, like it's the very last object in the entire universe keeping me tethered to the surface of the Earth. I should wash my face, drink some water. That will help. That much I can remember from my passing-for-normal days.

Slowly, cautiously, I inch my way to the bathroom. It's touch and go for a minute while I corner the bed, not a lot of excess floor space here at the good old Sea Breeze Lodge—*Asbury Park is still in its economic turnaround stage, or haven't you heard?*—and I stumble, collapse onto the bed for a second, wanting to disappear into it but remembering the original goal—*water!* flashing like a beacon inside my brain—and hoist myself back up and through the bathroom door.

But it turns out the bathroom is basically a black hole. Which is weird. Unexpected, I mean. Or—wait, the lights are off.

That's the problem. Yes, that makes much more sense, Lu.

I slap my hand along the wall beside the toilet, groping for the switch, *pat, pat, pat,* about as gentle as a bear under the influence of psychotropic drugs . . . *Pat. Flick.* The lights flip on. The bathroom is engulfed, there's a solar flare roaring to life around me. A wave of red washes over me—just the beer, again—and I steady myself, blink a few times.

Balance back, I open my eyes.

And then.

The room shifts, tilts again. Seems to collapse in on itself, an Escher painting come to life. I'm upside down, backward, swimming, spinning, spiraling off into the atmosphere. And it's not the beer. (I don't *think* it's the beer.)

No. It's definitely not.

It's the *mirror.*

There's something written—scrawled, really, like a ransom note or graffiti art, rushed and jagged and sinister. There's something scrawled in bright red lettering, the color of a fresh wound, the color of . . . a note. For me.

I stumble back, banging against the wall. This time it's definitely not the beer *or* anything else. This time, it makes perfect sense that I'd be knocked senseless, the universe inverting here in this tiny motel bathroom, because this time, there is a *message* for me, and the message says "*NOT A SUICIDE.*"

There's only one suicide that these words can be referring to. Only one that would mean anything to me.

Lucia:

How did my mother die?

THERE WAS A FOGGY, *murky blackness. I fell into it, backward, and then I was sinking, drowning. There was a rushing in my ears, roaring like the ocean, and suddenly the black is the Atlantic at some unnamed, deep-night hour . . .*

I am in Asbury Park, here and not-here, somehow. And through the moonlight, paper-white images bob, float, roll to the surface of the water, drifting toward the surf.

Bodies. Naked, carried in a slow, rhythmic sway to the shoreline, glowing and otherworldly. In the distance, there is a flashing light, alien blue. From here, from this not-space I currently occupy above the landscape, it appears to be a lighthouse. A lantern. A beacon. It looks to be one of those things.

But it's not. I know that.

Wreckers, *I think.*

One body is different than the rest. It's not the ghastly fish-belly white of the other corpses.

It's red.

But its hair is chestnut brown. Sensibly bobbed, and I know that haircut, I know every single strand on that head because I have almost the exact same haircut, the same head, the same face, myself. I keep my hair slightly *longer because isn't that what daughters are supposed to do? Rebel?*

I would get so angry when she'd finish the fancy shampoo! Why did I get so angry about such a small, stupid thing? How did I not realize how utterly, incredibly lucky I was to have a mother to finish our shared shampoo bottle in the first place?

That's whose body it is, without a doubt. My mother's. Dead. Bloodied and limp against the dark, hard-packed wet sand.

In the distance, I hear a jingle: coins, spoils being shaken and salvaged from the ruin. I feel a presence bearing down, creeping close. I hear the sharp whip of something unfurling, unfolding—a wing expanding, perhaps?—and from the corner of my eye there is the faintest of flickers, the quick release of a forked tail. It is followed by a howl, primal and wrenching. And as it echoes, it draws ever closer to my mother's body.

I try to speak, to form words, to force breath past my lips, but I'm coughing, I'm choking, my throat is seizing like a fist. The Devil, *I think.* Wreckers. *Be careful, Mom!*

But it doesn't matter, of course.

She's already dead.

AND THEN THERE'S A pounding. It's louder and more insistent than the low, ragged moans of my half-imagined Devil. My eyes flutter open. I'm staring at the Sea Breeze Lodge's water-stained, stucco ceiling. It is oddly bright. It occurs to me that I've been dreaming. There was no Devil. There were no wreckers. Not here, anyway. It was all in my head. The knocking, however, is all too real.

And good-freaking-*lord,* is it loud.

I roll over. The water glass on my nightstand is nearly full. All my good intentions: no match for the blackness, when it came. No wonder the inside of my head feels like a construction site.

"Coming!" I semi-shout, wincing as the syllables bounce against my skull. The clock next to my water glass reads 7:02.

Call time. Call time is soon. I should be grateful for whoever is banging away on the door. Certainly, I wasn't lucid enough to set an alarm last night. And even the garbage trucks failed to cut through my comatose state.

Basically, *I'm* wrecked, Lu.

I rise and the floor buckles under me. Or, that could be my knees. *Breathe.*

"Coming," I say again, more quietly this time, tugging my T-shirt down past my knees and shuffling to the door.

"Thought maybe you'd need an extra boost this morning."

It's Casey, shock of all shocks, posed in the doorway. She has an unfamiliar soft look on her face, as though, for the immediate moment at least, she doesn't actively dislike me. It's very unsettling, Lu. Particularly coming off of such a fitful night, such a horrific dream. She's holding a to-go cup of coffee in one hand and an economy-sized bottle of aspirin in the other, and she's got a jumbo bottle of water wedged against her, tucked between her elbow and her armpit.

"A cure for what ails you?" she says in my slack-jawed silence.

"Oh," I mumble, because *this is so weird* is not an appropriate response to an act of generosity, no matter how weird said generous act truly is.

"I did a run for the whole crew this morning." She sidles past me and into my room, closing the door with a definitive bang behind her. This revelation does not make the situation any less weird. The last time people were this nice to me was my mother's funeral. It was much more understandable then.

I accept the water and the aspirin with as much energy as I can muster, which turns out to be a surprising amount, tearing greedily into the medicine bottle and twisting off the water cap, guzzling down three pills and half of the water in one go. When I'm finished, I look up, a trickle of water running down my chin like I'm a feral animal of some kind. I wipe it with the back of my hand.

"Thanks," I manage.

"Last night was fun, huh?" she asks, as though we're not reenacting a bit from the theatre of the absurd together. "I think we're all feeling it today."

"Yeah." It seems I'm only capable of one-word responses. Thankfully, Casey doesn't seem to mind.

"Are you still feeling iffy about the paranormal stuff? Even after what you saw on the EMF readers and on the vid?" she goes on. "You can't be. Tell me you're not even, like, a smidge convinced." (The word *smidge* automatically engenders a bit of pity.) "You were great with the reader last night. I don't know if it was because you're such a skeptic or what, but you didn't flinch at all, even when the numbers started to climb."

"Don't call me a hero," I hear myself grumble.

Her smile is intact. *What is her angle? Is there an angle?* Is there something wrong with *me?* Why do I assume there has to be an angle? Rhetorical question, Lu. Shush.

"Cute." She takes a deep breath, like she's collecting herself. "Maybe I was a little hard on you because you were— *are*—Maggie's niece. Maybe I kind of held that against you."

"Maybe." Honesty is always appreciated. You know that about me.

"But if you can hold your own on the investigations, then we need you . . ." She trails off. Now that she's come out with all of that—whatever *that* was—she seems slightly abashed, drained.

"Um, great," I reply, because what else is there to say, really? Getting along is better than not getting along. Right?

"So—hey, can I just use your bathroom for a sec? I'm already checked out of my room and I'm *dying*." She does a little jig in place to demonstrate just how bad this dying experience is. It's actually quite jaunty for someone who claims to be hungover but, you know, she's a college girl, she probably has more experience with hangovers than we do. "Sure, of course." I point in the direction of the bathroom, but she's already on her way, doing that awkward shuffle around the corner of the bed because of the teeny-ness and weird layout of the room.

It's not until she closes the bathroom door that I remember. *NOT A SUICIDE.*

I go so rigid I almost drop the water bottle. "Wait!" I call.

But obviously, it's too late since she's already in there, and once you're in there, there's nothing to see *except* for the mirror, unless one happens to be exceptionally focused on the moldy shower curtain, which—why? And then I hear the toilet flush and it's well beyond too late. My heart pounds. Did she see it? What will she say? What will she *think*? Why was it there in the first place?

How did you die, Mom?

"Did you say something?" Casey is out of the bathroom now, wiping her hands against her gray cargo shorts. She does not wear the expression of a person who's just glimpsed a horrifying message scrawled in maybe-blood. But maybe she's just got a great poker face. I don't really know her, after all. And her behavior this morning has certainly called into question the things I thought I *did* know.

"I . . ." *How to go about this?* "Did you see anything in there?"

Her lips turn down. "Meaning . . . you didn't forget to flush, if that's what you're getting at? Don't worry, you did."

Ew. "No . . ." I shake my head. "I thought . . ." For lack of words, I push past her into the bathroom myself. Maybe the message was written in invisible ink. Maybe it's magic, and I'm the only one who can see it, like the boy who saw dead people in that Bruce Willis movie, the one with the twist that was totally untwist-y by the time I got around to seeing it. Maybe it was all in my head to begin with. There was that kooky dream, after all.

The mirror is empty. Clean.

Well, not *clean*, per se, not 100 percent, since house-keeping isn't high up on the priority list of the Sea Breeze Lounge's staff. But there's no message. No ominous red graf-fiti. *Definitely* no proof that I am not, in fact, completely and totally certifiable.

What is going on, Lucia?

People have been known to have severe mental break-downs after the death of a loved one. It is entirely possibly that I am full-on losing my mind. Maybe this is how it begins, Lu. Sign-mirages in the bathroom and drunken Devil-dreams and a sudden wavering in my heretofore-steadfast disbelief in paranormal phenomena.

I could very well be unraveling. And then what?

"Was there a bug or something in there before?" Casey's voice comes from over my shoulder. "I saw something in my shower last night, I swear it had, like, twenty legs. It went down the drain before I could pass out, thank *God*. Bugs are a million billion times creepier than *anything* supernatural I've seen, no lie."

I feel queasy, not only from the hangover. "You didn't see—there was, I don't know, something on the mirror last night. Or, that's what I thought, anyway. Maybe I was just too drunk. Maybe I was dreaming. Something . . . I don't know."

There it is again: *I don't know, I don't know, I don't know.* My brain is a loose thread that someone has tugged at, stitches of a sweater tangling into a trail of frayed yarn.

"On the mirror?" Casey finishes. She shakes her head. "Just that icky grease print that I'm guessing was there when you first checked in."

And there's that tightening in my throat again, that tingle that grows. It expands like a wet sponge. I cough, sputter, going red in the face. Stupid Jersey allergies. Just what I need right now. *I am allergic to this state, Lucia.*

"Easy there." Casey pats me on the back. She takes the water bottle from my hand, unscrews it, brings it to my lips. "Drink."

I do.

"Knock-knock." There's someone else, a boy someone else, at the door.

"It's open," Casey answers.

And then there's *the* boy someone else, Seth, pony-tail slicked back, looking fresh from the shower, T-shirt bearing Hans and Leia silhouettes with the phrases I LOVE YOU, and I KNOW above and below. He's holding a to-go cup that matches my own, which shouldn't be a surprise— Casey did say she bought for everyone. Maybe they went on the coffee run together, Lu. That's the party line, anyway, right? They are *Fantastic, Fearsome: NJ*'s very own Hans and Leia. Or they will be by the time the editing's done.

"You're not ready," Seth observes, his eyes grazing the hem of my T-shirt, which suddenly feels impossibly short, and also? It wouldn't be the worst thing if I were wearing a bra right now, Lu. I would not exactly mind that.

"It'll take me five minutes." Because I'm not one of Those Girls, the ones that primp, like Amanda, or even the ones that take the time to dye vivid blue streaks in their hair, like Casey. I'm nobody's Leia, which is why it doesn't matter that

Seth's seeing me like this. Though I could have stood to brush my teeth, maybe. Definitely.

"It's . . ." He glances at his geek watch, some kind of Bluetooth-y thing that connects via the "cloud" (What "cloud," Lu, and is it really any different than an EMF recorder? What sorcery is this that we live with?) "Seven eighteen. We've got to be out of here by seven forty-five if we want to get there by nine."

"Get there." Yes, nine, that sounds familiar, but my head (like my tongue) is still thick with cotton and I've blanked, absolutely, as to where we're going today. We're done with Asbury Park, but that's all I can remember.

NOT A SUICIDE. That tingling ball in the back of my throat. *Wreckers. And maybe the Devil himself.* A sweater, stitches falling out one by one.

"Overlook," Seth says. "Essex County. We're heading north. You're going to see a whole different Jersey."

"Overlook," I repeat. That's right. That's the next week of filming, that's our next location. Not the hotel from the *The Shining* (though what a *fantastic* coincidence!), but an asylum. Now defunct. A stark contrast to the boardwalks of the Jersey Shore. *Real Housewives* territory, Sopranos-land. *Joisey.*

"Meet you out there," Seth says, and then he's gone.

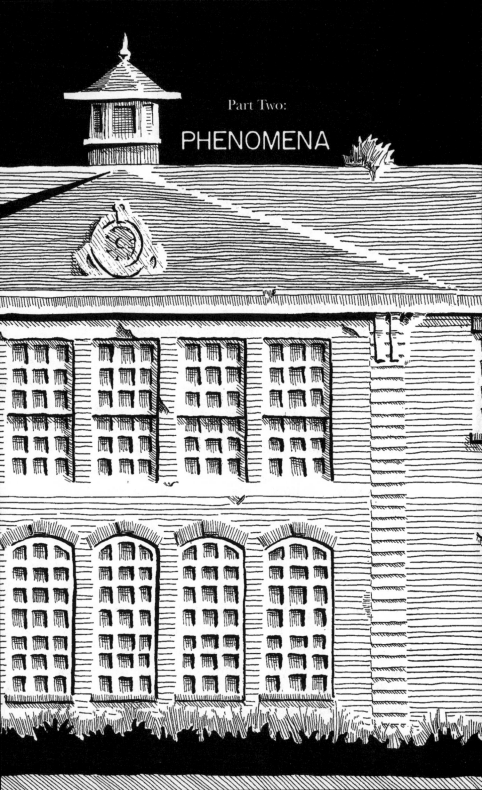

Part Two:

PHENOMENA

OVERLOOK INSANE ASYLUM (1895–1974)
Cedar Hill, NJ

History

In February of 1895, more than 300 acres of land were officially designated as the location of the Overlook Asylum, otherwise known as the Essex County Asylum for the Insane. Located in the idyllic, leafy hamlet of Cedar Hill, the facility housed mentally ill patients requiring daily care. The site was selected due to the town's eponymous hill; its remote, elevated location was believed to be beneficial for convalescence. The complex came to be known as Overlook, due to its location overlooking the Peckham River. The hospital quickly reached full capacity. By the 1940s, thousands of patients were housed at the facility at any given time, and the hospital was so large that it had its own train stop on the Caldwell Branch of the Erie Railroad.

But the asylum's patients never experienced the solace they were promised with admission. Indeed, the Overlook's patients were subject to appalling levels of neglect, including a horrific incident in 1917 where twenty-four patients were left to freeze to death in their own beds. The hospital is well-known for its heavily documented, invasive, and cruel treatments, including barbaric levels of EST (electroshock therapy), near-constant sedation, and intense hydrotherapy

consistent with "modern-day torture."* Post WWII, a
sharp influx in patient intake meant that the facilities
grew dangerously crowded. Coupled with lack of suf-
ficient personnel on duty, as many as 150 patients went
missing during that time (only a fraction of whom were
ultimately recovered).

The Kallikak Family
Perhaps the most famous (and famously mistreated) of
the Overlook's documented patients was Deborah Kallikak, descended from Martin Kallikak, whose rumored
dalliance with a "feeble-minded barmaid"* led to a lineage of supposedly developmentally disabled persons.
Deborah was admitted in 1910 and treated by the state's
leading eugenicists, who were granted temporary tenure
at Overlook for this particular case study. Deborah had
already birthed several equally stunted children before
arriving at the hospital, and administrators agreed that
such "morally questionable"* genes should not be per-
mitted to reproduce. Thus, in addition to her so-called
therapeutic treatments, Kallikak was subject to a radical
hysterectomy to ensure that she'd bear no other "feeble-
minded" children.

Closing and Beyond
Throughout the 1960s and '70s, the introduction of
new medications meant that mental hospitals and their
methodologies were quickly becoming outdated. The
number of patients that made their way to Overlook
plummeted drastically. In 1974, the Overlook Asylum
closed its doors for good.
    In 1993, part of the facility reopened as a traditional

medical hospital. Many of the buildings on the property, however, were abandoned and left to deteriorate.
Curious locals began to explore them and dozens of
local legends were born. For scores of North Jersey
teens, a visit to the Overlook site remains nothing less
than a rite of passage—going to the "Hilltop," as it is
still called by its numerous crashers, is a surefire way to
test your nerves and impress your friends.

Alleged Paranormal Activity
Countless rumors continue to circulate about the many
unexplainable occurrences that are known to have
taken place at Overlook. Tales are told of escaped luna-
tics roaming the hallways of the derelict buildings and
making their homes in the subterranean tunnels that per-
meate the facility's foundations. Although trespassing is
explicitly forbidden, ghost hunters and other paranormal
investigators have occasionally been granted permission
to explore the old buildings. They've reported incidents
of screaming voices yelling for them to "get out," and
sightings of ghostly children roaming the upper floors of
some of the buildings. Other trespassers speak of unexplainable strange mists, the sound of phantom footsteps,
and a wheelchair that seemingly moves about the hallways
on its own. The atmosphere itself is said to radiate a sense
of fear and foreboding. With ancient hospital beds, gur-
neys, and medical equipment strewn about the place, one
almost can't help but imagine what lurks behind closed
doors.

* *See also: haunted hospitals, asylum, Mother Leeds, Kallikak
family, Northern New Jersey*

TWELVE

"It's just so overdone." This is my refrain as Seth, Amanda, and I make our way down Route 10, passing signs for NORTH-FIELD AVE., TURTLE BACK ZOO, and THE RICHARD J. CODEY ARENA AT SOUTH MOUNTAIN.

"That's where the Devils practice," Seth says.

"Practices what? His kangaroo high jumps?" I ask.

"*Devils,*" Seth says, emphasizing the plural. And then he has to explain through my endless hangover about how the New Jersey NHL team is known as The *Devils,* which of course is generally the first thing people think of when they hear of The Jersey Devil, rather than this D-List mythical creature we're theoretically in search of—and Amanda has to hold back her hysterical laughter at my ridiculous naïveté.

We're driving together to Overlook, just the three of us. Seth is at the wheel because he's actually from Essex County, *Verona,* which is apparently a real place, separate from the setting of *Romeo and Juliet.* We've just hit a local diner—Jersey is *lousy* with diners—since we're in charge of craft services for the morning. The others all went ahead in either the SUV or Maggie's trailer, based on how, um, *dependent* Maggie was feeling about a given person at her time of departure.

Casey and Ivan are in the SUV. Do with that information what you will.

The rental car reeks of bacon and watery coffee, all balanced beside me in the backseat, but that's not why I'm grumpy. The bigger issue here is that I think the whole "haunted asylum" thing is derivative; I've been saying it since we first hit the road, an hour ago. Emotions are running surprisingly high on the topic, I must say.

"It's not *overdone*, it's a *trope*," Amanda repeats yet again. "It's a *classic*. It became classic for a reason. Tropes become tropes when they *ring true*." She's throwing lots of added emphasis into her dialogue for the sake of persuasion. (It's only half working.)

"Besides, are you saying that the 'creepy boardwalk' or 'beach-horror' tropes aren't just as overdone?" Seth puts in. "*Freaks? Carnival of Souls?* Come on—*Psycho Beach Party?* Or even that opening scene from *The Lost Boys?* With the couple making out in the car and then the top gets ripped right off?"

"Vintage Kiefer," I acknowledge. Jack Bauer with a peroxide mullet. Talk about *fantastic*. "Amazing, yes. And no, I am definitely not saying that. The difference is, I *like* the beach. So that was *fun for me*. Whereas, poking around in an abandoned mental hospital sounds like it will be the opposite of fun. For everyone. Not to mention totally cliché in the bad way."

At least, for people (like me, yes) who are creeped out by old medical equipment and other sharp objects. People who may or may not have witnessed a loved one with their wrists freshly slashed by an ostensibly sharp object. For example.

NOT A SUICIDE.

Yes, it's still on my mind. Understandably.

Seth veers off the main road into a so-called "jug handle turn." I'd never once even heard of a jug handle turn before arriving in New Jersey, Lu. But they're the highlight of the transportation infrastructure around these parts. Go figure. Also, there have been many McMansions. Neo-Grecian columns galore, circular driveways packed bumper to bumper with gleaming luxury cars. Tiny little mini-trees obviously freshly transplanted into pristine, Stepford-meets-Sopranos developments.

And the strip malls! Oh, the glory of the strip malls, Lucia. This is a whole new set of clichés, suburbia writ large. This is *Real Housewives* a-go-go territory. Frankly, it makes me wish we were going to be filming some to-be-bleeped-out table-flipping instead. You know, instead of rusted-out operating tables and moldy hydrotherapy tanks.

"I'm calling your bluff," Seth counters. "You're just having a rough morning after a late night. Which I get. We're all feeling it." He doesn't really look like he's feeling it. His eyes are clear and bright, making me crazy with envy. "But you still need to come clean."

"Come clean about *what?*" If only he knew the half of it. *NOT A SUICIDE.* What would Seth say to that, if I were to tell him the truth?

"There's no way you don't love a good insane asylum setting. You're too much of a maven of the genre not to." He gives me an appreciative glance in the rearview mirror, gray eyes gleaming, impossibly.

Maven. I can't say I've ever been called that before. It's a good word, I decide. I'll take it. "Thank you," I mutter. Grudgingly.

"Don't pout," he admonishes. "Come on. Do we need to

have a cast and crew movie night? *Gothika. Session 9. Grave Encounters. Nightmare on Elm Street 3. "*

"People go harsh on sequels, but *Elm Street 3* is *gold,"* I admit. Because: "Dream Warriors 4EVA," right, Lu? How many times have we watched that one? How many sleepovers, bottomless bowls of greasy stove-popped popcorn and waxy, sugary stalks of those satisfyingly plasticky strawberry Red Vines? Not Twizzlers. Never Twizzlers. *Please.* We are better than that.

"Exactly." Seth sounds self-satisfied from his perch behind the wheel. It's cute.

"*Girl, Interrupted,*" Amanda throws in. "I know, not a horror movie, but dudes, that scene with Brittany Murphy and the chicken? Gross." She shudders, and now I can't help but laugh.

"Spoiler alert!" I protest.

"Excuse me, but that movie came out in 1999," Amanda points out. "Angelina took an *Oscar* for it, which was probably, like, ninety-nine percent due to that fright wig they had her wear for the part. *God,* costuming can be such a cheat!"

I glance at the clock on the dashboard. "We're running a little late." Thirty minutes, to be precise. It's 9:30 now. People are going to be angsty about their breakfast.

"Eh, that's, like, the whole thing about filming," Amanda reassured me. "Lots of hurry-up-and-wait. Thirty minutes is within an acceptable window of our call time, especially since we're the ones bearing sustenance. Right now, I predict with ninety-nice percent certainty that Maggie is chain-smoking outside her trailer, watching Jane scream at Ernie about the dangers of backlighting."

She's right. I can picture it. "Poor Ernie."

And all at once we're heading up a hill—the place is called

Overlook, so a hill would make perfect sense—and all I see in front of us is the gentle slope of road and the gnarled trees lining it, low-hanging branches creeping toward us like tentacles. The car is dimmer now, and yes, I'll just cop to it, Lu: I feel uneasy. Hills can be bad news. And then we're at the top of the hill (*The House on Haunted Hill, The Haunting of Hill House, The Hills Have Eyes 1 & 2*), and practically in unison, as though we had planned it, the three of us gasp. Loudly.

It is a magnificent, glorious wreck. And I am immediately terrified.

"We're here," Seth says. "This is Overlook Asylum. What's left of it."

IF THERE'S A COMMON thread to my time in New Jersey, it's that much of this state has seen better days. And yes, I'm probably generalizing. I'll bet lots of the neighborhoods we drove past from Asbury Park to Cedar Hill are perfectly lovely and probably filled with very delightful and upstanding citizens. Probably very few ghosts.

WikiHaunts claims the Overlook was shut down in 1974, but the Internet claims a lot of things. This place looks like it was not so much *closed* as *condemned, abandoned, and left to rot in a postapocalyptic dystopia.* Perhaps in 1874, actually, or even earlier. Glancing at the jagged peaks of the crumbling stone façade, I worry about what it means, truly, that we're going to be sleeping here, or at least, that we're planning to spend the night.

Glancing around at the ruin, I think of the very pragmatic issues of building codes and safety violations. The grounds are sprawling, spanning the length of at least three football fields. (That's an approximation, Lu, obviously you get that the cross-country runners know nothing from team sports).

One massive main hall and various wings and outbuildings splintering out, classic gothic architecture . . . It's one part Hogwarts, two parts Grey Gardens, as envisioned by Guillermo del Toro.

There is a *clock tower*, Lucia.

I flatten my palm over my eyes and press closer to the car window. I catch movement, a dark shadow, at the very top of the turret. It's a bird, an enormous bird. It's far away, but it seems to be looking directly at the car, unblinking, as though it knows we're interlopers and it doesn't approve. Its head is white and its body is speckled brown. And yes, it's only a *bird*, but: *The Birds*, Lucia. And this one is nearly the same size as the rust-scarred clock, or at least, that's what perspective suggests. And it's looking right at us.

Right at *me*.

There's something in the bird's beak, something long and skinny like a branch or a leaf . . . or an animal's tail.

Yeah, an animal's tail.

Oh, vomit.

"Is that a *hawk*?" Amanda asks, her voice shrill. "Oh God, I think it is. A friggin' *hawk*, um, all gory with a rat tail in its mouth!"

She's right. That's exactly what it is. A *friggin' hawk*, Lu. With bloody rat parts hanging from its beak. My stomach lurches. Woozy, I open the back car door. Humid air sucks at me, pulling me from the cocoon of the car into the awful reality of . . . here. Of course, it would be silly to think I could *smell* the rat blood from all the way down on the ground, Lucia. It would be ridiculous.

And yet.

I gag.

Amanda remains in the front seat and shuts her eyes. She

shakes her head back and forth. "Please tell me that's not a *feral* hawk."

"I think technically the term is *wild*," Seth says. "And I don't think it'll bother us if we don't bother it. Birds of prey don't usually mess with creatures bigger than they are."

"Did you see The Birds*?"* Amanda practically shrieks. Even though she's obviously very close to freaking all the way out, I have to say: it's nice that her brain went to the same place that mine did. Silver linings and all, Lucia.

"That was a movie," Seth says calmly.

"*You're* the one who keeps telling us that movies reflect the truth," I point out. And if I sound ever so slightly smug about throwing his philosophy back in his face? Well. What can you do? Even if I don't *really* think that hawk is going to swoop down and peck our eyes out in the dead of night . . . still. It's not like I'm hoping it will stick around, be our mascot, let us dress it in silly T-shirts and feed it from our hands.

"Okay, every movie except *The Birds*," Seth jokes.

I'm not smiling. "It's creepy," I say. That rat tail, and those bloody feathers. It occurs to me that the hawk might be eating the rat for a very good reason. Because there are lots of rats to eat here. Hundreds, maybe. Thousands.

"I cannot believe we have to be here, like, overnight," Amanda says with a grimace. "*You* get the sleeping bag closest to the window in case you're wrong about hawky up there, Seth. You can be our canon fodder."

Sleeping bags. Hmm. I realize I haven't given much thought to sleeping arrangements. I was so busy not wanting to be at the asylum in the first place, it never occurred to me that there could be other, nonmental-patient-ghost-story-related horrors in store for our time here. So now I have at least three things to worry about:

- Possibly homicidal fowl
- The emotional trauma of spending a night in a defunct mental asylum
- And the all-too-real possibility of an awkward game of musical sleeping bags

Trouble. It always comes in threes. Don't tell me it's a cliché, Lu: tropes become tropes when they *ring true*, after all. I think I heard that somewhere.

THIRTEEN

"Are you guys with the TV show?"

I'm still staring at the hawk out of the corner of my eye, willing my stomach to settle, so the question catches me off guard.

When I look up, they're *right there*, two greasy-looking guys vaguely "our" age—that is, somewhere between Seth, Amanda, and my ages. They have wan skin and purplish shadows under their eyes. Taken all together, it is a scene only vaguely less unnerving than the hawk was.

"Um, yeah," I say after I recover. "We're with the show. *Fantastic, Fearsome.* We're PAs. Well, *we* are." I jerk my head toward Seth. "He's the talent. A Devil Hunter."

"Dude," the oilier of the two breathes. The word doesn't seem to call for a specific response, so I don't give one.

"That's cool," the second one agrees.

"Glad you think so," Seth says. His demeanor is friendly but wary, which I guess makes sense when you consider that a self-professed Devil Hunter has probably dealt with more than a few cuckoo paranormal fanatics and weirdos in his time. It's unclear what category Oily and Oilier fall into just yet.

"So, what are you guys doing here?" Amanda asks. "You must've seen the rest of the crew pull up. Were you, like, staking us out?" She gives me a look that says: *I wish our location schedule hadn't been leaked to* Variety *online.* I return one that says: *I'm pretty sure these guys haven't been reading* Variety *online, though.* Not that this makes their shifty, blurred-lens intensity any less discomfiting. Also, it's cool that we're communicating in looks, isn't it, Lu? Another check for the "normal" column. Yay.

"Yup," Oilier confirms. "I mean, not that we were staking you out. We had no idea anyone was coming or anything. But we saw the rest of the crew. They got here, like, half an hour ago. We talked to them and everything. And we even saw Maggie, real quick." This in the hushed, reverent tone generally reserved for sightings of Elvis. Or UFOs. Or, yes: ghosts. He seems to realize how much he's been babbling on and turns a shade of violet, almost like a character from *Willy Wonka.*

My eyes shift between the two. "So, if you didn't know we were going to be here . . ."

Now it's Oily's turn to blush. It doesn't do great things for his complexion, which is speckled with acne scars. "It's just a thing locals do. We camp out here, party on the grounds. Just to be able to say we made it onto the campus, maybe saw something supernatural."

"It's really such a big deal?"

Oilier straightens. "Yeah, I mean, it's not regularly patrolled or anything. But it's private property, and trespassing is strictly verboten. You never know when a security guard is gonna pop up."

"You guys are such total danger junkies, *obvs,*" Amanda cuts in with a smirk. "Life on the edge."

Fantastic, Fearsome had to apply for special permits to be able to shoot here, and *extra*-special paperwork for an overnight stay, so their story makes sense. But it's still pretty smirk-worthy.

Oily somehow, amazingly, completely misses her tone. "You know it," he says, corners of his own mouth turning up right back at her. He points to a small structure past the leftmost wing. It looks like it could have been a chicken coop or a public stockade, maybe a guillotine, once upon a time. Either/or/all of the above, really. "We do campfires over there," he says. "Especially around the seasonal equinoxes, when, like, supernatural charges are supposed to be even stronger in the air and stuff."

Now I have to bite my lip to keep from laughing.

"Maggie said she's going to tape a tour, that we can be on it if we sign releases," he goes on. "Like, on the show. Actually, she seemed kind of excited about the idea. I warned her that, you know, there'd be some, uh, leftovers from our partying left lying around in some places. Things that might not be suitable for the PG-13 crowd and stuff."

He actually *winks*. I hold back another giggle. But somehow it catches in my throat and then I'm coughing again, that weird and uncontrollable cough. Now *my* face is no doubt turning red. But this time, I detect a strange thought. It emerges from the back closets of my brain, half-formed . . .

You wish.

That's what the thought is. As in: you freaking wish you had anything rated R to show us. I see them rushing out to buy beer bottles; I see them pouring them out and fraying their labels—all to make them look enjoyed and discarded, all a vibe for our cameras. I'm 130 percent sure and then some. I don't know how, but I do: they're lying about the partying. I just know it.

For a moment, as my coughing dies down, there's a hum between the three of us that's almost palpable. *You're lying. You're lying. You're full of shit, and we both know it. So just, please . . . come on.*

And then I clear my throat and we all break the mutual staring contest.

"There," Oilier says. He points toward the clock tower. The hawk is gone now, finally. "That's where Mother Leeds killed herself."

"You must know all about that, if you're a Devil Hunter," Oily says.

He looks at Seth: it's a challenge.

"Mother Leeds was never in this hospital," Seth replies evenly. "She gave birth to the Devil in 1775. This place wasn't around then." He sounds bored. I don't blame him; he must get this sort of stuff on a regular basis. Like how doctors are always being asked to do armchair diagnoses at dinner parties.

"Well, duh." Oilier actually says *duh*, Lu, and it's amazing. "Not the *Mother* Mother Leeds."

"Are you high?" I ask, because it seems appropriate.

They ignore me. "Mrs. Kallikak," Oily says. "Believed to be a direct descendent of the Jersey Devil. *Also* believed to be retarded. The whole family was. That's what happens when you inbreed with monsters, I guess. They were locked up here, given electroshock therapy and other crazy treatments." He stiffens, lets his limbs jerk uncontrollably like he's being electrocuted. It's disturbingly convincing. *Lovely.* "*She* was kept in the clock tower room. The ticking drove her crazy. She jumped. *Goodbye, cruel world.*"

I swallow. *NOT A SUICIDE.* All at once, I realize I'm staring at Oily.

He raises an eyebrow. "Legend says they found her body just a few feet from here. We could be standing on an ancient, invisible bloodstain *as we speak.* You know, those molecules, they never completely evaporate."

"Gross," I hiss. I take a step back and grab the car for support, even though I hate myself for doing so. Mothers and self-harm, what can I say; he's hitting me where I live, Lu. I'm not too proud to admit it. But Amanda catches it, and even though our relationship—our *friendship!*—is still new, still fragile like a baby bird (not a hawk), she knows what I'm thinking; she knows why the surface of my skin is radiating discomfort like one giant itch.

"Save it for the cameras," she says. This both shuts the guys up and effectively saves me from a not-too-useful meltdown. Is this what it is to have normal female friendships again, Lu? Because it's nice. And then she's out of the car, all business, moving with purpose toward the main trailer. Thing One and Thing Two are hot on her heels. After a beat or two, Seth and I follow suit.

It's hard to say which of us is more reluctant. So we've got that in common, I guess.

It's better than nothing. Maybe.

Fantastic, Fearsome: NJ
Release Form—Performer Agreement

This Agreement is made as of the date indicated below between Filmmaker and Performer as follows;

1. Performer agrees to render services as an on-camera performer in connection with the production of the Video.
2. The term is in perpetuity, and the territory is worldwide.
3. Performer hereby grants to Filmmaker, its successors, and assigns the right to use and display Performer's likeness and performance as contained within the Video for any and all purposes and in any and all media channels, now known or hereafter devised.
4. Performer agrees to accept as full compensation for Performer's services and for the rights granted by Performer, the single payment defined below (if applicable).
5. Payment and receipt is hereby acknowledged, and Performer further agrees that Performer does not expect and will not pursue any further compensation for the services rendered and rights granted under this Agreement and Release.
6. I hereby release Filmmaker, its successors, and assigns from any and all claims, demands, and liabilities of any kind or nature whatsoever arising out of the aforementioned materials and the use thereof.
7. Filmmaker, its successors and assigns shall be the absolute owners of any and all photographs, film, Video, and other materials (and all rights therein, including the copyright) produced pursuant to this release. Performer further

agrees, subject to the provisions above, that Filmmaker may use Performer's photograph, and/or likeness in any manner and with whatever copy they choose. Performer understands that Filmmaker is not obligated to use Performer's image.

8. Performer represents that by signing this Agreement and Release, Performer fully intends to be legally bound to the terms stated within or, if Performer is under the age of 18 years, this Agreement and Release is being signed by Performer's parent or legal guardian who represents his/her agreement to the terms stated within and that Performer will be legally bound to such terms.

9. Performer acknowledges that the production is nonunion and holds the Filmmaker harmless for any claims relating to hiring the Performer on that basis.

Date _____

Signature of Performer/Guardian _____

Print Name of Performer/Guardian _____

Character/Role _____

Performer's Email & Physical Address_____

Payment Amount (if applicable) _____

Signature of Filmmaker _____

Print Name of Filmmaker _____

Title of Video _____

Important: Attach a scan/photo of Artist's driver's license or passport for age & identity verification. This Release Form template must not be modified or edited in any way.

FOURTEEN

The lighting isn't working. I've learned at least that much. I'm new to the reality TV game, sure, but by now I know enough that I can tell, here—three takes into the "asylum tour" segment—that the lighting isn't working for the camera. We're going to have to backtrack, start the scene from the top. Again. It turns out TV is tedious, Lucia. Shockingly so.

"Cut," Jane calls, her voice nasal and high-pitched, the way it gets when she's irritated, which is another thing I'm learning to suss out on my own. It's a questionable life skill, Lu. No real practical application once the summer is over.

Maggie collects herself before anyone else can notice. Say what you will about my aunt—legendary and brash and decidedly self-made in a boy's club, an industry overflowing with arrogant, entitled man-children—but she's one cool cat in the workplace. Maybe it was all of those pitch meetings, but this woman just does not get ruffled. Or if she does, she doesn't let it show. Now, *there's* a life skill I could apply in the real world.

"Is it the shadows, muffin?" Maggie asks, eyes twinkling. "Still giving you trouble?"

"You're a mind reader, Meg," Jane agrees. I think that she means this literally.

"Well, that, and the dust, pumpkin." Maggie winks. "Good for the woo-woo atmosphere. Bad for actual footage. It's dust if we're lucky. Asbestos if we're not. Spooky, yeah. But peanut, we need to be able to get good facial close-ups, cues, and expressions. If I can't look the camera in the eye, so to speak, I've lost the viewer."

She tips her head toward me to show that this information is mainly for the newbie's benefit, that she's not telling Jane or the crew anything they don't already know. And she's not. I'm the only one hanging on her every word; while she speaks, Casey furtively attacks her chin with a compact and a sponge; Hillary scowls in concentration at her video monitor; Amanda cranks and fiddles with a silver reflector—a *bounce board* or *b board*; production parlance is another skill I'm learning.

At 45 degrees the room is brighter. It may mean that Amanda is going to have to stand in that position for the next forty minutes or thirteen takes, whichever comes first. Poor thing. In these situations there's a certain benefit to presumed ignorance.

Lead-camera-guy Russ glances over Hillary's shoulder and waves at Jane. The three of them huddle in a brief conference. Sweat trickles down my back. There's no air-conditioning in the asylum, needless to say. Even with the windows pretty consistently shattered, cracked, or knocked out, it's stifling in here. The stone walls trap air like a cork-stopped bottle. Casey's basically chasing a dream with her pressed powder. It's going to be more like clumpy Play-Doh on her skin.

Russ fans his cap in front of his face. "Okay." He's in lead

camera mode, not to be taken lightly, and the energy in the
room responds, funnels toward him in one intangible snap.
"Lighting. Lee, Ernie."

The two step toward him: matching goatees and wire-
rimmed glasses. They are doing nothing to disabuse the
notion that they are, in fact, conjoined twins—if not actually
one person and/or interchangeable. Maybe this is easier for
them, the collective recognition. Forging an identity of one's
own, it's not for the weak. I know it.

"We need more lighting. Which means we need to find
a place to *hide* more lighting." Russ scans the room, pupils
flickering back and forth over pebbled surfaces. "The two-

hundred-watt flood lamps in
Maggie's trunk—they're on dim-
mers, right?"

Lee or maybe Ernie nods.

"Great. Go grab me two of
those, we'll tuck them . . ." His
eyes light on an object so woefully
shabby that its presence barely
registered to me when we first
stepped into the room. "Right
behind there."

It's a grandfather clock, believe
it or not. It's practically the size of
a small Redwood, nestled in the
far corner of the entry atrium.
Once upon a time, it must have
been grand, epic, majestic. Now
its face is yellowed, its body
gnawed to shreds, its pendulum
rusted off. Its glass panel is laced

with snarling cracks. It's a little bit sad, really, how something so elegant can deteriorate, crumble from the inside out, lose all its value . . . just from being left alone, in a corner, to rot.

I'm trying not to overidentify here, Lu. I promise. I mean, let's be real—it's a clock.

"There's no chance of that thing coming to life, ruining a take with some chimes or something, right?" Elena asks.

Russ scowls. "This *thing* hasn't chimed since the hospital's opening day, I don't think." He raps on the wood, producing a dull thud, like its surface is waterlogged. We hear a scratching sound from within. His knock has awakened something small nesting inside. Or some*things*.

Which is worse, Lu: rats that you can't see? Or bloodthirsty hawks that you *can*? Feels pretty lose-lose, if you ask me.

"Get the floodlights," Russ says again.

Ernie and Lee start checking their pockets.

Jane reaches for the coiled telephone-ish cord she always wears around her neck and unclips a set of keys from it. She tosses them to Ernie or Lee. "Should be unlocked," she says. "But just in case." Her face twists into a grimace as she turns to the clock. "This thing is rotting from the inside out," she observes. "But it'll at least work for as long as we need it to conceal the floodlights." She pauses. "I think."

There's one last *scritch-scratch* from inside the clock, as though the rats agree with her.

ASYLUM FOOTAGE—TAPE 7.12—OVERLOOK TOUR

FADE IN

EXT. OVERLOOK ASYLUM—DAY
WIDE SHOT

CAMERA PANS across the crumbling, decayed
buildings. We briefly glimpse a graffiti-
covered wall *(MOTHER LEEDS WUZ HERE LOLZ)*, some
patchy grass, and a few stubbed-out cigarettes
beside the remains of a hasty campfire, still
smoldering.

CLOSE-UP on MAGGIE at the double front doors of
the main building. An old set of thick, heavy
chains—cut, but not by our crew—dangles from
either side of the door frame.

MAGGIE STEPS FORWARD to the chains, LIFTS
THEM, and HOLDS THEM OUT to the camera, like a
sacrificial offering of sorts.

MAGGIE:
The Overlook Mental Asylum. Condemned amidst a
hailstorm of controversy in early 1974. These
days, it's little more than a party site
for thrill-seeking New Jersey teens. They come
here to prove their strength and so-called
"bravery."

(derisive snort)

They dare each other to trespass, maybe even
spend a night—hoping to catch a glimpse of the
tortured souls said to linger on the premises.

(straight at Camera One, laser-sharp)

It's too bad those patients would never know the
peace they so desperately craved when they first
checked in.

                                    FLASH CUTS:
(stock footage)
Cracked, grime-streaked hydrotherapy tubs.
Hospital beds with stained mattresses and
frayed restraints snaking out from their rusty
metal frames. An old-fashioned operating table
beside a tray of ancient, nasty-looking surgical
instruments.

CLOSE-UP on MAGGIE with ROD and GLEN (AKA OILY
AND OILIER) in the former basement ELECTROSHOCK
THERAPY ROOM. The boys look TWITCHY, ANXIOUS.
MAGGIE is IN HER ELEMENT, as always.

                    MAGGIE:
The "Juice Den," as it was known, or, more for-
mally, the Electroshock Therapy Treatment room.
    Electroshock Therapy, or EST, is still
practiced, of course, though far more judi-
ciously than it was during the heyday of

Overlook. Then, EST was so common that the hospital required not one but *two* backup generators, in case of an all-too-frequent blackout.

PAN to GLEN, who SWALLOWS, visibly wigged, and to ROD.

ROD:
Down here is where they'd drill little bits of your brains out, too.

(mimes drill-to-forehead with his fingers)

MAGGIE:
You're referring to a procedure known as the prefrontal lobotomy, Rod. And yes, that was very common at the Overlook. It leaves you docile, a shell of your former self. Here it was performed on any patient who presented a challenge to the doctors' authority or proved difficult to subdue.

(smiles wryly)

In other words, my little coconuts: The problem children were, for all intents and purposes, neutered.

MAGGIE SIDLES UP to the EST TABLE. She LIFTS a MEDIEVAL-looking METAL SKULLCAP up off of it, running a thoughtful finger along its surface.

She PLACES it carefully BACK ON THE TABLE, then
PATS the table like she's welcoming a guest.

MAGGIE (beckoning):
So. Who's first to take a ride? I promise it's
not locked and loaded. *Anymore* . . .

ROD and GLEN EXCHANGE an UNEASY GLANCE.

GLEN:
No, thank you.
This room is making me want to barf.

MAGGIE:
Barf. I see.
I had higher hopes for the two of you.
You were ballsy enough, staying over last night.

(clucks her tongue)

Shame. This is a waste of a release form,
honestly.

ROD RUNS HIS FINGERS THROUGH HIS HAIR, nervous.

ROD (defensive):
Sleeping outside on the front lawn is
different, you know? It's not the same, messing
around with old medical equipment and stuff.

MAGGIE takes a DEEP BREATH, moves SLOWLY,
DELIBERATELY toward ROD, until she's close

enough that she can REST HER HANDS ON HIS
SHOULDERS. She LOOKS him SQUARELY IN THE EYES,
not blinking.

MAGGIE:
(softly)

Rod. Please.
Now's not the time to lose it, bonbon.
You think anyone really cares that you
camped out at the Overlook overnight?
That's weak. And thanks to the legally binding
paperwork you've signed and submitted, that
weakness will be revealed to millions just as
soon as this season of *Fantastic, Fearsome* airs.

(conspiratorially, closer to him still)

September, by the way. Leading into
Halloween season. Our ratings go *haywire* in
Halloween season. It's amazing. Just wait.
Everyone you know's gonna be watching. I'm
sure they'll be thrilled to see you both on
TV, wussing out . . .

GLEN (rushed, in burst of adrenaline):
Okay!

(taking deep breaths, slightly calmer)

Okay. I'll do it.

GLEN all but LEAPS toward the EST TABLE,
GRABBING at the CAP to place it on his HEAD
himself. MAGGIE thrusts an ARM in front of him
to HALT him in his place.

                    MAGGIE:
                 (to the camera)

      Cut! Jane—where are you? Where's Jane?

                  (frustrated)

                   Damn it!

                JANE (OFFSCREEN):
           I'm here! What do you need?

                    MAGGIE:
      (clearly unaware the camera's still on her)

      Glen's in. He's doing the EST table. So we're
      gonna need some effects: flickering lights,
      crackling sounds . . . Other noises, maybe.
      Like muffled voices. Phantom footsteps, maybe?
      If you think it won't sound too hokey.

                JANE (OFFSCREEN):
        No, that'd be perfect. Not hokey at all.

                    MAGGIE:
      (yawns, stretches—still turned away from
                   the lens)

Talk to Russ—have him check in with Lee and
Ernie, Wade. Make sure Elena and Hillary are
                    looped in.

                (beat, an afterthought)

            Do we have a smoke machine?

                GLEN (OFFSCREEN):
    Smoke machine? What? I thought this show was
        about *real* hauntings and shit!

                (incredulous, angry)

    What's with all the props? That's *cheating*!

                    Maggie:
                (deep breath)

                    Well.
        I won't tell if you won't.

                                FADE TO BLACK

FIFTEEN

Rod and Glen manage to pull off their fifteen minutes of fame. That is, they succumb to Maggie's blackmail and somehow make it through the EST reenactment without yakking or fainting. My aunt is very good at her job, Lu.

Now Elena stands over me in the main atrium, hovering as I wrestle a snarl of cables from a large plastic bin. I'm sweaty from the effort. But Elena isn't concerned about that. She's got her mind on other things.

"No one cares about the cables, Winnie."

"Wade asked me to do this," I say, which is true. But I don't really want to push back. In the great mathematic equation of our production team, Elena > Winnie. Wade or no Wade.

"Right, no, yeah," Elena says. She pushes her short, shiny black hair back out of her eyes and glances at her ever-present clipboard. She's like a high school coach from the eighties or something. "I mean, cables, yeah. We'll get them for Wade. But the sun's going down and we need to get the criminal ward set up for the séance tonight."

Oh, that.

Did I forget to mention this little nugget, Lucia? Aunt Maggie's super-fun plan for our overnight? We're holding a séance in the old dorm of the *criminal ward* tonight. Because rustling up regular old garden-variety mental patient ghosts would just be too tame for our purposes. We need the ghosts *with a record.*

Let me be the first to say it: Bad Idea. Even a non-believer believes in some things, namely that certain sleeping (criminally insane) dogs should be left alone to lie, lie, lie. *Dormant.* But it's happening, Lu. And Elena is waiting for me to step away from the power cords and get cracking with the *setting up of the criminal ward.* And it occurs to me: I really have no idea whatsoever what that means, what it entails.

"Okay," I say. "So what can I do?"

"Dwyer ward," Elena says with the *obviously* part implied through tone. "Amanda is up there, staging. She'll show you what to do."

SO THAT, DEAR LUCIA, is how I come to be in the Dwyer ward, fourth floor, dormitory hall. It's a cavernous space with a rank, mildewy stench. Creaky, battered cots line the walls. It's what you'd expect from a wartime period drama. Some of the cots are broken or bent out of shape. The floors are cold and hard, slate and stone and ancient looking, and mottled with ominous-looking stains that time can't completely erase. Maybe Glen was onto something with his idea about molecules and blood.

If ever a place were *meant* to appear potentially haunted,

it's this one. Frankly, now that I'm here, I'm even less sure what needs to be done as far as staging goes. The creep factor here is already well above eleven.

"Is that a . . ." I move to the corner and peer more closely. "I'm sorry, but is that a *chipmunk nest* in the corner?" It's a pile of shredded rags and refuse. And it is speckled with all manner of mysterious . . . *stuff* I'd rather not identify more precisely.

"If we're lucky," Amanda chirps, cheerful as ever.

"And if we're not?"

She gives me a look like I should know better. "Rats, probably."

Yes, Lu: I *should* know better. "So what are you doing?" I ask. "Since this place is already plenty spooky, if you ask me."

"Windows," Amanda says. "Open 'em. Give me a hand."

I glance around. A few of the arched windows that line the room have been forced open. Paint chips and streaks in the dusty windowsills tell me that this has not been the simplest task. Amanda's forehead, too, is smudged with soot.

"Why?" I ask. Other than the fact that the hint of a cross breeze takes the space from *murderously stifling* to *intensely suffocating*. "How is this 'staging'?" When we staged the interview with Genie it was mostly about making sure all of her woo-woo-iest toys were right in frame beside her at all times.

To her credit, Amanda is patient. "*Darling*," she says, doing her best Maggie, "it's supposed to storm tonight. Thunder, lightning, heavy winds, the works."

"So opening the windows lets the dark and stormy in."

"Well, yeah. But it gets better than that."

This from Seth, who materializes in the far doorway like an apparition himself, trusty backpack in tow. "Opening the windows lets the *wind* in. And the shadows. And other tiny micro-movements that Maggie's cameras will pick up, that will give the appearance of 'supernatural phenomena' being picked up on film."

"The wind," I echo, a mix between skeptical and deflated. *Now* I get it. Unfortunately. "Shadows. So, things flicker and sway and the camera catches it. And then we pretend that it's ghosts." *Pretend.* That's the word that trips me up, every time.

"Pretty much," Amanda says.

"*Pretend* is a strong word," says Seth.

I sigh.

"I think you're looking at this all the wrong way," Amanda adds. "Reality TV isn't *journalism*, Winnie. No one watches *Fantastic, Fearsome* for veracity."

"*Veracity.* See, I know you're serious when you use your ten-dollar words."

"Shut it," Amanda says, "or you'll miss my brilliant point."

"Go on." I wave grandly. "Please."

"Reality TV is, at heart, *entertainment.* This isn't Ken Burns. It's not about *educating* the public or documenting the truth. It's about—"

"Grabbing ratings," Maggie's voice interrupts.

Seth and Amanda both jump. Maggie has materialized out of nowhere, too, appearing next to Seth without warning, and smiling like a Cheshire cat. Seth looks vaguely embarrassed, as though he were the one caught trash-talking our show. Amanda, on the other hand, mostly looks stunned.

"I didn't mean to follow your train of thought *out loud*, pumpkin pie," Maggie adds. "But you're right. And frankly, I wouldn't take it any other way. The truth is: it doesn't matter whether we're peddling the truth or not if we can't get the viewers to tune in. So we do what we have to do in order to make sure we're getting the attention we need. The attention we *deserve*," she clarifies.

"That, um, makes perfect sense," Amanda says, still sounding horrified and chastened. "You know I'm a fan. And a believer."

"Of course I know that, licorice whip." Maggie turns to me, her smile fading. "It's this one who's feeling very let down by it all. My darling flesh and blood." She lingers on the word *blood*, rolling it along her tongue like a dollop of cream.

I'm not sure how to counter that. She's not wrong. But why should it matter, if I'm so sure the paranormal is all a bunch of hooey in the first place?

Why indeed, Lu?

"Tough girl," Maggie says, her voice lower now. "That's what you want us to think."

I say nothing. Am I that transparent? Or is blood truly thicker than water?

Maggie's gaze softens. "You're drawn to horror movies, ghost stories, and other tales of monsters and boogeymen for the same reason we all are: *you like to play 'what if.'*"

Just as suddenly, her eyes are twin beams, headlights bearing down on me. I have to look away. "The thing about the *what-ifs*," she whispers, "is that they *are* all eminently possible.

It's Seth's argument, too. But staring at the floor, I see the mirror again. *NOT A SUICIDE.* Maggie seems so certain about so many things. Could she know the truth about that as well? She's waiting; the whole room is waiting, for me to say something. But I don't answer. There's a dull pounding in my temples.

"The show is just a show," Maggie continues. "It's fun. Entertainment. Amanda is right; that's our priority. In that way, it has nothing to do with what's *really* real out there. And it has nothing to do with the fact that there *is* a lot—a hell of a lot—*really* real, out there. You'll understand that, by the time our summer is over." Her eyes lock with mine again. "You'll see."

I swallow.

Maggie claps her hands together, and the chill is gone; the momentary trance is broken. "Now. Seth, you're setting up the ion counter, yes?"

"Yup." He nods, clearly grateful to be back on solid footing.

"I want infrared, too," she says. "My guess is this place is haunted enough that the ion counter will give us plenty, but just in case, the infrared can pick up any cold spots—the real ones, and the ones we get from all of our deliciously open windows."

The open windows, right. *Staging.* I aim to keep my face neutral, and think I've got it mostly under control. That is, until Maggie turns to address me directly once again.

"And you, my little peach cobbler," she says. "Once you're done with all of that onerous, unseemly window opening, maybe you'd like to join me in the basement? I could use a partner in crime down there."

Alone. With Maggie. This is the first time she's singled me out for a task. What does that mean?

"Sure," I say. My voice catches. I clear my throat before I go on. "What's in the basement?"

Maggie grins. "The records room. You up for it?"

And Lucia? It turns out: I am.

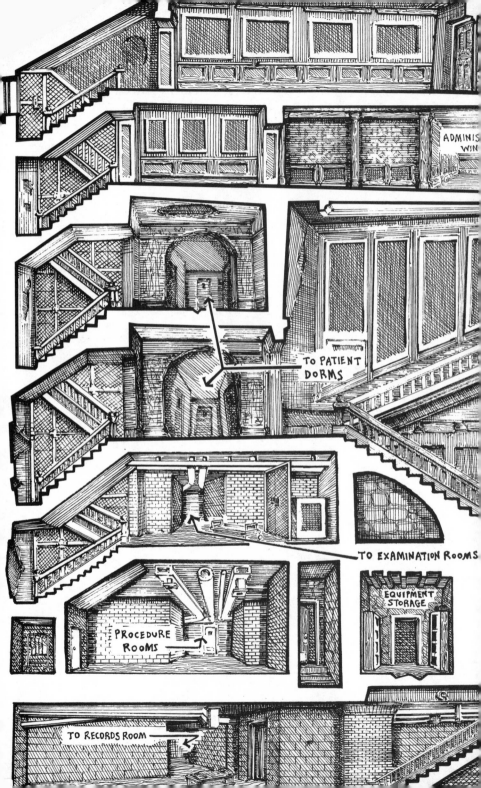

ADMINIS
WIN

TO PATIENT
DORMS

TO EXAMINATION ROOMS

EQUIPMENT
STORAGE

PROCEDURE
ROOMS

TO RECORDS ROOM

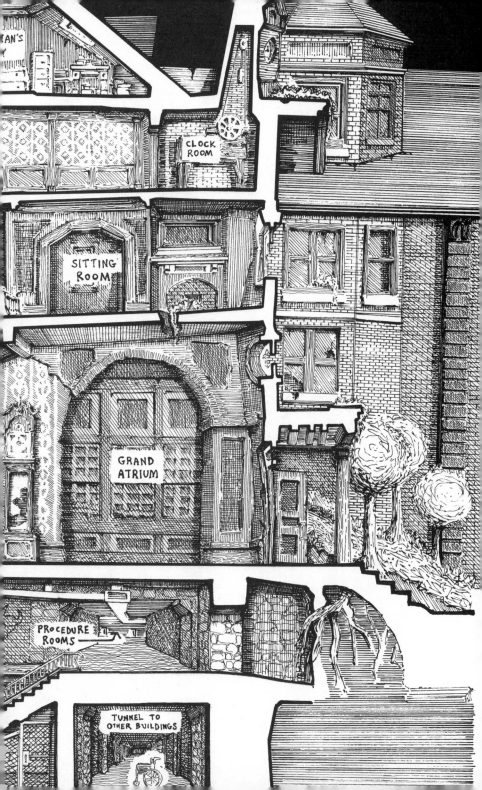

SIXTEEN

The thing about basements is: they're *all* creepy. If the "asylum" trope is a beaten horse, then the "creepy basement" is its desiccated corpse, beached and buzzing with flies. (Seth did call me a "maven.") And yet, Lu—this one feels creepi*er*, somehow.

Maybe I'm not being stalked by a shriveled madman as I navigate this maze; maybe I don't hear the constant refrain of Freddy's laughter echoing through the dank, dim corridors; maybe I'm not *actually* the Final Girl, the star-crossed heroine of some Tobe Hooper knockoff, played by Sarah Michelle Gellar or Jennifer Love Hewitt or some other former up-and-comer with two first names . . . (Side note: W*hy* do they always have two first names, Lu? Why?) Maybe I'm none of those things, because life is not a horror movie, not even *here*.

And yet. I feel a pull, a tug from inside. It's different. The sensation of this place, it burns from the inside out. It burns from beneath the ground, from within the walls.

Elena gave me an old set of schematics meant to provide a map of the basement floor plan. *Old* is the key adjective there. It's faded and missing important elements. She's covered the image in hasty chicken-scrawl, trying to fill in the blanks, but Wikipedia could only offer so much. Not even the county hall of records had the full basement layout. Such things are "not currently available." I should know. It was my job to research that, back in preproduction. Suddenly, I wish I'd worked harder at that, even knowing right now that it wouldn't have made any difference.

At this point the "map" is basically just a Rorschach guide to Elena's imagination.

It's interesting to look at, but it doesn't really help me when it comes to finding my way to the records room. Which is where I'm supposed to be meeting Maggie.

I haven't seen a window since four left turns ago. My eyes struggle against the unreliable buzz of a few bare bulbs dangling from the ceiling at random intervals. *No one is meant to be down here.* The thought forms, full and unbidden, in my mind. There's a reason the map is illegible. There's a reason the county records are incomplete. *Something is wrong here. Something in the earth has spoiled.* I can sense it, can smell it, can feel it coagulating at the back of my throat.

There's nothing down here but me. (And Maggie. But *where?*)

Right?

I'm losing it, Lucia. Down here in the belly of the beast. Which would not be inconsistent with typical horror movie tropes of the genre. All of those George Romero zombies roiling in the root cellar; those snarling Nosferatu cave-creatures from *The Descent.* All of those things, they came from underground. And now, me. I'm here, too.

There's a *pop!* and a flash, and the closest bulb to me snuffs out, leaving behind the faint aroma of sulfur.

And then I hear footsteps.

Oh God, oh God.

You're doubtful, I can tell. *Footsteps, Winn?*

But the sound, it's unmistakable: *left, right, left, right.* It's coming toward me from the darkness ahead, a slow, scraping sound along the floor. All I can imagine is a dull, lumbering figure in my mind's eye, something grotesque, gore-soaked. The golem. Frankenstein's monster. The hag in room 237. Something *returned* from the dead. Something that's doing what it can to bridge the chasm between the space it's left behind, and the place it's meant to inhabit.

Oh God, Oh Jesus, Lu, I'm really losing it this time—

There's a shattering sound. Another bulb a few yards up ahead blows. I bite back a shriek. The corridor is black.

Of course that's when I hear something *behind* me, too. I hear breathing. Steady, rhythmic. It's at the back of my neck, tracing airy snow angels at the nape of my neck.

I'm motionless.

A hand clamps down on my shoulder.

This time, I can't contain my scream. It's a very loud scream, Lu.

"My little strawberry cheesecake! Are you trying to give me a heart attack?"

When I dare to turn, it's Maggie (who else?). She looks confused and mildly amused, like this not-so-secret side of me is a pleasant not-such-a-surprise. Though . . . what was that in front of me?

"I wasn't," I stammer. "I mean, it wasn't. Dark down here. When I first came down. Or at least, not like this. There were some lightbulbs." I'm babbling, and Maggie's smile grows wider. I take a breath and start again. "Some bulbs just blew out. I wasn't deliberately skulking around down here in the pitch black."

Because *that* would be weird, Lu.

Maggie is dragging large box behind her. I flush with renewed embarrassment. *That* was the scraping sound I heard. Chalk it up to acoustics that it seemed to be coming from the abyss *up* the hall. She taps it with the toe of her sneaker, bright red Converse. "A receptacle for the records." She shrugs, suddenly seeming a good five years younger than her age. "It was light, but bulky. I got sick of carrying it in my hands." She demonstrates, edges her foot forward to show me how she shoved it along in tiny sliding kicks.

"Bulky." The word feels foreign in my mouth. I lean against the wall for support. *"God."*

"No such thing, cheddar biscuit," Maggie says, perhaps not getting that *she* almost gave *me* a heart attack. "Sorry. He's not paranormal. Just made-up."

I sigh. "Of course." This, at least, does not come as a surprise.

Maggie claps her hands together, bright and alert. It's up to me to recover, to find some way to get to snap out of it and get to her level. "So," she says, 115 percent no-nonsense. "The records room."

I wave the schematics at her. "I couldn't find it."

She sniffs, barely dignifying the old paper. "We don't need that. It's right there." She pauses a moment, closes her eyes, as if breathing in every horrible fetid thing that may or may not be down here. Then she pulls her phone out of her pocket, swipes a few times until the hallway is illuminated with some kind of flashlight app. She sweeps the beam along the walls until I see it:

A door. A heavy industrial door.

She was right, Lu. It was *right there*, in front of my face, that door, and I managed to miss it. But she figured it out, innately, in the pitch black . . . somehow.

I know how I sound, Lucia. But she did. That's that.

"We're here," I say, feeling dumb but not able to hold back from stating the obvious.

"That we are, my little chocolate eclair." She steps forward, rattles the doorknob. It fights her for a moment, but then the knob clicks and twists, and the slowly swings in and open. From where I stand, the doorway is nothing but cobwebs. Nothing about it is remotely inviting.

Maggie moves back, gestures. "After you."

I can't deny Maggie, apparently. I shove the cobwebs aside and plow through.

PATIENT INTAKE FORM

June 22nd, 1905

NAME: Marie Kallikak

DOB: Feb 1885*

*exact age unknown

MARITAL STATUS: Unwed*

*patient arrived at Overlook with child, seemingly six or seven months along. She could not or would not communicate the identity of the baby's father.

RELIGION: None stated.

OCCUPATION: None stated. She is believed to be irregularly employed as a housecleaner, as indicated by her signatory.

EDUCATION: None that is known or demonstrated.

HANDICAPS: Descended from the "feeble-minded" Kallikak lineage, as first identified by H. Goddard. Functionally dumb, minimally literate. Subject is able to communicate through crude drawings. She is known to use "grunting sounds," as per Woodale, below, on occasion.

WARDSHIP: Kallikak was admitted at the request of her guardian, Calvin Woodale, for whom she performs occasional housekeeping and cookery duties. No other living relatives have been identified. Whether this is due to Kallikak's diminished mental capacities remains unclear, but falls beyond the purview of our hospital.

CHIEF COMPLAINT: Woodale reports that in the last year, Kallikak has experienced recent bouts of fits, once every month, culminating in prolonged periods of unconsciousness. According to Woodale, as of the last two months, they have increased, coming multiple times a week. Somnambulistic episodes ihave always been reported in the last two months. Woodale explains that she has been known to "draw" in her sleepwalking deliriums. Her etchings, though crude, are alarming. The vast preponderance depict childbirth. The infant is consistently rendered with two distinct characteristics: horns and a forked tongue.*

*figs. 1a, 1b, attached

Woodale believes that Kallikak is telling us that her unborn child is, in fact, a devil.

"Whether she be insane, or be pregnant with a demon, attention must be paid," is his final analysis. This institution is inclined to agree.

DIAGNOSIS & TREATMENT: In progress.

SEVENTEEN

I toss the onion-skin-thin papers to the top of the pile beside me.

Needless to say, it does not end well for Marie Kallikak. You may have guessed that yourself. And she's not the only one. The hospital records are studded with reference to "hysterical" women of "feeble mind," many of whom are—*surprise, surprise*—at least distantly related to the Kallikaks. Of all the female wackadoos to be admitted to Overlook, the Kallikaks were hit the hardest, both in terms of harsh diagnoses and harsher "treatments." There are at least ten in the stack I've unearthed, so fragile and old that they threaten to dissolve in my fingertips.

I'm being careful, Lu. If I had actual kid gloves, you can bet I'd be wearing them. Ten Kallikak women here—maybe fifteen, twenty total. And those are just the ones that are documented! Which probably means there are more. Maybe twenty doesn't sound like a lot, but when you stop to think about how they were all related, it hits you: *The Overlook was basically wiping out an entire bloodline.*

The question is: Why?

"It's because they were different," Maggie says, interrupting my reverie. I'm kind of getting used to her being able to read my mind. Even if I'm *not* willing to admit that it involves anything other than intuition. We're family, after all.

"It's because they were 'simple,'" I say, harsher than I mean. "Although, I don't know who these ladies pissed off so badly. You have to hand it to their enemies . . . They were devoted to systematically butchering Kallikak brains until there was nothing but oatmeal left."

"Vividly put." Maggie scoots over to me so that we're side by side on the dank concrete floor. She sifts through the papers, plucks one of Marie Kallikak's drawings between two fingers and lays it gently between us. "Do you see?" She jabs a pointer at the picture. "Horns. A forked tongue."

"I know; she thought her baby was a demon." (Lu: I never said these ladies *weren't* crazy, just that they maybe deserved a bit more compassion, is all.)

"She did. But more to the point—she thought *she was possessed*. To reproduce with a demon requires demonic blood."

"Not according to *Rosemary's Baby*."

Maggie laughs. "Touché. But that was a movie. Fiction, remember?"

"Ah, yes. Whereas this is *real life*." My thoughts turn to Seth. I wonder what he and Casey are doing right now.

"I can see you'll need a little more convincing, my little blondie bar. That's fine. I've got some time. Not too much time, but some."

My ears prick up at that. *Not too much time*. Like there's an unspoken deadline in place. But a deadline for what?

"The thing is, though," my aunt continues, "even if *you*

don't believe it, *she* did. Marie Kallikak thought she was possessed by a demon. And that was enough for the doctors." She
shakes her head. "It always is, for men in power."

"What do you mean?"

Maggie is so self-assured, she practically *drips* with confidence. It would never occur to me that she'd go all "I am
woman, hear me roar." Mainly because she'd never have to.
She just roars. Note to self already taken, Lu: *Must roar more.*

"*I mean,* history is lousy with women being labeled 'fragile,'
or 'hysterical,' or even—more often than not—'insane,'
particularly when they're claiming to have some sort of otherworldly ability. People in power—traditionally, men—fear
women with *actual* power." She arches an eyebrow. "As well
they should."

I turn toward the pile of records.

"These women weren't strong *enough,*" Maggie continues
in my ear. "They didn't have enough mastery of their powers.
They behaved . . . well, not *foolishly.* But rather, they *were*
foolish. As you say, they were simple. That was their downfall.
Sometimes, a little subterfuge is necessary. Sometimes, one
has to fly below the radar. Or hide in plain sight."

When I whirl to face her, she winks at me, briefly obscuring
one of those eyes that could so easily pass for my own mother's.

Hide in plain sight.

"If powerful—*literally* powerful—women are always tar-
geted, then what's the point of owning up to any sort of
power at all?" I say, though I'm not sure if I'm arguing or
agreeing with her. "Isn't that just asking for trouble?"

"We live in different times now, Winnie. Modern times. I
don't have to tell you that. Entertainment is paramount. You
could even argue that the *most* powerful people in our world
today are the ones who control the message."

She has a point. "Still, there are other, less dangerous ways to brand yourself," I say. "You could be a house flipper or an antiques picker. A maniacal dance coach."

"*Hiding in plain sight,*" Maggie says again, wagging a finger this time for emphasis. She seems to think I'm going to get it, that it's all going to click, if she just keeps repeating herself. The joke's on her. She sighs. "I knew you'd be tough to turn, oatmeal cookie, but now? Even after what you've seen, what you've felt? Since you've been here, with us? You still think the paranormal is bullshit?"

I shrug. I wish I didn't feel so guilty, so conflicted and unsure.

"Well, that's disappointing," she murmurs as if I'd spoken out loud. "I do still hope you'll come around. I chose this . . . shall we say, *genre* of television, because it's real to me. It allows me to do my work. But of course, viewers don't suspect a thing. They just want a good show."

My work. There's that hint again, that suggestion of an agenda, a time line . . . things to come. Distant warning bells sound in the recesses of my mind. How can someone be both vague and crystal clear at the same time? Because that's just what Maggie is doing. What really went on between my mom and Maggie?

NOT A SUICIDE.

The paranormal can't be real, or Mom would be reaching out to me. She'd want me to know the truth. It's the only thought I can cling to.

"Did it ever occur to you, sweet pea, that there's a *reason* human beings—*mortals,* I should say, regular old, vanilla-bean-standard *people*—are drawn to tales of the supernatural? A reason they're *obsessed,* truly, with the notion of magic, of power, of life on the Other Side? Where do you think those fables came from, after all? *Human beings are not innately imaginative creatures,* I can assure you. They didn't make those things up."

"They did." I'm steadfast. It's so simple. There can be no other explanation. I simply refuse to accept it. *La-la-la, can't hear you, Maggie.* I know, Lu: immature. "And anyway, not *all* people like horror and fantasy."

"The good ones do," Maggie says. And I can't argue with that.

So we're at a standoff, Maggie and I. She stands, hands on hips, and starts to pace the room as though her footsteps will spur my imminent "come to Jesus" moment. Then she pauses, bends her knees, squatting so that we're eye to eye. And it's my mother's eyes, again, liquid and searching, fixed on me. Peering at me through Maggie's face. Around me, the room begins to buzz, that scratching sensation tightening in the back of my throat.

"Okay, Winnifred," Maggie says. Her voice is different now; she's dropped the snack-food-nickname lilt. "Look at me. You don't think you'll ever come around?"

I do look at her. A thought takes hold like a fishhook in the folds of my brain, worms its way into my bloodstream. *It is possible. It is possible. It is possible.* The words wrap themselves around my tongue and burrow into my lips until I have no choice but to speak them out loud.

"It's possible," I say. But out loud it sounds foreign, watery, and far away.

Maggie practically squawks with glee. "I'm *thrilled* to hear you say that!" She claps her hands together like an organ grinder's monkey. In the dim light of the cellar, her gaze is devilish and full of mischief.

"Um, *what the hell just happened?*" That tickle in my throat comes back. Before I even have time to be embarrassed, I dissolve into a coughing fit. Maggie rushes over, thumps me on the back a few times until I've got it under control again.

"What *was* that?" I gasp as soon as I can speak clearly again. "I mean, I *felt* all those words, those thoughts, I mean, like when you were asking me. When you were *looking* at me. Right then, I meant what I was saying . . . but I don't know why those words came out. It was like I was . . . I don't know, in a trance or something."

Maggie nods her head, wry. "Or something." She shrugs.

Something. What the hell is *something*, Lu?

"What *was* that?" I ask again, hoarse.

"*That*," Maggie says, "was my magic. Let's just call it the power of persuasion. I've always had it, for as long as I can remember. Your mother's magic was different, of course. But she had powers, too."

Your mother's magic. My head spins, blood rushes to my face, the floor drops out beneath me, turns to quicksand. *Your mother's magic.*

Your mother's magic.

NOT A SUICIDE.

What is going on?

But Maggie's not finished. She reaches out, smoothes my hair off of my forehead.

"The Leader women are *all* powerful, Winnie. All of us."

All of us. Us.

"What are you saying?" I ask in that underwater, distant voice again.

"I'm saying, Winnie, that you have magic, too."

EIGHTEEN

The fact is, I've always been basically a good girl. But that doesn't mean I've never made a mistake.

Nobody's perfect.

Remember that time I got caught "trespassing" on the Rainers' property?

You know how I get when I run. I space out; I'm in a zone. It's not usually an issue. I mean, where we live, people are mostly relaxed, mostly normal. No one gets all up in arms about their personal "estates." But the Rainers were new to the neighborhood. And they mostly kept to themselves.

I was fourteen. I thought I was running in a nature preserve, that I'd somehow discovered the holy grail of off-roading. I thought, foolishly, that the trail I found was an as-yet-undiscovered slice of Zen. I hopped over a spiky patch of onion grass and there it was: a thin path forged in the red-dish dirt through the azaleas and canary violets.

I was alive that morning, Lucia. You know that feeling? You're not a runner, you won't do it "unless someone's chasing you," but I know that sailing is like that for you.

When you're breathing and the blood is pumping and happiness is suddenly not abstract or an idea, but something solid and miraculous you can hold in one fist? Yeah, *that* feeling. I miss it, these days.

I had no idea it wasn't public property. The energy, the rhythmic pounding of my soles, the dull throb in my quads . . . I was caught up. It was a good run, a good day, and I had no idea I was doing anything wrong.

Like I said, the Rainers hadn't introduced themselves to any of us, which was slightly strange but not too-too weird. We're not, like, a welcome-wagon-block-party neighborhood or anything (do those even exist these days, Lucia?).

It turns out they were not very neighborly.

They were territorial, and I was on their territory.

As I would soon learn, they had security cameras installed. All over their property. Every square inch was under surveillance. Creepy, yes. Creepier: the way I found out, long after my run, when the doorbell rang that night.

It was late by doorbell-ringing standards, nine-ish, and we weren't expecting anyone because, you know, nine on a weeknight, who would we be expecting?

Mrs. Rainer introduced herself, loudly enough that her voice carried to the second floor, where I could hear her through my open bedroom door. Mr. Rainer was quieter, gruffer. At first, I wasn't listening closely—why would I?—but after I heard the kitchen rattles of drinks being poured and chairs being pulled out, my ears perked up.

"Trespassing . . ."

"Video . . ."

"Fines . . ."

Mr. Rainer mostly hung back but Missus had quite a bit to say. Some of it pretty threatening. From my nervous perch on my bed, I could hear my mother's voice creep higher and higher, indignant.

"Clearly, it was an accident," she said, her voice razor wire. "She was out jogging. I'm sure my daughter had no intention of trespassing on your private property."

"There is a sign," Mrs. Rainer said. "On the edge of the property line."

"She runs cross-country," Mom said. "She was zoned out, you know teens. I'm sure she overlooked the sign, accidentally. But she didn't disturb the property, did she? She didn't take anything or destroy anything?"

The silence that followed indicated a reluctant agreement.

"So I don't see why we can't all just agree that this was a harmless, innocent mistake. It won't happen again. There's no reason we should have to pay a fine. We're neighbors. I don't see why we can't be neighborly about this." Mom was getting quieter and quieter, her usual MO right before true rage took over. Dad was out, a late seminar to teach, office hours, something like that, something we never paid attention to. I remember thinking it was a shame he wasn't home, since he was the only one who could calm my mother in these situations. She didn't get worked up often. But when she did—watch out.

When Mom spoke again, her voice had an odd singsong feel to it. Not unlike the tone Maggie used with me, Lucia, when she managed to bend my thoughts to her own in the basement, just before. It was hypnotic, like that. *Just* like that.

"I see no reason why we shouldn't just forget all about this," Mom said.

It was a suggestion, but it carried the weight of unwavering authority. In that moment, I *knew*: the Rainers were going to agree.

It didn't make sense, of course—they'd been up in arms since they'd arrived. There'd been mention of a lawyer. Maybe they wanted to make an example out of me. There was no earthly reason to assume they were going to back down.

I held my breath.

"So," Mom said. "Do we agree to forget?"

Mr. Rainer cleared his mouth. "Forget what?" he asked. He wasn't kidding, the way people do when they've agreed to drop something or get over it. His tone told me he meant it literally. He had no idea what my mother was referring to at all. They'd both forgotten it. They'd blanked on the entire reason for their visit in the first place.

My mother laughed, hearty and full, and thanked them for coming by. She told them she was so glad they'd had a chance to get to know each other, now that we were all neighbors. They agreed. And the kicker: as she opened the front door, she added, "I hope we'll see you around the neighborhood. My daughter's on the cross-country team. You might catch her out on one of her training runs these days." And then, conspiratorially: "You'll recognize her. She's a beauty, just like her mother."

They laughed, too.

She said goodbye, closed the door behind them.

We never spoke of the Rainers' visit directly, though my mother paused in the hallway after letting them out. I heard her sigh and I just knew: *she* knew I'd overheard every word. But she didn't mention it to me. And as far as I know, Lu, I don't think she ever mentioned it to my father, either. What would he have said, if he knew? Did he know? Did he think she could—she would—do it again?

I tried not to think about it. I paid attention to property lines. I tried not to think about this strange, unfathomable thing that my mother had done. Because: You know what,

Lu? It wasn't the first time she'd done something I couldn't explain or understand.

It wasn't the first time that I forced myself to decide: it's better not to believe.

"YOU'RE REMEMBERING SOMETHING. I can see it on your face."

Maggie surveys me, lips pursed. Her expression is somewhere between curious and pleased.

I shake my head. But the echo of my mother's voice lingers. *My mother's power.* How can a truth be both inconceivable and incontrovertible, Lu? How does that even work? Because this one is. I don't believe in magic, not at all . . . this gift that my mother had, this . . . yes, it was like a sort of Midas Touch, an ability to strike certain thoughts from people's minds when necessary.

But it wasn't *magic.* It was . . . psychological skill, a talent for persuasion and rhetoric—the kind of talent a violin prodigy has. The kind of talent that appears miraculous to those without it. That's how I always explained it myself. She could make people go along with anything she wanted, Lucia. You remember that, don't you? You joked about it all the time. It came in handy on some parent-teacher nights, on those (rare) occasions that some inexperienced math teacher had an unflattering thought or two about my class participation.

But it wasn't *magic.*

The cinder-block walls shift closer to me, sifting up dust as they tighten around me. I breathe in quickly; the room's getting smaller and I can't get any air and I'm *choking*, Lu, I'm *drowning*, which doesn't feel real but then again, neither did *magic,* and it turns out I was wrong about that, maybe—

"Close your eyes." Maggie's hands are on my shoulders

heavy and commanding. I do as she says and the room steadies, my breathing slows to a normal pace. The sensation of collapsing into a black hole begins to fade. My yearning to disbelieve does not.

"My mother didn't have any powers," I say, once I can breathe again. "*No one* has any powers. And there's no such thing as ghosts, either."

"Your eyes are telling me a different story, pop rock."

I want to close them again, just to spite her. But that would be immature. I want to show her that I'm strong, that I'm grown up. I want her to call me Winnifred again.

She made me change my mind. She made me believe what she wanted me to believe. To think what she wanted me to think.

I can't deny it. But I can't believe it.

So where does that leave me, Lu?

My mom and her sister had shared power. And then they were estranged. And now my mother is dead.

Where does that leave me?

"Your *magic*," I sputter. "Your powers." Maggie looks at me, waiting for me to go on. "If you *do* have powers, why the staging, then? Why did we have to rig the Dwyer ward? Why can't you just . . . show what you *say* it is?"

Maggie sighs. There's sadness, maybe even regret in her eyes. "I'm not a demon myself, you know." She pauses. "I have a useful ability to help others to . . . shall we say, *see things my way*. My sister, on the other hand, was good at getting people to forget things she didn't want them to know." The sadness melts away and there's a hint of a smile. "I'm *certain* you were aware of that."

I say nothing.

She goes on. "Our powers were linked, related. That's the way these things tend to work. I suspect your skill, when it's

revealed, will be connected to ours in some way, too. That's
assuming it hasn't already begun to show itself to you?"

I glare back at her. "How many times do I have to say it? *I
have no skill*. No *power*. No *magic*. Neither did my mother. And
neither do you." I swallow. *"There is no such thing . . ."* The last
angry words are lost as something bubbles in my throat like a
bee sting. I begin to cough.

I begin to cough.

I tell a lie to Maggie. And I begin to cough.

Lucia.

I cough when I lie. I *cough*.

But it's more. Since I've been here, I cough *at* a lie.

When Maggie talked Jane into pushing the shooting
schedule, way back in Asbury Park. When Ivan took Amanda's Jersey Devil story for his own. When those greasy boys
tried to convince us they'd been partying hard at the Overlook before we got there. Each time, my throat caught. And
each time, I sensed that they weren't telling the truth.

I sway. Maggie grabs me by an elbow, guides me to a wall,
props me up. I feel like a paper doll. I mean, I'm not an idiot.
I can read between the lines, Lu. I understand the pattern,
here. Our family's skills are connected.

Our powers are connected.

Because of course, we do, actually, have powers.

There is magic, Mom. There is. *So where are you?*

I need you.

My throat burns, and I choke the thought down. I'm not
ready to admit anything. I can't, I won't let Maggie see me flinch.

"The staging is for the show," Maggie says, apparently
continuing our conversation, pretending like I'm not in the
throes of a nervous breakdown. Like this sort of conversation
is normal, garden-variety for her. (Maybe it is, Lucia.) "The

presence here is real—all too real, buttercup—and I know that you feel it. But for our show, we need a little spectacle. We need *ratings*. We can't rely on what we can't control. We need to be able to shake things up, to make things happen on camera that will guarantee viewers."

Satisfied that I'm able to stand, she puts her hands back on her hips. "I'm only in charge of the show, not of the forces within these walls. Not yet, anyway. That's where my team—the camera crew, the production people, *not* the Devil Hunters—comes in. We get our job done. And then I can go back to what's important. Like everything we're learning down here."

Not yet, anyway.

And then I can go back to what's important.

I skate past those phrases, shove them aside for now, and straighten. "Down here," I hiss at her. "You mean, all these records about crazy women being tortured for their delusional beliefs? That kind of shit happens all over the place, all through history. You said so yourself. There's no evidence . . ." I cough, pause, clear my throat. It's a curious feeling, having your own subconscious calling you out for a little white lie, Lucia. "There's nothing," I say, less forcefully this time.

I'm thinking of the bathroom mirror in my hotel room.

Again, Maggie is right in tune with me, even in my silence. "Your mother wasn't as comfortable with her magic as I am, Winnie. And that was her downfall. She didn't embrace them . . . and she let that drive her mad." She peers at me, expectant. Sighing, she hugs her elbows to her chest. "That's how we lost her."

That's how we lost her.

As in: *that's why she killed herself.*

But. I can't forget those words.

NOT A SUICIDE.

Maggie is saying that my mother's rejection of her own—I trip over the word, even in my mind—*powers* was what swept her to the brink. What pushed her, ultimately, to leave me. My mother's estranged sister is truly telling me this. And as far as my own internal lie detector is concerned, she means it. She's either telling me the truth, or she *thinks* she is.

But . . . What if Maggie's not *quite* right? What if, maybe, it wasn't the pressure of rejecting her powers that drove my mother crazy? What if it she tried to embrace them . . . and *that* drove her mad? After all, I have that memory of the Rainers. And I have others. I can see it, Mom using her magic. Maybe she was flexing her muscles, so to speak, experimenting. But trying to keep it hidden at the same time. Maybe?

I don't know what to think.

I am close, Lucia, so close to asking Maggie for the truth, to confiding her, to letting the words pour out, a waterfall of confusion. But Maggie has an agenda of her own, one that's hers alone. *That*, at least, is clear. So what if I can't trust her?

Maggie fills the silence herself. "Being plugged in to the supernatural has its advantages," she says. "Some very practical. Some very *lucrative.* Do you think I'd have been able to build the *Fantastic, Fearsome* empire without it?"

She's waiting for me to answer. She's gone from talking about her sister's death to her own success in a happy heartbeat.

I turn away, afraid I'll explode if I don't. "Yes, how *fantastic,*" I mutter. "You got to meet Tim Gunn at least year's Emmys. Hooray for you! You own the mansion next to Jennifer Aniston in Malibu. You have a pocket dog that only eats sashimi straight from Nobu." (That last point is rhetorical, so at least I don't cough.) "I'm glad this thing is working for you. But if it's what *drove my mother to suicide*, maybe you could understand why I'm, I don't know, *reluctant* to embrace the darkness within."

So it's out: all the ugly blackness of my confusion. I thought letting go would help me feel relieved, unburdened. But I just feel worse. I feel *alone*. I guess . . . well, I guess there was a part of me that secretly hoped I'd be able to connect with Maggie, after all. I lost my mother. I left my best friend behind. Who do I have now, Lu?

"Um, hey. I hope I'm not interrupting anything."

Maggie and I both turn to the doorway. It's Casey, wide-eyed. She's dying to know what she walked in on. I wonder how much she heard.

"Not at all!" Maggie and I say in perfect unison, and even through the doubt and anguish, I feel a frisson of satisfaction that in this, at least, we are united. I am not *utterly* alone.

Casey tries to hide her disappointment. "Well, Maggie, uh, Jane needs you in the trailer. She has some dailies she wants you to look at before we finish setting up for the séance." She turns to me. There's a sparkle in her eyes. "And Elena wants you to help Amanda stage the turret room. She wants sleeping bags for Seth and me set up there. Alone. I guess Seth requested it?"

"Whatever," I say. "Sure." I brush past her, wanting to be away from my aunt, *wanting* to be alone.

It's only as I'm groping my way back down the dim hallway that I realize: my throat is tingling again. Seth didn't request to be bunked with Casey. Of course he didn't. Casey was lying to me. And I could totally tell.

It's a strange feeling, Lu.

And maybe . . . it's a *powerful* feeling, too?

NINETEEN

I wish I could tell you that the "turret room" wasn't romantic.

But God—even with the smell of mildew, the crumbling stonework . . . even with the knowledge that this space used to be a clock tower, where the guards kept watch on their fragile charges . . . Even knowing these things, this round room with the vaulted ceiling holds more than a little bit of charm.

I admit it: I wouldn't mind spending the night here with the guy of my dreams, Lucia. If that guy existed, I mean. *(Shush, you.)* Amanda and I unroll two standard-issue sleeping bags, tucking them against one wall.

"Are you sure they need to be so close together?" I ask. Coziness is one thing, but the two sleeping bags practically overlap, they're so tightly laid out. It seems . . . excessive.

Amanda shoots me a knowing look, but kindly keeps her mouth shut.

"It looks weirdly tight, I know," Hillary chimes in. "But the camera angle will be pulled in, so we'll create the effect of a smaller space." She makes a goofy face. "Jane said, 'love nest.' So that's the vibe we're going for."

I fight the urge to vomit. Hillary peeks over her shoulder. "Wade should be up here soon to set up the infrared cameras. That way we can catch all of their movements, even in the dark."

"Aces." I try to sound casual, but bark the word.

Amanda giggles.

Elena shambles in, toting a skinny floor fan that's almost taller than she is. With a grunt, she sets it down just off to one side of the sleeping bags. "We're going to plant mics near their heads. Make sure Wade runs an extension cord up here, too, for the fan. I want it on full blast tonight. We want it to be freezing up here."

"We do?" I ask.

Elena waves Amanda and me away from the sleeping bags, hunches over them for a closer look. She frowns at the zipper on one, then whips a Swiss Army knife from her back pocket and jabs at the lining until the zip pops off into her hand. She turns to me. "Winnie, there are some wool blankets in the large PA trailer. I want you to grab one for up here—but only one." She smiles. "That way, they'll have to snuggle."

Hillary gives an appreciative grin. *"Love nest."*

Lu: save it. It's not jealousy. I'm just sick of the fakeness of this "reality" bullshit.

Elena raises her eyebrows at me, probably wondering why I'm just standing there with a scowl. "Come on; we've got to finish with this room so we can deal with the séance equipment. Time's a-wasting. Winnie: the blankets. And I think Jane picked up some flowers, too."

"Flowers?"

"For us to leave on Casey's pillow. You know, from 'Seth.'" At my expression, she laughs. "Whatever. I know it's not news to you: you know you can't believe everything you see on reality TV."

I shake my head. "Try, *anything*."

Elena laughs harder. "Just do it. Then set up lunch in the waterboarding room."

I roll my eyes. Amanda doesn't miss it. "Bet you never thought you'd have a reason to say *those* words," she says to Elena.

Elena eyes the sleeping bags. "I do love my job."

Well, one of us has to, Lu.

ASYLUM FOOTAGE—TAPE 7.23—SÈANCE

INT. OVERLOOK ASYLUM—NIGHT

TRACKING SHOT

CAMERA FOLLOWS MAGGIE as she moves through a doorway into the cavernous darkness of the Dwyer ward. Curtains are drawn and lights are down—we're using NIGHT CAM lighting here for the greenish, extra-eerie vibe. The curtains SWAY a bit in the evening breeze, giving the sense that anything could be LURKING in any corner . . .

Maggie's FOOTSTEPS ECHO as she leads us to a ROUND TABLE draped in a weblike crocheted covering, very boho-goth.

CLOSE-UP on MAGGIE as she sits. She makes eye contact with the camera and grins.

MAGGIE:
The Dwyer ward. Where the most dangerous patients were housed. The criminally insane.

(dramatic pause)

How many of their spirits still linger in this tainted space? We'll know soon enough.

TURNS to CAMERA LEFT, PAN to show the DEVIL HUNTERS in full regalia (IVAN has his special infrared goggles on for effect), WINNIE alongside them, looking small and nervous, vulnerable.

MAGGIE:
Tonight, on *Fantastic, Fearsome: New Jersey,* we're holding a good, old fashioned séance.

(beat)

Tonight, we're going to talk to the dead.

EVERYTHING IS SPOOKIER IN the dark, Lu. That's just a fact. I totally get why Maggie wanted to hold the séance at night. Communing with the Great Beyond just wouldn't be the same with sunlight streaming through the windows. Gathered around this Hot-Topic-Halloween macramé tablecloth, listening to the intermittent buzzing of Ivan's infrared goggles . . . Well, in this setting, who's to say we *aren't* going to reach out and touch some criminally insane spirit?

Russ adjusts something on his camera. "Rolling!"

"Ivan," Maggie says. "How many séances has your team participated in?"

He's directly to her left at the table. Casey is on Maggie's opposite side. Seth is next to Casey, and I'm sandwiched between Ivan and Seth.

One big, happy ghost-hunting family.

Ivan's been prepped for this; we all have—Elena is a tyrant of a script supervisor, emphasis on *script*—but he flubs his line, anyway. "Um, a bunch. Like ten, maybe? But wait, no . . . that's fifteen, but only if you're counting the investigations, too. And, uh, you know—all séances are investigations, but not all investigations are séances. Like in math."

Seth groans. Casey makes a repulsed face, like she's caught a whiff of something foul. Maggie just looks baffled. Poor Ivan. Really, the question should have gone to Seth, but something about Ivan being a little younger, a little too eager, has Jane thinking he's going to be the breakout comic relief of this season. She wants more footage with him showcased. Good thing she's not sitting in on this taping.

"Cut." Russ's voice is strained.

We break for a minute. Maggie has a very solemn, very brief heart-to-heart with the Hunters, and we go again, with Seth in the driver's seat this time. He knows exactly how many séances the Hunters have conducted (eight, officially), delivers the Ivan lines smoothly, and you can feel the relief radiating from Russ. This time Ivan has only a quick one-liner to throw in, and the fact that his timing is a little off makes the comic relief angle that much more comical, and all is well in the *Fantastic, Fearsome* world again.

Meaning: we're all set to commune with the dead.

All cynicism aside, Lu (if you can manage it), it's been a long few months for me. Followed by a weird few weeks.

And then, today, there was that interesting thing I learned. That in fact, not only is the supernatural most likely real, but that I myself am a part of it.

I have a power of my own.

All day, preparing for this shoot, I've been turning the facts around and around in my brain. It's basically an insanity merry-go-round in there now. I've tried to chalk my spastic coughing fits up to some wicked Jersey hay fever, but Lucia . . . *my power is lie detecting.* So it's hard to keep lying to myself, under the circumstances.

On the plus side, I finally know what irony means.

And now . . . we've made it through Maggie's preamble and are ready to go forward with this scene. And it's dark in here, and it's spooky, and Ivan's infrared goggles are humming away, and the night breeze glides through the open windows—carrying with it the scent of rot—and my skin prickles with anticipation, and my throat is clear and open and strong, and all of that means that *we're doing this* . . . and that I have no reason to think that we can't or won't get exactly what we want out of this moment.

I shiver.

NOT A SUICIDE.

If we can do this, Lucia? If we can talk to the dead? Does that mean I'll be able to speak with my mother again, someday? Does that mean I'll get some answers?

Maggie thinks so. That's what she told me, when she insisted that the team *needed* me on camera for this séance. She thinks my magic is vital to the success of the scene . . . and that once our séance has succeeded, I'll be that much closer to having my mom back, again.

I know: she played me like a fiddle. *Long shot.* But I have to take it. So here I am.

My aunt places her hands flat on the table. Chunky silver rings glint in the moonlight. It's a slightly hippie-dippie touch; she hasn't gone full Madam Marie gypsy medium, not quite, but she's certainly getting into character, here. But then, that's why she's the best at what she does. She knows how to put on a show.

"We are here at the Overlook Asylum to commune with the spirits of their lost patients," Maggie says. Her voice is smoky, her cadence musical. "We sit at the traditional round table to symbolize the circle of life . . . and afterlife." She looks at Casey. "Casey, the bread."

Hillary hands Casey a cutting board with a loaf of bread, just out of frame. Casey stretches delicately—girl's been practicing her angles—and places it in the center of the table.

"Simple, natural, aromatic food," Casey intones. She's trying to match Maggie's gravitas. Not doing a very good job of it, I have to say. Still, the scene has been set and the effects are working. The ambiance is in high gear, in spite of Casey's Jersey accent. Anyway, they can always loop that over in post. Amanda told me that.

"Winnie, the candles." Maggie slides a box of wooden matches my way.

I wonder, fleetingly, if Amanda resents that I'm in front of the camera right now. Probably not, she's not that way. If anything, she's excited for me. I know Casey resents it, and probably Ivan and Seth are wondering about the special treatment. It's not something I asked for. But they wouldn't have believed me if I'd told them the truth: Maggie wants me here because of my gift. She wants to see what I can do. She *needs* it.

It's a little too early to say whether or not the camera loves me, Lu. Or if it even likes me really. But I try not to worry about that. Dutifully, I light the three candles at the center of the table. They're long, tapered, pale-yellow beeswax set in appropriately tarnished pewter candlesticks. Amanda scoured four different flea markets to find them, and they're perfect, like something you'd use to murder someone in an Agatha Christie novel. The matches take a moment to catch, but then the flame ignites, casting a shimmery halo around my fingertips. I lean forward and *one, two, three,* the candles spark and the room takes on a hazy tint.

I catch Seth's eye over the candles. I must say . . . he gives good haze. I can't help but let my glance linger.

This moment, *our* moment, is not lost on Casey. She eagerly chimes in. "Three is considered a charmed number in attracting spirits, and the candles project warmth and light, which will bring them to us."

Smarty-pants.

Maggie opens a dark file folder and slides a few pages out. "I have here some of the original records concerning the Kallikak sisters. They were among the most mistreated of the Overlook patients. I'd like us to channel our energies toward them in particular." She holds up one sheet. "It will help to have a visual image on which to focus your thoughts."

I recognize the image from our time downstairs. Marie Kallikak. She's only a few years older than I am. Her outfit is old-fashioned—possibly older even than the era in which the picture was taken—a long white Victorian-style nightgown with a high neck and a row of tiny buttons up the front. The photo is black and white, of course, stained murky sepia with age. Marie's curls are wild with neglect. Her eyes are inky pools set against shadowed hollows.

Looking at the picture, something comes over me. I

squirm in my seat. Marie's eyes bore into mine. Everything about this woman's face tells me that she needs our help.

And every cell of my body tells me that despite every effort to pretend otherwise, despite my reluctance to accept the truth . . .

I wonder if I might be able to give her what she needs. Her spirit, anyway. If it's really still here. If it really needs help.

It makes no sense. None of it makes sense. But I can't deny what I feel.

Hope.

NOT A SUICIDE.

Whatever it was that killed my mother, I wasn't able to help her. But maybe I'll be able to help someone else?

I look up, away from the photo to find that Seth is looking back at me again. He's smiling again. I smile back. Again. Another moment, Lu? Maybe. There's no point in lying about this, either, because coughing would break the scene.

"It's time," Maggie says. The lights dim. *Thanks, Amanda.* I imagine how the five of us must look, huddled around this table, the candles flickering like something alive, beckoning.

"Let us join hands." Maggie is totally in character now. She brings it, turns on her full-force medium mode. And yet she *believes.*

Ivan's hand is warm and sweaty. Casey's is softer than I would have expected, and trembling slightly. She's up again next. Her big paranormal moment . . .

She closes her eyes. "Our beloved Marie Kallikak, we bring you gifts from life into death. Come to us, Marie, and move among us."

A hush falls over the table as we await a reply. I'll admit it, Lucia—even I'm straining to make out any creak, any whisper. I bow my head slightly, thinking that supplication, maybe, is a way to draw a skittish spirit out.

Nothing.

There's quick movement under the table, and Casey squeezes my palm—a weirdly intimate gesture—and I realize that Maggie has given her a kick. She takes another breath, tries again. "Marie, we are here for you. Come to us. We want to know the truth of your time at Overlook, and the circumstances of your death. Yours, and your sisters."

In the silence that ensues, I realize I've been holding my breath. I let it go at the same time as curtains just behind Maggie flutter.

Casey inhales sharply. "Did you guys feel that?"

Ivan and Seth nod.

"It's freezing in here, all of a sudden," Ivan says, offering himself up as our exposition jockey. It's clunky, yeah, but sometimes you need it, Lu. This is TV.

Maggie nods, serene. Her eyes are still closed. "This is good, this means that we have company. The thermal imaging camera will confirm a spike in the levels later. But for now, let's concentrate on sending our friend some energy, so he or she will feel comfortable talking to us."

Again we bow our heads. I feel it, our collective energy, crackling and snaking from palm to palm. I feel it grow. Because, Lucia: I want her to come to us. To speak to us. I want to communicate with Marie. I want to know that it can be done. And I do want to help her. I want to know what happened in this hospital.

Talk to us, I think. The thought blazes in my mind, so bright and loud it must be shining right through my skull. *Talk to me.*

That's when I hear it. Three quick, sharp raps.

Beside me, Casey gasps. Her fingernails dig into my palm.

She's here, I think, and I believe it. *Marie is here.*

TWENTY

If this were a movie, I'd be easy to cast, Lu. It's so obvious, my part: daughter of the True Believer, blood descendent. Skeptic. Pop-culture "maven," emotionally detached, always ready with a quip or deflection. I can see the cattle call they'd hold for auditions, a roundup of all the C-list ex-Disney starlets, the ones who weren't hospitalized for "exhaustion" just yet. She'd have a fake eating disorder, and a side-boob problem.

It's so clichéd, Lucia. So *undignified*.

But worse, the script itself: nonbeliever Slowly Comes Around, develops Power, learns of Lineage Link to the Super-natural. Gets Overeager During a Séance. Develops False Sense of Confidence, along with an Ill-Advised Curiosity. All tied to Desperate Desire to Talk to Dead Mother Just One More Time.

Not to mention: she's all caught up in the moment, in the plummeting temperature and the fluctuating meters and the phantom knocks on the table, and somehow loses sight of that timeless truism we all *know*. Which is: That *girl cannot allow herself to be swept up, to get distracted. That girl, that reluctant archetype?*

She is the Final Girl.

That girl, our Final Girl, she'll have a moment, usually at the halfway point of the movie, where she suddenly assumes all is going to be fine and dandy, a-okay.

It will be none of those things.

That moment is a *turning point*, Lucia, and some movies are better at it than others. In *Nightmare on Elm Street*, it's when Nancy pulls the hat out of her dream and into reality, assuming tactile evidence of Fred Kruger's existence will persuade her mother of his existence. (It doesn't.) In *The Shining*, it's just after Danny meets the woman in room 237, though one would argue that Wendy harbors no such illusions of Things Being Even Remotely Okay at that point in the movie. (They're not.) If nothing else, Wendy assumes Jack will agree to leave the Overlook. (*The Overlook! The Overlook, Lu!*)

But he doesn't, of course. And things get so, so much worse.

Anyway, the heroine has a pivotal moment of belief. (Is it grandiose to assert oneself as the heroine in one's own movie? Or just the obvious conclusion?) That moment allows her to think she can conquer what's to come. And maybe she can. Usually, she does.

In the movies, anyway.

But not without steep sacrifice. Not without a price.

Point being: things will get worse—*much* worse—before they get better. For the Final Girl. I know that. My better self knows that all too well. But still, in the moment, I forget. I *am* the cliché. I get swept up. I forget the underlying truth, the stakes: if the paranormal is real and I have a power, then the rest of the myths may be real, too. Including the ghosts.

Including the Jersey Devil himself.

* * *

MARIE KALLIKAK IS HERE; I just know it. She's answered our summoning; she's here to chat. She has things she wants to tell us, Lu.

Again: three quick raps.

I shiver, glance up, flick my eyes around the table, confirming that the sounds weren't only in my head. Maggie's eyes are still lidded at half-mast. Seth's head is cocked to one side, ready to absorb what Marie has to share. Casey's eyes are shut so tightly her entire face is a road map of tense wrinkles. She looks like a panicked shar-pei. Next to me, Ivan's face is slack, drained of color.

Okay, so, yeah. Not just in my head.

Without breaking our circle, Maggie clicks on a dictaphone-ish thing that she operates with a remote pedal beneath her chair. It makes a grinding sound that is comforting and also otherworldly at the same time.

"Marie, if this is you, please give us a sign."

Yes, please do. I am breathless.

And then.

Two of our three candles go out, plunging us further into shadow. A squeak escapes from Ivan.

"We know you were treated cruelly here, Marie," Maggie continues. "We know you have secrets. Please, Marie—share your nightmare with us. Share it, so you can be free of it."

Silence. At my side, Ivan twitches.

Share it, so you can be free of it. Is that how these things work? If that's right, maybe my mother can share and be free, too. Maybe she can free *me*.

Casey sighs.

"Do not be afraid. We want to know your story. We want to bring justice to you, for your family."

Silence. Still.

And then. *And then.*

There is a beat, and the third candle goes out.

All at once the room is near pitch-black. The curtains we hung earlier block out all but the faintest tendrils of moonlight. The only sounds are the clicking of Maggie's recorder and our breathing. A breeze skates along the back of my neck. Is it colder in here? The readers will confirm later, of course, but I don't think I'll need to check their results. Ivan's palm is slicker in my own. I want to break away, to wipe off my hand, but that's verboten during the séance. We can't break the circle, our channel, our bond.

That's when I hear it again: three short taps.

"Thank you, Marie, for acknowledging us. Can you knock once for *yes* and two for *no*? Perhaps we can talk that way?"

I don't realize I'm holding my breath until the response comes:

Knock.

Yes.

She is here. She wants to talk to us.

"Wonderful. So: First of all, are you Marie Kallikak?"

Knock.

"Were you imprisoned in this hospital?"

Knock.

"Against your will."

A pause, not unlike a hesitation. *Knock.*

"And were you subjected to unconventional treatments? Invasive therapies?"

Knock. Another pause, for clarity this time. *Knock. Yes and yes.*

"Why were you committed, Marie?"

We wait.

Nothing.

The air swirls with a hot, active pulse. The darkness grows darker, still.

I feel warm breath on the back of my neck.

Marie? I think.

Knock.

My stomach falls open. *Who put you here? Who imprisoned you?*

"Marie?" It's Maggie.

I don't know if she senses that I'm somehow speaking with Marie—probably she does, she's Maggie, after all—but she can feel the hesitation, she feels the jagged break in the energy streaking through the air. Marie is still here. Marie is still talking. But not to Maggie.

To *me.*

Turning point. This is my turning point, Lucia.

A thought, warm and soft like a faded comforter, curls around the edges of my brain: *keep going, Winnie.*

It's Seth. He's with us, he's with me, inside my thoughts. He *knows.*

I don't ask how this is happening; I just draw that comforter against me, hold it close as I can.

Emboldened, I sit straighter in my chair, tighten my grip on Ivan's and Casey's hands. "Who put you in here, Marie?" I ask, aloud this time.

In the dark, I feel a jerk on our circle. It's coming from Maggie, who's tensed in her seat. A crack of thunder explodes outside, violent and unexpected, even though we'd talked about the possibility of rain all day.

Beside me, Ivan gasps. "What's happening?" he whispers.

I feel a flash, a wave of pity for him because I know, Lu, that he's not a True Believer. I know he's been lying since the day we met and probably even earlier than that; I know all those things with dead certainty, and because I do,

I know how his heart must be clawing to escape his chest right about now.

What *is* happening?

I think I know that, too, Lu.

"She's with us," I whisper through clenched teeth. *"She's inside Maggie."*

Outside, there's a silent flash of lightning, an alien ultraviolet, and Maggie convulses again, flailing, breaking the chain of clasped hands.

"Don't break the circle!" Casey shrieks, but of course it's too late. Maggie is jittering in her seat like she's having a seizure, like she's been electrocuted, *like she's been possessed by the devil,* and the storm thrashes outside in angry sympathy. Her body swoops forward, a rag doll, one slender arm sweeping across the table as a gust of wind explodes through the room.

The candles turn over.

I smell smoke, bitter and acrid. Casey shrieks again, and Ivan lets out a small whimper. But that mental blanket is back, sliding over my shoulders this time, as though Seth's arms are actually around me.

Let her speak, he says. *Let Marie tell us what she needs to say.*

I'm trying, I answer. *I'm waiting.*

There's a pop of embers on the tablecloth; the wicks must still be hot.

Maggie heaves one last involuntary gasp, head flung back, and then collapses like a bag of bones onto the table, barely missing the candles.

At that, Casey full-on screams. Then it's bedlam: she's leaping up and flicking on the camping lanterns placed strategically around the room. She grabs a sneaker from one foot and slams it down on the table, smothering the last of the tiny sparks.

Jane materializes in the doorway like a phantom, backlit. "What the *fuck* is going on here?"

"You tell us!" Casey demands, almost sobbing. She's sweaty and truly terrified. "Everything was going *fine*—Marie was here, she was talking to us and everything!—and then Winnie just, like, *took over*, and then Maggie was, um, *possessed* or something!"

She dissolves into weeping.

Ivan maneuvers around the table to place a tentative, reassuring hand on her shoulder. You know she's a mess, Lucia, because she totally lets him. I hear another set of footsteps approach; it's Amanda, hands on hips, eyes full of concern. She would have been watching us on the monitor. I have to wonder what it all looked like from where she sat.

She raises all the lights in the room, does something with the curtains so that the rain outside stays outside.

Jane rushes to Maggie. She props Maggie up gently, waves a hand in front of her face. Slowly, Maggie blinks back to life.

Her eyes flutter open. She glances around the room, fuzzy, and then homes in on me like a heat-seeking missile.

"Well, well, well." She gives a crooked grin. "My little Sour Patch Kid has some dynamite, buried deep in there."

Casey bristles at that, but Seth draws forward, waiting.

There is the weirdest energy in this room right now, Lu. And some of that's because of *me*. I'm proud, too. I admit it. Because: Can you even?

"So," Maggie goes on. "What'd she say?"

"Who, Marie?" I'm confused. "You heard it all."

She wags a finger at me. "Dearie. I meant *after* I went all whirling dervish. The candles. The fire." At our collective blank stare, she sighs in exasperation. "Winnie, you I can excuse, you're new to this. But the rest of you—have you forgotten all of your training?"

Casey blinks several times. A flash of recognition crosses her face. She shakes Ivan's hand away, collects herself with a sniff, and starts to sift through the candle ashes.

"Is there a method to the madness?" Maggie asks, her voice a singsong.

Casey's eyes widen. She nods, awed, backing away. "There is." She clears the candle fragments out of the way. Now it's my turn for awe. The air seeps out of the room. All I can see is that tiny swatch of table, where the cloth was pulled away in all the commotion.

Marie's final message to us. To *me*.

She has left us a missive, amidst the smoke and ashes. The burn marks are hazy and jagged, of course. This communicating with the dead is an imperfect science. But nonetheless, the words are there. They're scorched into the wood in plain sight.

Mther Leds.

Leeds.

Mama.

TWENTY-ONE

We don't speak about the séance before we turn in for the night, not really, even though we're all obviously thinking about nothing but.

Casey starts to say something in the immediate after-math—of course it would be Casey, Lu—babbling about how Genie's going to *freak* when she hears about this. Maggie just cuts her off. ("*Genie's* not your boss now, little Ring Pop. *I* am.") Then she takes about a million and five pictures of the scorch marks with her iPhone. She's all business now. She instructs Hillary and Russ to film the living shit out of the room from every possible angle, and tells the rest of us to "marinate on it."

Well, I can do that. A little quiet time is not the worst idea. So we separate. Casey steps outside "for some fresh air" and no one bothers to point out that it's raining, and that she's obviously going to call Genie. (The Odditorium, Lucia: How irrelevant does it seem right now?) Amanda and I set up our sleeping bags in what was probably once a small intake office just off the cavernous entry vestibule. The rest of the crew is sprawled out, tucked away in different corners anywhere that isn't a full-on, asbestos-thick health hazard—and taking shifts on the various equipment set up throughout. Amanda and I were deemed "expendable" for these wee hours, which is a lucky break, considering.

Soon enough, I'm cocooned in a brand-new-from-Target-on-Route-10, extra-thick-nylon sleeping bag, blinking madly at the darkened ceiling, thoughts running like a hamster on an exercise wheel.

Mther Leds. Leeds. Mama.

Mother.

NOT A SUICIDE.

Is there a connection? No, of course not. I know the lore as well as any Hunter now: Mother Leeds gave birth to the Jersey Devil, according to the legend. And the Kallikak women believed themselves to be possessed by the Devil. By *a* devil, anyway. Marie believes that Mother Leeds was the cause of her own persecution.

Maggie seems to believe that, too.

But I don't see how any of that could be related to . . . whatever it was that happened to my mother.

The questions turn over again and again. I don't have any good answers. Maggie might; she probably does—but she's not talking. At least, not yet. So once again, Lu, it's just me, alone with my thoughts.

For a minute or two, that is.

Then I hear the clock chime.

It's loud. It splits the silence in two. It splits *time* in two, into: *before* and *after*, into *real* and *unreal*, into *here* and *not*.

The clock is chiming. The once-majestic grandfather clock we found in the lobby. The one with rats or mice nesting inside. The one that was old, rotted out, and completely defunct.

The one that was broken.

Amanda snaps awake next to me. She sits straight up in her sleeping bag, groping for her phone. When she flicks on the flashlight app, her face is a ghostly gleam of cheekbones and shadow. "What the hell was that?"

"The clock, I think. I'm pretty sure. That big one from the front hall."

"The broken clock?" Amanda blinks at me.

"Yes. Well, apparently not so broken." I sit up, too, and start unzipping myself from my bag. It's freezing in here. "I don't know."

Amanda quickly pulls her hair into a knot and ropes it into place with an elastic from around her wrist. "If only that were the weirdest thing that's happened today. I take it you're coming around on the whole, 'believing in the paranormal' thing?"

"No comment."

As if to punctuate me, the chiming ceases abruptly. The sudden silence that follows is almost eerier.

"You guys hear that?" a voice asks.

Amanda shrieks. She flies out of her sleeping bag. When she realizes it's Seth, peeking in on us, she pulls her tank top down and hitches up her pajama bottoms. "Seriously, *what the hell?*"

"Sorry," Seth says, but his eyes are dancing like he's actually a little bit amused. "I didn't mean to startle you guys."

"You knew we were probably sleeping," Amanda points out.

"But then, the clock . . . I assumed it'd woken you up."

"So naturally, it made perfect sense to *creep up on us in the dead of night.*" She glances at her phone again. "Whatever. Anyway. Apology accepted. It's four in the morning. What could you possibly want?"

Seth runs his fingers through his hair, which I just at this moment realize is swinging free of its usual ponytail. It's very bouncy, Lucia, even though we've all been playing it a little fast and loose with the personal hygiene these days. (Production life! It's a grind.) I bet it even smells good, too, in that boy-shampoo way.

Oh, right: Seth was *in my brain* earlier this evening.

Speaking of the weirdest things that happened tonight. It makes me feel a little bit naked, standing in front of him now. But not necessarily in a bad way.

Share it, so you can be free of it.

Weird, weirder, weirdest.

"I was, uh, looking for more of the little dictaphone tapes. For the recorders upstairs."

Isn't it charmingly *retro*, all of this quaint, analog technology the Hunters use? They seem to think it's more reliable than a lot of the "newfangled" machinery. Or at least, that there's value to be had in using the two together. Hence, tiny little cassette tapes, stacked in plastic shoe boxes, labeled diligently and filed away for posterity. They make digital dictaphones these days, Lucia. But our Hunters won't have any of that.

Amanda yawns and narrows her eyes. "Didn't we give you, like, a million before you went up there?"

"Maybe not a million," Seth says. "Maybe more like ten. But something bizarre is going on with them upstairs."

"More bizarre than smoke signals from Marie Kallikak?" she counters. "More bizarre than a dead clock suddenly springing back to life?"

Seth shrugs. "Kind of the same bizarre, I guess."

I find my voice. "Bizarre like how?"

He shakes his head. "You're not going to believe this . . ."

"Really?" I cut him off. "That's your line after the séance?" That gets a smile. I smile back.

"Touché. Well, it was like the second the clock started going off, the tapes went crazy. The machine was going, but it snapped off, started doing that auto-rewind thing like when it gets to the end of a tape."

"Maybe it *was* the end of a tape," Amanda suggests dryly.

Seth frowns. "It wasn't. I was monitoring. Casey and I both were. We were up, taking turns."

"Oh, you were *up. Together.*"

He completely ignores her coy tone, which makes me much happier than it should. "We tried the backup tapes, but one snapped, and the others came all unspooled in the machine."

Weird, weirder, weirdest.

"Very *Outer Limits*," Amanda says. "Maggie will be thrilled."

"He's not lying," I say. I know this, now. "Whatever's going on with the tapes, *he* doesn't have a non-supernatural explanation for it."

Seth gestures to me while looking at Amanda, as if to say: *Listen to this girl. She's one of us now.* But he is saying it. To me.

"If you can't beat 'em, join 'em," I murmur out loud. I turn to Amanda. "But first, get 'em more tapes." I dig into the backpack on the floor beside my sleeping bag for the key ring. "In the back of the SUV. Maybe under that big-box crate of Ding Dongs."

Amanda pouts. "It's so dark and creepy out there!"

"It's pretty dark and creepy in *here*," I point out. I toss the keys at her. "Meet us in the turret room. We need to get back to Casey, anyway." I hate to say it, but it's the truth. She probably shouldn't be alone for too long, with all the strange stuff going on. That's just Horror Movie Rules 101.

I turn back to Seth, who nods. I tell myself: that's just chivalry, good manners, not, like, proof of romantic feelings for Casey. Myself wants to believe that.

"In the meantime—" I start, trying to put away thoughts of romance when there's for-real more important stuff going on—"Seth, I want to hear what you got on record, before everything went all *fantastic* up there."

AN UPDATE ON THE turret room for you, Lucia: it's still all kinds of lovey-dovey. You wouldn't expect that from, you know, an *abandoned insane asylum*, but the fact is: we PAs get the job done. I do, truly, wish I weren't wondering about the romance factor of the turret room as I make my way upstairs, right behind Seth, I wish I could say I was 156 percent focused on the fact that Seth's found some potentially extremely persuasive paranormal evidence up there . . . but I can't. I can't tell a lie, Lucia. Not these days, not anymore.

I scan the room in tiny little birdlike pecks that I stash away for future analysis.

The two sleeping bags: shoved together the way Elena predicted they would be when she jiggered the zippers. The flowers: gathered and set in a cloudy old vase that looks like it *could* be from the days of Overlook's first incarnation. In the corner: clothes, discarded. Mind you, they must have been exchanged for sleepwear at *some* point, as Seth and Casey are both currently fully dressed. But nonetheless, Lu: *clothes*, tossed in a corner as though they might have pulled off in a rush, in a heat, thrown aside carelessly. Boy *and* girl clothes, in a tangle that can't help suggest an embrace. On top of the pile, like an afterthought: a blue, lace-edged bra. It's just a few shades lighter than the Day-Glo hair that tickles Casey's cheekbones.

Oh *God*. Casey's bra, thrown across Seth's cargo shorts.

And Casey: surveying me steadily. Seeing me seeing the space, knowing exactly what I'm wondering, what conclusions I'm drawing. She holds my gaze and grins. Then her eyes move to Seth.

"Dude, Winnie, did Seth *tell* you about the tapes?" Ivan pops up behind Seth and me, bounding into the room like a puppy, shattering the mood.

I give my throat a tentative clearing, check the pipes as it were, and evaluate: he's genuinely excited, genuinely freaked.

So. Ivan believes fully in whatever strangeness was happening. *Is* happening. That's . . . different. Useful to know.

"Yeah, he told us," I reply. "Amanda went out for more tapes. But in the meantime, I want to hear what's on the ones you've been running."

"Nothing, probably," Casey says. She sounds impatient.

"Meaning, you don't think anything paranormal is going on?" I ask. But really I'm wondering if she just wants to kick us all out so she can be alone with Seth again.

"*Meaning*, the tape freaked out and vomited itself out of the recorder. *Tapes*, in fact. All ten of them. So I kind of don't think we're gonna hear *anything* on them. They're probably ruined."

She has a point, but I'm not going to admit it. "But you haven't actually *listened*, yet? You haven't even tried to play them back?"

"We wanted to wait until you were here," Seth clarifies, shooting a look at Casey. "I mean . . . we wanted to wait until everyone was here to hear it."

"Everyone." I speak slowly, deliberately. "Okay."

Since when am I *everyone*, Lu?

TWENTY-TWO

My hands are shaky as I spring the cassette player open, nestle the tiny plastic tape inside. It takes me two tries to snap the machine shut again. As it closes, finally, I feel Seth's palm brush against my back. Then it's gone.

"Ugh, please. You're not going to be able to make anything out," Casey whines.

"Quiet." I don't say it nicely. It's the dead of night and I'm learning all sorts of new and terrifying things about myself and my family. Forgive me if I'm a touch grouchy, Lu.

"We already tried it, like, twelve times," she insists.

"Shush," Seth says, firm, and that does the trick.

Clack whirrrrr. The machine clicks into motion, spinning time backward. After having handed over the new tapes, Amanda has retreated to the doorway, eyes glued to her phone.

"Are you filming this?" Ivan asks her, his voice as shaky as my hands.

"I am," she assures him.

"Who *cares*?" I cut in, startling everyone, even myself, with the force of my own voice. Slowly, more deliberately now: "I mean come on: *Who cares?* Hillary and Russ bugged this place to the rafters. We're getting it, okay? We're getting it all. Now *shut up.*"

The whirring stops. There's silence in the space between the five of us. The tape hitches, begins to spool again, ready to reveal its secrets. For an agonizing moment, there is nothing. It is emptiness so round and overwhelming it crushes my throat, my ribs, the space behind my ears. Behind me, I hear Casey take a breath, hear her wind up for another round of *told you so,* and imagine though I can't actually see it, the silencing glance Seth gives her. His hand is on my back again.

I'm paralyzed.

From the machine: a series of hums, a pop of static . . . a buzz like white noise between radio frequencies.

It's nothing, it's really nothing, *and I was dumb, I was naïve, I was hopeful enough to think that any of this could actually mean someth—*

"SSSS . . . Shhh . . . SS . . . Susan."

In my head, in that inner space just behind my eyes, the world fractures into tiny glittering pieces.

From the tape: "*SSSusan. SUSAN.*"

Susan.

My mother's name.

"Uh, did everyone hear that?" Amanda asks, her voice shrill.

I hold my breath, wait for the confirmation.

"I think it said *Susan,*" Ivan offers.

"Great," Casey says, snippy. "So who's Susan?"

I am in another black hole, but I find my voice. It is clogged, not with lies or their detection, but with sand. "My mother."

The other four turn rapid-fire, away from the tape and

to me, radiating confusion, fear, I can't tell what else. Seth's
eyes are searching.

Clack. Whirr. The tape isn't finished.

"The Devil. The Devil."

Amanda shrieks.

"The Devil the Devil the Devil the Devil the Dev—"

Abruptly, the sound halts, its absence sharp as gunfire. I
flinch. The machine's lid pops open. The tape juts up, self-
ejecting, somehow, unspooling in a hectic trail of tangled
ribbon. I reach to extract the cassette from the mountain of
tape. Before I can stop, the ribbon catches, shreds.

"Are you *crazy?*" Casey shouts at me. "Now we can't listen
to it!"

I'm paralyzed again, clutching the cassette.

"We couldn't listen to it at all until Winnie got here," Seth
points out.

Casey makes a face like he's so stupid it physically pains
her. "Oh, so you think the tape only played because of
Winnie? *For* Winnie?"

Seth nods. He doesn't blink. "Well, yeah. Yes."

Susan. The Devil.

I shake my head. My mother wasn't the Devil. If that's
what the voice even meant. My mother wore striped pink-
and-green socks in the winter because she said it made her
cheerier. My mother wouldn't eat watermelon because it
was "too watery"; she preferred "brighter" fruits like canta-
loupe and pineapple. My mother read forensic mysteries and
watched TV modeling competitions and freaked out when
my father made their bed "wrong." My mother loved thun-
derstorms and cloudless sunshine and nothing in between,
weather-wise, though when pressed she'd concede that snow
days were at least good for reading.

She loved hardwood floors and vintage perfume bottles. She loved brand-new pink erasers, fireworks, and crafts-fair beaded jewelry. And she loved my father. And me.

My mother was many things, some of which I'm only now beginning to learn about. Maybe, just maybe, she was magical. (She certainly was to me.) But she was not the Devil.

I bite my lip. "Everyone heard that, right? *Susan? The Devil?*"

Nods all around, no hesitation.

"Dude," Ivan breathes. "What did your mother have to do with the Jersey Devil?"

"*Nothing.* God!" But: *something.* Something, yet. My thoughts are a tidal wave. What what what? *Think, Winnie.* But I can't. Not clearly. It's all a jumble. The words scorched on the table: *Mther Leds. Leeds. Mama.* My mother's maiden name: *Leader. Susan Leader.* The Wikihaunts page: *Mother Leeds.*

My aunt: *"The Leader women are all powerful, Winnie. All of us."*

Aunt Maggie, "hiding in plain sight."

What would my mother have to hide from? What did all those other women—the Kallikaks, the Leeds-descended—have to hide from?

The message on the mirror: there one moment; wiped clean, tabula rasa, the next.

Even if my mother *did* have powers, she wasn't the *Devil.* Devils don't dip their pancakes into syrup, bite by bite, instead of pouring it over the whole stack. Devils don't protect their daughters from evil neighbors. Devils don't protect their daughters with magic . . .

I squeeze my eyes shut. Marie Kallikak believed herself to be possessed by the Devil. Whether or not that was true, it destroyed her. From the outside in.

NOT A SUICIDE.

But who would have hurt my mother? I couldn't think of a single person. My mother loved *people*. Until this very day I'd chalked up her powers to her being an exceptional people-person. And everyone, *everyone*, loved my mother.

That leaves one other possibility.

I hear Seth sigh beside me, know he is coming to the same conclusion I am, know he has his own reasons for feeling conflicted. I know every nuance of his thought process, stitched into the cadence of that breath. I don't stop to think about how I know all that, just now.

People claim to see the Jersey Devil up and about, all the time, Lu. *It touched Amanda's mother, once.* And that was just the one, the most personal, of the anecdotes I'd heard. The New Jersey Devil. It lives, it breathes, it walks among us, to this day yet.

This idea makes more sense to me than the idea that my mother committed suicide. That she voluntarily abandoned me, abandoned my dad.

How badly do I want to believe those words in the mirror? So badly it hurts, really *hurts*, in a palpable, aching way, Lu. I'm letting any last semblance of reason slip away from me. I know that. I know it's wrong. But it's too late. The glimmer, the spark is there:

What if she didn't kill herself?

What if the Devil *killed my mother, instead?*

TWENTY-THREE

"Wait. This is weird." Casey gnaws at a lower lip.

I try—and fail—to hide my disdain. "Yes," I say, flat. "*This* is weird. Just this. Nothing else leading up to this one particular moment. Like, say, *everything that's happened up until now.*"

I feel bad (sort of) the moment the words leave my mouth, worse (not that much worse) as Casey's cheeks redden slightly. But then Amanda giggles, high-pitched and nervous, and Casey recovers. That sour-lemon façade is back, all puckered disapproval, and my sympathy evaporates. Screw it.

"I just meant," Casey continues, her voice barbed, "that we're the only ones awake. Where's the rest of the crew? Why didn't they hear the clock?"

To her credit, that's not a bad point, but it just doesn't seem important right now. I shrug. "Maybe it's more sound-proofed, where they're sleeping. Maybe they sleep deeper because they're older, because they have more responsibility here, because they're all on prescription downers." I take a deep breath. "Maybe the clock didn't want them to wake up—maybe it just wanted us."

I said that. *I said that, Lucia.*

And I meant it, too.

Seth takes note. His face is alert, like a forest animal sensing an unwelcome presence in the woods.

Casey rolls her eyes. "And this from the chick who doesn't believe in the first place."

"I don't care what you think," I say, and my voice is steady. "But you're right; this is weird. There's something weird going on here. We all heard that tape. That was *my mother's name*, and then—the Devil. And then that writing on the mirror—"

"What writing on the mirror?" Amanda cuts in, and I remember that I'm the only one who saw that, that no one else knows. *NOT A SUICIDE.*

"Nothing, forget it," I say, shaking my head. The room tilts, shifts dangerously, along with all the things I thought were true. There's only one person who may have the answers I need. "I'm going to talk to Maggie."

"I'll come with you," Seth says instantly. And even though it's private, even though my family is the last thing I want to let Seth in on before I know the whole truth myself, it feels good, safe and warm, like that cozy mental comforter that he should want to follow. And so I nod at him, short and sincere. Grateful.

"You can't *go*," Casey sputters. To Seth, obviously, not me. "Elena wanted us to *spend the night up here*. She wants footage." She pauses, taking everyone else in, then plows forward in a softer voice, with Meaningful Eyes. "Of *us*."

Seth shrugs. "Don't worry about it. There's plenty of footage. I'm sure we got it." He reaches for my hand, and the room closes in on me. "Come on, Winnie. I think Maggie's in the basement, in the records room."

"Bring your phone and keep the video *on*," Amanda instructs.

I nod, stumble after Seth, my mind a tornado.

The Devil. My mother. Suicide. Or not?

And also—wait.

What did he mean, *plenty of footage?*

I know, I know—*so not the issue, Winn, focus now!*

But still: Plenty of footage of *what*, Lu?

INTERVIEW FOOTAGE—SETH JARVIS—TAPE 5.8—CASEY ROMANCE?

SETH:
What are the tapes from the turret room going
to *show*? Come on. Does it matter? Maggie can
make this footage look like anything she wants
it to, right?

(laughs, a beat)

Huh? Winnie? Why would I worry about what
Winnie thinks? Seriously? This is what you guys
want to talk about? Whatever you want, it's all
there for you. Check out the footage for yourself.

FADE OUT

ONCE WE'RE DOWN IN the basement, it's easy to see how Maggie could have missed the clock chiming. Back in the dank underground labyrinth, the concrete walls block out anything but what's right there, right now: our footsteps and breathing. Seth charts the course down the hallway, lighting our way with his phone flashlight, the little red light on his touch screen assuring me that he's taking seriously Amanda's insistence on filming *everything*. I'm relieved that Seth is relatively sure-footed, stable, and confident.

I am the opposite of stable and confident. In many ways.

He turns left, and that's when we hear it: murmurings, rolling and indistinct. It's Maggie, and maybe . . . Russ?

Without warning, Seth stops short. I stumble into him, sending him through the door and into the records room, tripping over my own feet right behind him until we're both sheepish and fidgety but at least standing straight. It's all very *Heeere's Johnny!* except neither of us is wielding an ax.

Maggie looks us over. "Hi," she says wryly.

The room is dark, the only light coming from two portable lanterns resting against opposite far walls. Russ has a camera mounted, trained on Maggie and the wall behind her. She's holding what appears to be the mother of all glow sticks, glimmering neon phosphorescence. She's streaking it and its electric glow across the wall like graffiti.

"UV light wand," she explains, catching me gaping. "Looking for traces of psychic residue. That's 'ghost footprints' to you, applejack. Think of this as a spiritual crime scene."

I gesture toward a luminescent splotch along the wall. "Looks like you found some."

She grins slowly. "Oh, yeah. The basement is a hot spot. We're thinking maybe a secret dungeon, maybe whatever was going on with Marie and the other Kallikaks, was going on here."

My stomach drops. The wall is practically dripping with Day-Glo, fierce and intense, demanding we stare.

A spiritual crime *spree*, basically.

"If I'm right," she supplies, "things were pretty gruesome down here."

We've all used and heard the phrase "my blood ran cold," because of course, it's the most obvious, the most cliché of all possible clichés, so I won't say that's what happens, Lucia. I won't say it, but you'll know. And it isn't just my blood; it's my bones, my flesh, my cells . . . every molecule in my being turned to solid ice. Because that wall . . . it represents an atrocity that may or may not be connected to my mother. To me.

The glow begins to fade. And then it trails off, into a corner, melting behind a stash of age-battered boxes, half eaten by mold.

"What's that?" I ask, not sure I want to know the answer.

"That's the best part."

With flair for the camera, she slides the ancient boxes out of the way, stirring up dust. I see it: speckled with the last few lingering drops of neon residue—as if the ghosts were shaking off their boots in a doorway—is a hidden cache in the floor.

"Jesus *Christ!*" Seth explodes.

I'm so startled my knees buckle. I'd almost forgotten he was there.

"You're filming, right?" Maggie asks him, and Seth nods. "Good. We'll be able to choose between your tape and Russ's. Shaky-cam might work better for effect." She thinks for a moment. "Can you do the scream again?"

"What?" Seth is truly puzzled. "Maybe. I guess?" He looks doubtful. "It'll probably sound fake."

"Just try," she encourages.

So he does, like six or seven times, and each time I have

to pretend to be startled again, so that by the end I'm feeling like a marionette. The bad news is that I'm not less freaked out than I was the first time.

Finally, Maggie is satisfied that we got it. With another Mona Lisa smile, she crouches down, fiddles with the latch on the door. That sharp, acrid stench grows stronger. With a wet, heavy *thump* the hatch opens.

"Anything inside?" Even Russ sounds excited.

"Oh, yes." Maggie reaches long, sinewy arms down and retrieves a crate, crusted in dirt and bursting with water-logged papers. Gingerly, she thumbs through the materials.

"Oh, my pretties," she breathes. "I think we've found the mother lode."

"Records?" Russ asks.

"Records. Patient intake forms. Evaluations. But not the ones a doctor would *want* you to see. These were the *real* records, I think. The ones that documented all the stuff Marie Kallikak was trying to tell us about."

The mother lode. Just like that, I forget all about my original reason for tracking Maggie down. This box is more important than all that. Maybe even the key. The mirror, the tape . . . whatever they were hinting at, maybe this box will shed some light. Maggie seems to hear my thoughts, as has become typical. Waves me over. "These are a mess. Take this upstairs, and find Amanda. *As carefully as you can*, I want you to take the papers out, wipe them down, lay them out to dry. Then maybe we can get a look at what they're saying."

"Yes. *Of course*." I lift the crate. It's heavy. I grunt, protesting when Seth holds his arms out to take it from me, an offering.

"I can do it," I insist.

"I know you can," he says, and because I can tell that he means it, I let him do it for me, anyway.

We're heading out when Russell calls to Maggie from behind the camera. "Amazing find, Boss Lady. Anything else down there?"

"Nope. Just that one box, marshmallow fluff," she trills. "But it's plenty."

The cough bubbles up, rumbles in the back of my throat. I'm able to hold it at bay, to play at normal, but just barely. Because, Lu, here's the thing:

Maggie was *lying* just now.

TWENTY-FOUR

The first mile of a run always hurts. Achy joints, tight muscles, the idea that I could be somewhere, anywhere, other than outside. I make a deal with myself to get it done. Tell myself: *it's just the one mile. If you're not down for it after that, you can go home.*

I don't mean it. Not really. And I never go home.

They say it takes ten minutes for the human body to adjust to a differentiated state. (Who are *they*? I don't know. I'm not the boss of these things, Lu.) About ten minutes to fall asleep. Ten to feel full when you're eating. And ten minutes for me to lose myself in this morning run, to breathe in the dawn, absorb it like armor I'll carry with me through the day. Ten minutes for the burn in my flesh to fuel me, to feel part of me, to remind me that *yes, I know how to do this, my body was built for this.* Ten minutes for that muscle memory to reassure me: in some things, I am strong.

By ten minutes in, running feels more natural than not running, more natural than breathing. That's when I know that one mile would never, could never be enough. Before this summer, I thought *that* was my superpower.

Of course, before this summer, I thought I'd understood my mother. My teen angst was always so mild, Lucia—what did we have to rage against? Except for that one time, when Mom suggested ever so gently that bangs were a bad idea. She'd been there, done that. (She was right.) Then my mother died and *became* my teen angst.

One mile. One point twelve. One point sixty-five.

No turning back.

The South Mountain Reservation unfolds beneath me, dirt paths beckoning underneath a brilliant canopy of summer forest green. My footfalls are even, sure, as though I've been here, traced this route before.

Unbelievably, Maggie gave the peanut gallery the morning off. She and the lead team are meeting to review footage, scan it against the scripts, re-break story lines and rethink that which needs rethinking. It works out well. I have some rethinking to do of my own.

Two miles.

It's warm in spite of last night's chill, slightly humid in spite of the thunderstorm, and the boundary between the summer air and my own sweat-slick skin is permeable. Like I can't even trust the way that I inhabit my body. There are a lot of things I can't trust, Lu. People, too, apparently. Maybe even my own aunt.

Just when I was starting to maybe warm to her, starting to let my defenses down and let someone new in.

So where does that leave me?

The path curves, crisscrosses, spirals off in either direction around the slope of a hill. I'm good at hills. I lock in my pace, start moving up, up, up. *Two point twenty-five miles.*

I'd wanted to go to her, finally. To unburden myself of the mirage of the motel mirror, to admit that she was right: *yes, I am a Leader woman. Yes, I have a power.* Yes, there is a thing that I can do that other humans can't. Yes, I believe. But she *lied.* She lied to me, and I know it. So how can I believe *her?*

Two point five miles. Three.

My muscles are molten lava. My bones are titanium. I am a machine, and I am on a mission.

This subconscious mission carries me through the woods, up a well-trod path, through a clearing. It takes me to the only place, the only person who could possibly make sense of the chaos building inside me right now.

I crash through a scrub of underbrush, twigs snapping beneath my feet. Skid to a graceless halt, run the back of one hand against my forehead so it comes back streaked with dirt. Take deep breaths, bouncing back and forth on my toes. *Reset. Relax. Come back to now.*

"Hi," comes the greeting. Soft, but not surprised. Like he's been expecting me.

Maybe he has.

I say, "I need to talk to you."

. . .

Genie—

She came to find me this morning at Turtle Back Rock. Just like you predicted, like I hoped she would. I made a whole point of telling everyone exactly what I was going to do with the morning off. "Going to get some footage of that place, it's an Essex County landmark," etc., etc.

Honestly, I hate feeling like I'm lying to her—hasn't the girl been through enough?—but I know, I know, we've got a bigger purpose going on here.

It's a rock that looks like a turtle shell, tucked away in the reservation. Kind of a touristy thing. People assume: mystical. (But they're right in this case.)

The energy there, you don't even need the EMF readers to know that something's in the air. Mystical's one word for it.

It's not like she knows Jersey, or the reservation, but she found me, anyway. I think it was almost a subconscious thing, the way she came to me, just found me while she was out running. That's gotta count for something. She came bounding through the trees, the look on her face saying she was almost surprised to see where her feet had taken her.

But only almost.

Her eyes said on some level she meant to end up here, with me. She needed to talk to me, which you know is exactly what we were hoping for.

"What is this place?" she asked.

I told her about Turtle Back Rock, like how people say it was a former site of ritual sacrifice, and she told me that people always say that about weird rock formations in the woods. She smiled, but it didn't make it all the way to her eyes.

After a minute, she looked like she'd come to a decision or something. Her exact words: "Maggie thinks I might have a . . . I don't know, a power, or something." She gave me a look like she was waiting for me to break out laughing, right in her face.

Meanwhile, all I wanted to do was cheer. She admitted she'd come around. Her face showed relief, but there was still a little bit of sorrow, or, I don't know, suspicion or disappointment in her eyes. And when I told her that Casey isn't psychic, not even the tiniest bit, she lit up with a smile like the sun.

I could tell, she was struggling to find a way to ask me something, to pick exactly the right words. I wanted to tell her: there are no wrong words, but it felt like interrupting her could wreck it all.

In the end, she kept it simple: "I need your help."

I said, "Of course I'll help you. Whatever you need." I tried to make my whole body communicate that to her. Like so the words were almost secondary. She's tentative, obviously. Questioning things. And really, really confused. Can you blame her? But something's changed. She's changed.

And that means: we're finally getting close to getting what we want.

TWENTY-FIVE

The gates of hell are real, Lu. We're filming there at dusk tonight, before we head off to the Pine Barrens, for the final show location. From what I understand, they're not *actual* gates: false advertising if you ask me. (Who ever asks me?) But it is a very real gateway to some supernatural realm. Cue *X-Files* theme in a minor key. It's a Hellmouth, basically. As far as I can tell. Tell Joss Whedon he was wrong about Sunnydale, after all.

The whole crew is there now, setting up shots and getting establishing footage. Lots to do before the sun sets, don't you know. Everyone is very busy.

Everyone except for Seth and me.

I don't know if our request was more apt to be taken seriously by Maggie in the first place coming from the mouth of a legit Devil Hunter himself. Probably it was. But Seth was smooth, too. With everyone heading off to Clifton (bet you would never have guessed that the gates of Hell were located in Passaic County, NJ, huh, Lu?), it was the perfect chance to do some digging. It was our moment to try to figure out what exactly Maggie was keeping from everyone in the hidey-hole under the Overlook records room.

"All of those papers we laid out to dry," he said to her. "Let Winn and me log them while people are setting up for tonight. It might not be a bad thing to have a Hunter on them, too. For, you know, interpretation and stuff." Great reasoning, truly. Best of all: not a lie. I would know.

"Fair enough, my little Almond Joys," Maggie agreed. Did she look, maybe . . . even a little bit *proud* of me? I thought she did. I wished I could be happy about that. But, you know—betrayal and deception, all that stuff. It gets in the way of the happy thoughts, sometimes.

Casey was annoyed, of course. "What about *our* story line?"

Oh, right. What about that? However I personally felt about that Seth-Casey faux-mance Jane and Elena were so desperately concocting was largely irrelevant.

Jane was puzzled at first. "You *want* to stay here to work with Winnie, rather than come with us—with *Maggie*—to scout the Gates of Hell?"

But then she laughed and turned to Amanda, who was holding her ever-present iPhone aloft. "Did you get that?"

Always the same question, the same concern. *Did you get that? Did you get it? If a tree falls in the forest, and no one catches it on film, did it really happen?*

From behind the phone, Amanda curled her mouth up in a little smirk that was meant just for me. "Seth chooses to stay behind with Winnie. Casey's not happy about it." Dispassionate, like she was ordering a cup of coffee or reporting on the weather. Then, to Jane again, as if Casey, Seth, and I aren't standing right there: "A love triangle. That's what you're getting at, right?"

"Oh, yeah. Love triangle trumps straightforward romance every time." Jane sounds downright thrilled. *"Drama."*

Casey stormed off, either out of anger or embarrassment or both. Seth just shrugged, as if to say: *let's forget what isn't real and focus on what is.* I'm not sure how unreal the triangle situation is to Casey—or yes, Lu, even how I might feel about it—but he's right. What's real is everything I believed wasn't. *Drama* is the name of the game, after all. So, off everyone else went, too.

OF COURSE, THE FLIP side of our clever scheming is that now Seth and I actually have to pore over the moldy old documents. We've spent the last three hours photographing anything that could possibly be good television, making notes that Elena will be able to incorporate into her scripts. Now we're spread out across a folding table, leafing and scanning and flagging and, occasionally, sneezing because of the mold.

"These reports are horrible," I remark.

Neither of us has spoken in a while. Not much to say. Because the reports *are* horrible. Insofar as they depict actual horror. It is not an exaggeration. Page after page detailing "feebleminded" patients, most of whom were Kallikak women. They were studied like lab rats, strapped down to beds and pumped with outrageous doses of experimental drugs. If they were lucky, they were given treatments like the waterboard-y "hydrotherapy," or strung up in straitjackets and thrown in padded isolation rooms. This, so as not to be "a danger to themselves and others." To be lucky, Overlook style, you received semi-regular electroshock therapy. Most of the time, short-term memory loss occurred. A little bit of temporary disorientation, if it went well.

Unlucky meant you were just flat-out lobotomized.

I stare, dumbfounded, at a picture of one such subject, bone-thin and dressed in a filthy, tattered nightshirt. Her legs are covered in dark spots. It could be the age of the photograph. Or it could be she's riddled with bruises. Her dark hair hangs uncut and unwashed over her shoulders. Most striking about the image, though, is her dead gaze. It's not just flat. It's truly lifeless, unseeing.

And the telltale dual scars: small and round like bullet holes, branded on her forehead.

This is worse than any image my mind has conjured of a New Jersey Devil or the wrecked passengers of the SS *Morro*. This is sickening.

"It's torn." I show Seth. A large chunk of the lower left corner is missing, effectively amputating the subject below the knee.

He scoots his chair closer to mine, leans in. I can smell his shampoo again, something woodsy and fresh. He breathes sharply as the image registers.

Then he says, "Thank God."

"What?" It wasn't the reaction I expected. No one should be thanking any gods for what this photograph reveals.

He raises an index finger, then dives underneath the table to his ghostbuster pack. When he emerges, he's waving something in front of me: a corner of paper, thick like the photograph, ripped along its edge in a pattern that matches the picture in front of me. "*Thank God*, because I don't think this scrap would've made any sense without the rest of the photo."

He takes the picture from me and flips it facedown on the table, lines up the missing corner. There's writing on it.

Handwriting. Maggie's handwriting.

My heart thumps and my skin does that prickle that tells

me something's Happening, that this moment is Important. It's not supernatural—or if it is, it's the kind of supernatural that everybody has, at least a little bit.

"Where did you get that?"

It wasn't in the papers we unloaded from the box. But I think I already know the answer.

"I'm a paranormal investigator, Winn," he says. Forget what you think about the first part, Lu; he isn't lying, and that's what's important. It's the way he says my name like that, the way he shortens it like he knows me in a special way . . . Well. Something could be Happening, Lucia. I'm just saying.

"I'm trained—"

I give him an eyebrow.

"—okay, not trained, *per se*, but I'm *experienced* in surveying a scene. I'm always looking for clues."

"So you found . . ."

"I found exactly what Maggie didn't want us to find. This photo. The *other* thing that was in the cache in the basement floor. The thing you said she lied to us about."

"How?" He is basically my hero. My knight in shining armor. I don't even care if it's "unfeminist," Lu, it's just a fact. He looks slightly embarrassed, like my gushy expression is too much.

"I assumed she wanted to keep it close to her. I looked in the most obvious place."

"Her bag?" Maggie carries a giant satchel with ten zillion flaps and buckles that comes from some Spanish designer whose name I couldn't pronounce if I tried. Honestly, if he located this scrap from in that thing, I'm extra impressed.

He makes a *pssht* sound. "God, no. That's *too* obvious." Now he blushes, adorably. "It was . . . uh, in one of the inner pockets of her suitcase. With her underwear."

"You went through my aunt's underwear. You're a . . . trouper."

"Hey, you said you think something weird is going on. I'm all about weird somethings."

He puts a hand on my shoulder, palm radiating warmth, then looks ten kinds of awkward about it and takes it away. I want him to put it back again. But there are more important things—I think—at hand right now.

"Right." I take a deep breath. "So this says . . . *Amelia Leeder.* Spelled with two *e*s. But Maggie thinks . . ." It takes me a minute to decipher the penmanship. ". . . My great-great-great-great grandmother? Lots of 'greats,' anyway."

"And look." Seth points. "There's an arrow. Marie Kallikak was Amelia's ancestor?"

Name chg? I read, squinting again at Maggie's shorthand, which even Jane complains about. "So I guess at some point the Kallikaks became the Leeders. But why?"

"The Kallikaks thought they were rebirthing the Jersey Devil. At least some of them did, as we know. Meaning they were resurrecting the Leeds lineage."

"So they reclaimed the name?" It's another piece of the puzzle, to be sure, but it's not nearly the whole picture. "I still don't get it, though. Why would *this* picture be something Maggie needed to hide?"

"Well . . ." For a moment, Seth looks uncomfortable, twisting in his seat. That prickle lights on my skin again, that non-magical extra sense that says: *everything is about to change.*

"There's one more thing. That might help explain it. But I thought you should be the first to have a look." He's having a hard time looking me directly in the eyes.

The hairs on the back of my neck are at attention now. "Why?"

He fishes in his bag again, comes up with a slim white envelope. "Just—here." He shoves it at me. "Sorry. Maybe I should've given this to you earlier, like, first thing this morning or whatever. But I was nervous. I mean, I was worried it would upset you."

Alarm bells ring, shrill and alert, in the back of my mind. "Why would it . . ."

I trail off as the writing on the envelope comes into crisp, razor-sharp focus. *Meg*, it says. The ink is a deep, fluid blue. The handwriting is long and spindly. Graceful, in a homespun way.

The handwriting on the envelope is my mother's, *Lu.*

Dear Meg:

I should have written this letter—or a letter, any letter—ages ago, I know. I shouldn't have let you be the one to break the silence, shouldn't have let it come to this, shouldn't have let us become such strangers to each other. Regardless of what's come to pass, we are sisters, above all.

But I felt that pulling away was my only option. It wasn't— it isn't—that I don't love you. Of course I love you. And I miss you more than you could know.

Meg, it's that I worry. I worry about you, as I have since we were silly, stupid teenagers, when you first decided to explore the boundaries of your magic, and delved so deeply into our family history.

Just because there are things we can do, doesn't mean that we should, Meg. I said it then—even then! Even so young and reckless! I'm all the more certain of it the more distance I have.

Our powers are a gift we don't fully understand, left over magic from the Devil himself. Our powers are all that remain of him, since his banishment from our realm.

You choose to embrace your power, to use it for personal gain. I try not to judge. (You may not believe that, but it's true.) But as I told you, I fear we'll upset our delicate harmony with the natural world. It's what keeps us safe. Think of our ancestors, Meg. Mother Leeds: driven mad by raging towns-folk. Leeder women: burned at the stake. And the most tragic: the Kallikaks, trying to hide behind a false name, afforded a brief respite of anonymity: discovered and committed to that asylum. I say the most tragic because they probably were ill, Meg. They paid dearly for their blood ties.

We all pay dearly for our ties, Meg.

The Garden State is dangerous territory for us. Our family line was nearly wiped out at the Overlook. But why should I have to remind you of this?

"Maggie Leader." You're clever as ever, hiding in plain sight and reclaiming the family name. But there's a family burden, too. That burden is why I had to break away. I have Winnie to protect. I pray she never knows of our ancestry, that she lives her life peacefully, with no awareness of a power borne of demon. I grapple with it every day. And I know you do, too.

Above all, I grapple with trying to forgive you for your own choices. I am willing now. This is what I'm doing. So I hope, truly, that you'll forgive me in return for my silence all these years. It was the only way I could see to keep my daughter safe. And I hope that you'll forgive me now, when I say this:

I implore you, Meg. I beg of you with every bit of love I carry for you and for Winnie in my heart:

Do not do this.

Do not go back to New Jersey. Let sleeping Devils lie.

Wherever the Devil may be, he is a phantom. As he should be.

You've built an empire from your parlor tricks. Let that be enough. The Devil and his legacy have been a cancer on our family, on our mothers and sisters, our grandmothers, our aunts. The Devil has all but destroyed the Leader women, Meg. And if you go down this path, I fear that he will destroy you.

Am I hurt? Do I have a right to be? You emerge after a decade of estrangement—years I spent aching with loss—with your phone call. Your request. That takes some audacity, sister. But I understand you. I know you. I love you.

And if you feel the same way about me, you will understand why I must deny you.

I can't be a part of this, Meg.

I can't help you do this.

I can't and I won't.

My throat is thick. Tears blur my vision as my mind flutters high above. I don't realize I'm clutching the letter in a death grip until Seth gently pries my fingers open, setting it back down on the table.

I find my voice through the fog of confusion and pain. "The date. It was . . . She wrote this two weeks before she killed herself." Lower, a near-whisper, now: "She didn't leave a note. For me or my dad, I mean. But she wrote to *Maggie?*"

Seth finds a bottle of water someplace—his bag? I don't know, one minute there's nothing and the next I'm unscrewing the cap and guzzling it down like I've been trapped in the desert for weeks. Seth is patient, quiet, watching me with cautious sympathy that I'm just too tired to resent.

I take a deep breath and hand the bottle back. "She didn't *want* her power. She didn't want me to have one. What if . . ." I look up at him, my tears fracturing his face into a kaleidoscope. "Do you think it was the powers that made her kill herself? That she just couldn't cope with it?

Oh, God." My stomach lurches. "Whatever Maggie's planning to do . . . summon the Devil? What if *that's* why my mom killed herself? She just couldn't live with it, like just didn't want to be around for the consequences?"

"And leave you?" Seth shakes his head. "You read that letter yourself, Winn. Your mother would have done *anything* to protect you. She wouldn't have checked out if she thought you were in danger." He rests a hand on my knee. "You *know* that."

NOT A SUICIDE. I close my eyes and the mirror-words are in front of me again.

I do know that. I think. But there were so many other things I thought I knew, too, Lucia. And I was wrong about almost all of them. Still, I know what he's going to say. I know even though it's hurting him. I know before he can force the words out.

"What if . . ." His voice cracks and he looks away. The room is closing in on me, my vision narrowing to a dark pinpoint.

Seth swallows and tries again. "Winn, what if your mother was murdered?"

FADE IN

EXT. GATES OF HELL—NIGHT
WIDE SHOT

CAMERA PANS over a shadowy tunnel. Spooky in the
twilight. SOUNDS of water trickling, some creepy
graffiti . . . standard "scary tunnel" fare.

MAGGIE steps into frame.

MAGGIE:
The Devil's portal. The Gates of Hell.

(pauses, smiling)

Kind of a letdown, at first glance.

(sweeps her hand toward the tunnel—CAMERA PANS
across smoke-stained brick, spray-painted
obscenities, and other mysterious, more ominous
stains)

The name has been assigned to countless arch-
ways, doors, and tunnels all across the globe.

(BECKONS, wanders FARTHER INTO THE TUNNEL)

MAGGIE (CON'T):
This opening leads to a series of interconnected
passageways—theoretically created as storm
sewers.

(beat)

But we here at *Fantastic, Fearsome* know better.
And even if there weren't any fantastic
phenomena to record, The Gates of Hell are
hardly benign.

The tunnel is suddenly SUBMERGED IN BLACK.
Then, just as suddenly, eerie green NIGHT-VISION
CAM lights up the frame.

MAGGIE:
So you see: Not ten steps into this cavernous
network, natural light *completely vanishes.*
Of course, all paranormal hot spots come with
defensive explanations. The Gates of Hell are
no different. According to town records, the
tunnel system was originally built to manage
runoff from a nearby brook.

(shakes her head with a smirk)

These days, one heavy rainfall and the trickle
inside becomes a deadly torrent.

CLOSE-UP on Maggie's FACE, backlit so her
features are HEAVILY SHADOWED.

MAGGIE:

Legends abound of the terrors that locals have
found here . . . Mutilated carcasses, skulls
that glow . . . And perhaps most horrifying,
remnants of those who stumbled inside and never
returned. A shoe. A hat. A severed limb.

(beat)

And we want answers. That's why we're here. And
we may very well reset the bar for "horror."
Because we're going to summon the Jersey Devil
himself.

CUT

IVAN SNICKERS, WHICH TOTALLY undercuts the Big Dramatic
Moment Maggie is going for. He doesn't even try to hold
it in.

"*Cut!*" Russ yells, sounding pissed off enough for Ivan to
pull himself together.

"Oh my *God*," Casey grumbles. "How many times are we
gonna have to do this scene?"

I'm on her side for once. We've already had to do four
extra takes because of weird issues with the sound, which
Maggie chalked up to the woo-woo energy of this place. Too
bad for Casey *and* me that Maggie was for real. This time.
Even if it wasn't the place that was screwing with our elec-
tronics, she believes that it was.

My own new parlor trick is so handy, Lu. But the fact that
I haven't coughed in a while, that I haven't felt that sting
in my throat, is a little troubling. Everyone here is being

truthful, at least as far as feeling a certain way about this place. These feelings range from bored (the camera and sound crew) to scared shitless (me). It's not the place, even, for me, Lu. It's that my aunt may have killed my mother.

That.

It's just a theory I'm working on, Lu. We'll see if it pans out. But Seth was right; it's all too possible that *someone* killed her. It makes a *little* more sense (when you accept that none of this, really, makes any sense at all) than her killing herself. So if my mother was murdered, then right now, Maggie's at the top of the list of suspects. She's basically the whole list, actually, as far as human beings go. The other possible suspect is the New Jersey Devil, but apparently he's trapped in this tunnel. And in spite of my newly-opened mind, I'm still not quite ready to go to Devil-on-Mother killings yet.

No, Maggie is looking likelier by the second. Why the hell else would she have lied about the box from the records room? Why else would she have appeared on the scene and then—*oh, hey, how about that?!*—just days later, my mom decided to off herself?

Why else? Why else? Why else?

I've given the matter some thought.

Occam's razor. Dad taught me all about that, once. It means that the simplest solution is generally the correct one. Maggie either killed my mother herself, or somehow spurred her into committing suicide, threatening to stir up magic and other stuff my mom wanted to keep buried away. Either way, she's far from blameless. Either way, she's keeping something from me.

And now, she wants to summon the Jersey Devil?

According to her letter, my mom thought that was a bad idea with a capital TERRIBLE. Like the kind of bad idea people *die* over. Literally.

I'm with Mom on this one.

We have to shut this down. *I* do. Even if I have to do it all on my own. Other people here just don't seem to . . . *get* the urgency at hand, Lucia. Like Ivan, for one. He's still giggling, even through the death glares that Casey is shooting his way.

"Why is this funny to you?" I snap. Nothing about this is funny at all. It's deadly serious. And it's *my life.*

Ivan rolls his eyes at me, sort-of-but-not-really apologetic. "I'm sorry. Raise the Devil, though?" He snickers again. "I can't even . . ."

"Summon," Maggie corrects him. "*Raising* the Devil implies that he's dead, or somehow gone. But he's close. It explains—all the sightings, and yada yada."

I almost have to snicker, myself. *And yada yada. She just* yada-yada'd *the Devil.* My nerves crackle. For Maggie, this is a game, a puzzle to be solved. My mom, her sister, has already been forgotten. She doesn't even attempt to care about the loss, about what I'm feeling. And right now, she just looks annoyed with Ivan for being such an idiot. "Summoning involves bringing him from wherever he's at, to where we are. Get it?"

"Yeah, but here's the thing." (At least he stands up to Maggie; give him credit for that, Lu.) "We've been tracking the Devil for years—"

"—Um, *we've* been tracking the Devil for years. *You've* been tracking him for months," Casey interjects. "Barely."

"Whatever. So, now we're just going to snap our fingers and bring him here?"

"It's a *smidge* more complicated than that, Butterfinger," Maggie says. "But I've got a spell. Miss Marie Kallikak was kind enough to leave it for us in the records room."

Was she, now? I swallow, tentative: she's telling the truth. Just one more thing Maggie hid from the rest of us after digging up that box. I take another quick mental inventory of where we stand.

My mother didn't want Maggie to summon the Jersey Devil.

My mother is now dead.

Maggie is preparing to summon the Devil.

"A spell. Coolio." Ivan is still not convinced, but he's trying to work up the requisite enthusiasm, sort of. "I mean, what have we got to lose?"

Personally? Not a lot. Mom's already gone. So, yeah.

He brightens. "Then again, if it works? You're gonna *kill it* in the ratings. We'll all be stars."

Elena grins. "Reality Emmy, baby."

She just wants to wear a pretty dress, maybe be seated next to the latest cast of *Top Chef*. Besides, for Elena, this was only ever really about television, and not anything fantastical at all. But Lu: we know Maggie is *long* past any concerns with ratings. *Kill it* has a richer meaning in her case.

Maggie whips around to me. Her eyes blaze and for once, they don't remind me of my mother's. Too much has happened for that. And besides, my mother never looked at me this way. "Oh, my little raspberry tarts," she says, her grin wolfish, "you have no idea. An *Emmy?*"

She laughs, like the idea of an award is so far beneath her that it's amusing. "That's just for starters, kiddos." She looks around.

"Are we all ready to raise some Hell?"

Part Three:

INVOCATION

Clinton road is just two yellow lines parallel and unbroken, sprawling before the windshield, lit by twin beams from the SUV headlights. "The map thingy says this is . . . a detour," I mention, casual.

Seth is behind the wheel. He's stuck pretty close since showing me the letter. I'll admit that most of what I know about guys, I get from movies or TV, both of which suggest that the typical guy would have fled the scene the minute I unloaded my bag of possibly paranormal mommy issues on him. You know, all, *chicks be crazy, am-I-right?* But Seth, he's . . . well, he's *here.* Not only physically present (which is a lot, itself), but that he's just completely tuned in, in a way I didn't know anyone who wasn't *you* even could be.

He looks at me a lot, Lucia. I mean, not in a creepy way, though I'm not used to it all, and so it's not *not*-unsettling. But he looks at me like I'm a radio station he can't quite hear, like he's focusing all of his brain waves on filtering out my static and just plugging right into my energy. And I'm letting him.

Well, right now, he's actually looking at the road. But then he glances my way.

"The Barrens is southeast from Essex County," I say. "We're going . . . north."

"North*west*, actually," Seth clarifies. "And we're not *going*. We're *there*. Passaic. I wanted you to see Clinton Road. It's just a *slight* detour. We'll still make it to the Barrens in plenty of time."

The Barrens, aka: the Pine Barrens. The birthplace of the Jersey Devil. Maggie did some hokey little voodoo incense-burning back at the Gates of Hell for the sake of the cameras, chanted an invocation or two, but that was unreal reality. According to her, the Barrens is where the *real* magic happens, where the Devil's essence lingers. It's only logical that our season finale would be staged there.

Amanda's got the larger van, and she's driving carpool for the Hunters. Elena's got the trailer, with the rest of the crew. Maggie and Jane are in Maggie's car, high priestesses set apart from the commoners in high style.

I wonder if Jane knows anything about Maggie's true plans. And what would it mean, really, either way?

"How did you talk Maggie into letting us go off on our own again, anyway?" I ask.

"It was easy. I told her the truth." He says it like it's the simplest thing in the world. But, no. He couldn't have told her the *truth*. "Well, not the *entire* truth," he amends. "I mean, I didn't tell her you suspect her of murdering your mother. Obviously."

"Obviously." Because how awkward would *that* be?

"Just that you'd read about Clinton Road, and you wanted to see it before we headed back down to the Barrens. I played up the whole, 'you'd want an experienced Hunter with you, I know the roads,' *yada yada . . .*" He does his best Maggie here, and I even crack a smile.

"Still, though. Just the two of us." I'm not sure what I'm *really* asking, here.

"Fewer bodies equals less energetic interference with whatever's going on, psychically, at the location." (It's not *quite* the answer I was hoping for, to be honest. But I know *he's* being honest, so that feels good.) "But, you know— that's mostly crap. Good enough excuse for Maggie. Mostly I just thought it made more sense for it just to be, you know . . . you and me."

And as you might guess, butterflies swarm in my chest in a frantic flurry like I'm Snow Fucking White because that *was* the answer I was hoping for, *obviously*, Lu, but I try to keep still and play it cool.

He reaches like he's going for the radio, but feints, rests his hand over mine in my lap. The butterflies throw a wild dance party.

"Honestly, it wasn't such a hard sell. I don't know if this is good news, or not . . ."

I sigh, ignoring his lingering hand, and failing. "When is it *ever* good news?"

"Right, well. She was psyched when I told her you were interested in checking out Clinton Road. Like, she was really into the fact that you were getting into something, you know, *fantastic*, all on your own."

I think about that for a minute, let it settle.

"How does it help Maggie, for you to be a believer?" he asks.

Good question. "I mean, I don't know, really. But she called my mother asking for *something*," I remind him. "And whatever it was, my mother said no." My stomach churns in tune with the spinning in my brain. Between that and the butterflies, there's a lot going on inside me. "Maybe she's hoping I'll say yes."

We're both silenced by the thought. Seth doesn't take his hand from mine, and now I'm no longer nervous or self-conscious; I'm comforted.

Leafy trees rise up on either side of the road, speeding past us in a lush blur. Seth slows the car a little. The trees come into sharper focus, begin to take shape. Backlit by the full moon (did I mention the full moon, Lu? How perfect, right?), their branches creep like tentacles, reaching for us. Though I'm not sorry that we're here, that we're venturing down Clinton Road, I'm extra glad that Seth is part of *we*, here.

"We're close to the reservoir now," Seth says.

Reservoirs. The site of many a *Law & Order* opening teaser. Campy, yes. But still creepy. I decide to focus on the *camp* side of things. "What's the dumbest rumor you've heard about this road?"

"Oh God. People say all kinds of stupid shit about it. There's an old iron smelter left over from the eighteenth century, out in a clearing in the woods. People like to say it's a former pagan temple. You know, and that there are some loony fringe cults that conduct ritual sacrifices out there, today."

"Ah, the old 'sacrificial altar in the woods.' Classic. Like Turtle Back Rock, sort of."

"Exactly. Or, uh, there are stories, of weird hybrid animals roaming the woods. Not the Devil. Leftover mutants from a zoo that closed down in the seventies."

"Sure." I think I read that in a Margaret Atwood novel, once.

He sneaks another quick look at me again, out of the corner of his eye. "This road *is* haunted, though. The Hunters, we know. The overpass we're coming up on now is called the Ghost Boy Bridge. People have seen an apparition wandering here. A kid dressed in old-time clothes."

"A ghost boy," I say dryly.

"Yeah." He laughs. "And if you throw a coin off the bridge, the story goes that the ghost boy will toss it back to you."

Playing catch with the dead. Fun times. We're firmly back in *camp* territory, now, which makes me more comfortable. "So, have you ever seen him?"

Seth's face goes rigid, like I've hit a nerve. Great. *Forget "comfortable."*

"Not the ghost boy himself, no. But the Hunters, we believe . . . we believe that the bridge is a conduit, that it attracts wandering spirits. Not *just* that boy. And it's, like . . . well, it's personalized, is the best way I can describe it. The spirit that you're connected to is the spirit you'll find there."

His expression can only mean one thing. "So, whose spirit did you find?"

He takes a breath. "My grandmother's. She died when I was eleven. We were really close, I don't know, maybe that's weird, but we were."

"It's not weird; it's cute." Wait—did I say that? Flirting: I am bad at it.

Seth doesn't notice, though. "My older cousin, thought he was a badass, and he had a license, you know? So he took us—there were a bunch of us, it's a big family—he took all the cousins out here one afternoon. We didn't tell our parents. We all tossed coins over the bridge, for Nana."

I'm hanging on his every word. Seeing as how he went on to be a Devil Hunter and all. I have to assume there was *some* evidence, somewhere along the way, in worlds beyond our own.

"She didn't throw any back," he adds.

"Oh." And surprisingly, I'm *surprised*. I'm picturing little-boy Seth, sad and dejected, and I want to scoop now-Seth into a tight hug. But I have to settle for flipping my hand over and giving his a squeeze. He squeezes back, doesn't let go.

And . . . now we're holding hands.

"But I came back the next day. On my bike. I didn't tell anyone. And there was something waiting for me."

My skin tingles. "What was it?"

"This is going to sound dumb, I know, but it was a thimble. And it *wasn't* there the day before." He pauses, like he's waiting for me to laugh or to deny what he's saying. But I don't. Because there are way more implausible things in this universe (and the next one) than a thimble that was sent to you from another freaking dimension. I never thought I'd say that, Lu, but I sure as hell mean it, now.

"And my grandmother," he goes on, "she was a seam-stress, and she used to fix up our clothes. So I *knew* it was the thimble she used. She had tiny fingers. I mean, it had to be hers. One hundred percent." He swallows, eyes squarely on the road. "I'm sure you think I'm insane."

"No, definitely not." *Definitely. Not.* "It was a thimble that was the same size as your grandma's fingers. And it wasn't there the day before. I'm sure it *was* her message to you." *Stranger things have happened. And recently.*

He shakes his head, seems more relieved than I would have expected at that validation from me. Emboldened, I give his hand a squeeze. He winds his fingers through mine, and now our grip is tight, real.

And I want to *faint*, Lu, I want to curl up and die from happiness, right here and now (though maybe not literally, there's been way too much literal death going on around us, all the time, since moment one). I just want to wrap this moment around me like that Seth-comforter that exists in my head and cuddle up inside of it.

But then, in my peripheral vision, a flash of warning-yellow blooms, a road sign with the double bendy lines saying we are about to go around a blind curve. Seth cuts the wheel one-handed I hear a shriek, high-pitched and drawn. And everything changes.

It is otherwordly and horrible, that scream. It is animal-*like*, not quite animal. It is wounded, feral. But it also sounds familiar, in a surreal way. And then the sound thins out, stretches to a tenor that's identifiably human, but no less pained. It lowers, still as intense. Not only identifiably human, but recognizable . . .

My stomach clutches.

I must squeeze Seth's hand again, too hard this time, because he flinches, and the car swerves, and then *I* scream, which would be embarrassing if my blood weren't *pounding* in my temples. The next second, a second that feels like a lifetime, Seth regains some control of the car. He brakes, pulls over, flicks the hazards on. Turns to me.

"What is it?"

What is it? How can he ask that? Unless . . .

I stare at him. "You didn't hear that? The scream? The . . . moaning?"

His face is a blank. "I heard *you* scream, Winnie."

My throat is open, clear. He's telling the truth. *Was it all in my head?*

"What did it sound like?" he prompts.

I shake my head. I don't want to think about it, but I also can't get the echo to stop ringing in my ears. "It was . . . awful. Like something in insane amounts of pain."

"Maybe those reports of the mutant animals are truer than we thought."

He's so willing to believe me that it makes the next thing I have to say that much easier. "It *sounded* like an animal," I tell him. "But it wasn't. I think . . . I think it was a human being, in torture."

That *wail*. Its familiarity. My stomach hitches.

"Seth," I say. My voice is a ragged whisper. I start again: "That sound I heard was *my mother*."

Seth's whole body goes taught.

"Do you think I'm hearing things? Do you think I'm crazy?" I ask. "I mean, if that really happened, you would have heard it, too."

"Not necessarily."

"So you believe me?" I press.

Seth hazards a glance at me, quick but direct. "Winnie," he says, "I believe you."

I believe me, too.

TWENTY-SEVEN

I wasn't actually scared by *The Blair Witch Project*, if you'll recall, Lu—too slow-paced, too heavy on one-note atmosphere, and not enough Actual Stuff Happening; plus, we were long past the time when its viral marketing, "OMG is this really *real?*" thing actually had some people fooled. I wasn't scared by the original *Evil Dead*, either. Low-budget, over-the-top, all the cheesy effects and the Evil Molesting Tree of Bad Touching. Maybe there was a context problem happening—I was seeing it too late, it had already become a parody of itself. Was anyone *ever* truly frightened by that movie? I mean, I was glad to see it. I had a great time that afternoon—remember? We ate those cheese puffs that stained your mom's mohair throw traffic-cone orange, and I took the blame because we thought your mom wouldn't come down on me the way she would on her own daughter (and we were right).

That movie's part of the canon. Also, the canon of you and me, Lu.

But, I mean, it wasn't *scary*.

The Pine Barrens are scary.

Lu, if there was ever really a Blair Witch, I'd bet my money that she hung out here. Like maybe if she and the Jersey Devil even used to go steady or something, this was their make-out spot. Humor as deflection, I know: back to my old parlor tricks. But I'm not joking. Maybe it's because of how I've had my eyes opened since joining up with the *Fantastic* team; I know, now, that there *are* some things that go bump in the night. And worse. Maybe that's why the shadows cast by the towering pine trees just don't feel so harmless, Lucia, why their spindly branches are more like skeleton bones to me now. Before we watched horror movies, Lu, we read fairy tales. And in those stories, bad things always happen to little girls who wandered off into the woods.

I believe that bad things happen in these woods, too.

SETH STEERS THE CAR through thick underbrush. I wonder how he can even make out a road, or even a clear path, beneath us. Our headlights reflect nothing but the bumpy grain of tree trunks at close range, and the occasional flicker of a firefly.

"We should be close," he says.

"How can you tell?"

"Don't forget, I'm a Devil Hunter," he says. "I've been to the Barrens before."

"Even still. Everything looks the same here. Creepy tree, creepy tree, creepier tree. Oh! Creepy bush. That's different."

Seth offers an appreciative smile, which is about the best feeling ever, even with the lingering confusion of what happened near ghost-boy bridge, even with the faintest trace of my mother's (was it her?) agonized shriek echoing in my mind. "Annnd . . . creepy clearing in the woods!" He uses a game-show announcer voice.

"With bonus terrifying *Sleepaway Camp*–style cabins!" I'm like the girl who turns the letters, or carries the briefcase, depending what channel you're watching. Yes, I try to sound chipper, but Lu, did I mention the cabins? Apparently, there are people in this world who *want* to hang out in the Barrens for days—and nights—on end. Maggie has booked just one of several available cabin sites dotted across the area.

But the clearing is empty, now. Though we can see that Maggie and the rest have been here—her car is parked in front of us, and tire tracks lead off farther, past the semi-circle of small, rustic buildings. Two of Ernie's lanterns sit on either side of the low stairs leading to the cabin in the very middle. That must be Maggie's. Seth pulls us in right alongside Maggie's car and cuts the engine. I step out of the car and—

"*BOO!*"

A figure leaps out at me. And I can't help it, Lu, I let loose with the loudest, shrillest, girliest scream I've got. I honestly didn't know I had it in me. I realize I'm shaking, and not because of the night chill. Why does it get so freaking cold at night in Jersey?

"Ha! Gotcha!"

And there's Ivan, cackling with glee, totally pleased with himself for scaring the bejeezus out of me. I'm embarrassed. And my heart is still racing, despite the threat of danger obviously being passed.

"What the hell, man? Are you trying to give us a heart attack?" Seth is out of the car and he sounds angry; he *is* angry, which I have to admit makes me feel better.

"Dude, you're a Hunter. What happened to your nerves of steel?" Ivan grins like a moron. "You got here just in time."

Good. I'd rather keep busy, keep my body occupied so

my brain doesn't have time to churn over all the questions stomping through it. "I assume everyone's setting up for the big invocation tomorrow?"

"Nah, that's done," Ivan says. "Mostly. Now the rest of the grown-ups are putting together a shot list. Amanda and Casey will be back in a little bit. We're off for a little while." He waggles his eyebrows. "Who's up for some ghost stories around the campfire? I think Amanda even got marshmallows to roast."

"You're *so* original," I mutter. But again: keeping busy. It actually sounds more fun than the alternative: being alone in one of these cabins. "Let me just throw my stuff down somewhere. I want to dig up a sweatshirt."

"You, Amanda, and Casey have that cabin there." Ivan points to the cabin two down to the left from Maggie's. "I think they unpacked a sleeping bag for you, but you know, you can take whatever bed you want that isn't already claimed."

I want to say, *thanks, boss,* but I remember at the very last second that it's totally not Ivan's fault that I feel this way, like the inside of my body is trying to crawl to the outside of my skin. He doesn't know what happened to my mother. He doesn't know what we found at Overlook. He doesn't know about the Dead Man's Curve. So instead, I manage to shrug, neutral as I can.

"I'll be right back," I tell the boys.

Ivan cackles. "Dude! I *know* you've seen *Scream!* You know better than to tell us you'll 'be right back.'"

I shrug again, lighter this time. He's right, I do know better than that. It's, like, the number one rule of horror movies. Or maybe number two, right after "don't read from the diary in the basement," or "don't have sex when there's a psycho killer wandering around." *God,* Lu, come to think of it, we should probably publish a handbook or something. But you know what? Fuck it, Lucia. Fuck all of it.

"I'll be right back." I say it again, louder. Pointed, this time. Because whatever's going on here, I'm already right smack in the middle of it. It's already happening, all around me.

Whatever's going on, it's probably already too late to worry about rules.

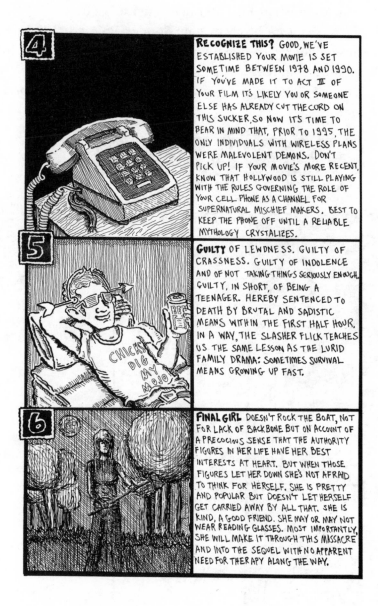

4 RECOGNIZE THIS? GOOD, WE'VE ESTABLISHED YOUR MOVIE IS SET SOMETIME BETWEEN 1978 AND 1990. IF YOU'VE MADE IT TO ACT III OF YOUR FILM IT'S LIKELY YOU OR SOMEONE ELSE HAS ALREADY CUT THE CORD ON THIS SUCKER, SO NOW IT'S TIME TO BEAR IN MIND THAT, PRIOR TO 1995, THE ONLY INDIVIDUALS WITH WIRELESS PLANS WERE MALEVOLENT DEMONS. DON'T PICK UP! IF YOUR MOVIE'S MORE RECENT, KNOW THAT HOLLYWOOD IS STILL PLAYING WITH THE RULES GOVERNING THE ROLE OF YOUR CELL PHONE AS A CHANNEL FOR SUPERNATURAL MISCHIEF MAKERS. BEST TO KEEP THE PHONE OFF UNTIL A RELIABLE MYTHOLOGY CRYSTALIZES.

5 GUILTY OF LEWDNESS. GUILTY OF CRASSNESS. GUILTY OF INDOLENCE AND OF NOT TAKING THINGS SERIOUSLY ENOUGH. GUILTY, IN SHORT, OF BEING A TEENAGER. HEREBY SENTENCED TO DEATH BY BRUTAL AND SADISTIC MEANS WITHIN THE FIRST HALF HOUR. IN A WAY, THE SLASHER FLICK TEACHES US THE SAME LESSON AS THE LURID FAMILY DRAMA: SOMETIMES SURVIVAL MEANS GROWING UP FAST.

6 FINAL GIRL DOESN'T ROCK THE BOAT, NOT FOR LACK OF BACKBONE BUT ON ACCOUNT OF A PRECOCIOUS SENSE THAT THE AUTHORITY FIGURES IN HER LIFE HAVE HER BEST INTERESTS AT HEART. BUT WHEN THOSE FIGURES LET HER DOWN SHE'S NOT AFRAID TO THINK FOR HERSELF. SHE IS PRETTY AND POPULAR BUT DOESN'T LET HERSELF GET CARRIED AWAY BY ALL THAT. SHE IS KIND, A GOOD FRIEND. SHE MAY OR MAY NOT WEAR READING GLASSES. MOST IMPORTANTLY, SHE WILL MAKE IT THROUGH THIS MASSACRE AND INTO THE SEQUEL WITH NO APPARENT NEED FOR THERAPY ALONG THE WAY.

TWENTY-EIGHT

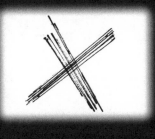

think the inside of the cabin couldn't possibly be worse—
s in, spookier, ickier, more Spartan—than the outside. But
t is.

A flick of the light switch in the corner illuminates a single,
bare bulb swaying from a frayed rope in the center of the
room. I sweep my eyes across the rest of the cabin: four sets of
bowing, metal-framed bunk beds that have seen better days;
flimsy mattresses sagging like deflated balloons. Amanda and
Casey have chosen caddy-corner bottom bunks, their telltale
bags rest at the foot of each bed. Amanda's is a sleek nylon
printed duffel that she no doubt bought someplace LA trendy
that I wouldn't even know how to pronounce. Casey's got a
smaller, slightly less ratty version of Ivan's and Seth's ghost
hunter packs in a vaguely feminine, goth, purplish color.

Amanda left a sleeping bag for me on the bunk next to
hers. I move to the bed, drop my own bag (functional oversized backpack, black-and-white stripes that make it slightly
"fun," but not in a shopping, girlie, I-get-my-nails-done-regu-
larly kind of way). Taking care to avoid whacking my head on

the edge of the top bunk, I flop down, feel the mattress sink underneath me.

This'll be a comfy night's sleep.

But I don't have time to think too much about it, because suddenly, there's a ripple in the air. I pause. Listening. *There. Just there.*

I see it rather than hear it. But more than that, I sense it with my whole being.

There's a flicker.

Flicker.

The bulb overhead dims and then glows brighter again. My spine stiffens. In that moment, in the split-second blackness, I hear footsteps. Footsteps, and a high-pitched giggle.

It's just Ivan, I tell myself. *Dorking out again.* I try to push aside the thought that really, though, it sounds nothing like Ivan.

The light buzzes again, a sudden strobe in the tiny cabin, and another sound comes, sharp as a thunderclap: The door to the cabin banging open, shut.

I curl my fingers around the mattress edge, breathing cautiously, listening for . . . what?

There's nothing out there, Winn.

But it's not the truth.

There's something. Somewhere.

And whatever it is, I'm in the middle of it.

Yes, true.

I've almost got myself convinced that my imagination is running wild with stress, I've almost got my breathing down to its normal pace again, when I stand to unroll my sleeping bag. The knotted elastic straps give me trouble for a minute; they're stubborn, and I tug. A fingernail catches on the fabric and tears at the quick.

"Damn." Blood wells around the jagged nail edge. I suck

on my finger for a second, taste copper. More carefully now, I unwind the straps. The sleeping bag uncurls. I move to slide it farther in place on the mattress . . . when something stops me.

Two somethings. Wait . . . three.

Three . . . are they cards? Pieces of paper? Peeking out from the top fold of the bag. Dread washes over me as I reach for them.

They're photos, like the ones we found at the Overlook.

Marie Kallikak. My mother. And me.

My breath catches. It's *me.*

Where did this picture come from? It's a moment I remember, at The Stone Pony. In front of me is a boy that I know is Seth, although all you can see in the picture is the back of his head. I remember that conversation. I remember how talking to him made me feel, alive and light. You can see it, in the picture, on my face. My eyes are bright, Lu, in a way they haven't been since my mother died.

It's a nice picture. Under different circumstances, I might be happy to see it.

These are not those circumstances.

Marie's and my mother's pictures have been scratched, defaced with harsh, jagged Xs over where their eyes should be.

Mine's been marked up, too.

Sweeping crosshatches scrape the landscape of my face. Like, whoever did this wanted to erase me from existence completely. It was done with viciousness, with intent. And there's writing, too. Underneath, in pen so heavy the paper's nearly torn in some places:

You're next.

TWENTY-NINE

Shaking with rage (and okay, let's admit it, Lu—a little bit of fear, too), I burst out of the cabin.

"What *is* this?" I shout, thrusting the photos toward Ivan and Seth. I move quickly down the steps, get right in Ivan's face, so close I get a whiff of the gunk he puts in his hair to make it extra-puffy.

His eyes go wide; he puts his hands up, not smiling. "What's *what*? Calm down, Winnie." He steps back. He's startled. "I didn't do anything."

"Sure." I wave the photos at him. "Just another *joke*, right? The same way it was a hilarious joke to jump out at us in the dark."

"*God*, no. I mean, I'm sorry about that! Bad call, fine. But I don't know what the hell that is."

"Take a look." I shove them into his hands, and watch as he shuffles through all three. His face goes slack, the way it did at the séance. His cheeks turn a shade paler.

"What is it?" Seth asks, concerned.

"Show him," I say.

Ivan hands the pictures to Seth. His reaction is less measured than Ivan's was. "What the fuck?"

I stare at them both, evaluating. I swallow, my senses poised to detect that creeping cough. "You *really* have no idea where these came from? Neither of you?"

They shake their heads, emphatic. They're both legitimately surprised by the photos. They're telling the truth. And they're scared. Or Ivan is, anyway.

"What is going on, Winnie?" he asks. His voice quavers and I have to remind myself: he was a nonbeliever, too. The fear in his tone right now is for real.

Seth and I share a glance, coming to an agreement. Time for brutal honesty. Seth steps in. "We think Winnie's mother's death wasn't a suicide."

"Winnie's mother *killed herself?*"

Whoops, Lu. I forgot that this wasn't exactly common knowledge. Poor guy's getting a lot of information, all at once.

"Well, that was the thinking. Until now," I say. What else would I have thought? Having been the one who found her, in a very suicide-ish state. I push the image away, out, as far as it will go.

Ivan looks like he's going to be sick. "And there's a connection between her and Marie Kallikak. And the Jersey Devil."

I sigh. "Yup."

"And Maggie wants to raise the Devil?"

"Yup."

"So Maggie may have . . . what?" Ivan's mind is clearly racing, scrambling to piece everything together. If only it were that easy.

"I don't know," I admit, grim. "Let's just say I've got a lot of questions."

"So what now?" he asks. His eyes are darting, furtive. I wonder if he's thinking of hopping into one of the cars outside and getting the hell out of here. That would probably be the best idea. Cowards survive in horror movies, Lu. (Though with thrillers it's a little iffier.)

I take a deep breath. "I think we're going to have to dig for answers." I look at Ivan. "Do you think we have, I don't know, like twenty minutes before the girls come back?"

He nods.

"Get your ghost-busting pack," I tell Seth. "There's gotta be some way—some*one*—to ask."

LEAVE IT TO A Devil Hunter to have a lead on calling the Great Beyond collect. Seth is like a paranormal Boy Scout: always prepared. Moments later, we're huddled around a small votive candle, the tiny flame lighting Ivan's fingertips glowing orange red.

"So what are we even, uh, calling here?" Ivan asks, whispering, even though it's just the three of us here.

I shrug. "Not sure. Just generally calling out, I guess. To see if there are any spirits out there who can help provide the answers we need. We all agree that there's psychic energy all around us, all the time, right?" I glance around, am met with nods.

Yes, we're all finally on that same page, Lucia. We've come a long way, baby.

"Okay. So somewhere in that energy is something that can help us. Imagine it's like, a spiritual SOS."

"Perfect analogy," Seth says. He has his iPhone out, and he's tapping, scrolling through the screen. Finally, he stops, gives a satisfied head shake. "Got it."

I'm incredulous. "No kidding. There's an app for that?"

Seth tries to smile, but it falters. "Even the undead had to embrace the digital age, eventually." He beckons. "Ivan, bring the candle closer. Winnie, here's the incantation. How's your Latin?"

I give him a look. "Um, seriously? Nonexistent. Clearly. You were expecting otherwise?"

He shrugs. "I don't know, I mean, you *are* a Leader, right?" I roll my eyes and he goes on. "It doesn't matter, there's a transliteration here, too. Just read along with me. Sound it out the best you can. Ivan, you too. The more energy involved, the stronger our signal."

"Like a psychic cell tower," Ivan says. Even though it's funny, it's not a joke; it's the truth, and no one laughs.

We shuffle together until we're so close our shoulders touch. Huddled around the iPhone screen, we read the choppy dialect out loud as best we can. I'm as skeptical as Ivan right now, as the old Winnie. But I cling to my hope. Our voices start out tentative. Still, they grow stronger as we go along, until we're reciting loudly, confidently. In unison, as though we planned it. As we come to the end of the incantation, a breeze picks up, swirling around the back of my neck.

We're doing it. Something is happening. I look up, lock eyes with the boys. They feel it, too.

"Winnie." It's time. One by one, Seth hands me the photos: Marie, my mother, and then me. I hold them to the flame each on its own and breathe deeply as they catch fire, dissolve into ash. The chemical smell of their burn lingers in the air between us.

And then it's over.

The night stills. Crickets chirp around us.

"Now what?" Ivan asks, after a beat.

"I think," I say, hesitant, "now we wait."

"Do you know what we're waiting for?"

"I really, really don't. But I have a feeling we'll know it when we see it."

But there's nothing. A big, fat, empty nothing.

And then, just behind me, a rustle.

"Know what?" It's Amanda, breathless and rosy-cheeked. Leaves and twigs crackle under her feet as she approaches. She sniffs. "What's that smell? Were you burning something?"

"Uh . . ." I start.

"Yeah! You know, just a little pagan ritual to kick off the Devil hunt in style," Ivan jumps in, so smooth I want to hug him because, yes, Lu, Amanda is my friend and yes, she deserves the truth. But maybe I need some time to figure out what the truth even *is*, really, before I drag anyone else into it. Besides, Ivan isn't exactly lying.

Things are getting very complicated, Lucia.

"Staying in character. I like it," Amanda says, approving. "On that note, Casey's got a Ouija board in our bunk, too. Wanna play?"

And I nod yes without even really hearing the question, and the boys do, too, and then we're heading toward the cabin. Ivan's candle is still smoldering in his hands, and fine, why not, *on that note, staying in character,* and all of that, sure. But really, Lu, by this point all I'm thinking is: we are so far past Ouija boards, my friends.

BATSTO VILLAGE
The Pine Barrens, NJ

The national historic site of Batsto Village is located in the Wharton State Forest region of Southern New Jersey. Some archaeologists have even uncovered evidence of prehistoric life in the area. But savvy paranormal investigators know the village as a literal ghost town.

Batsto Iron Works was founded by Charles Read in 1766, where bog ore was mined from the riverbanks. In 1770, business great John Cox became part owner, advancing to full owner in 1773. During the time of the Revolutionary War, Batsto was a manufacturer of supplies for the continental army.

But by the mid-1800s, iron production was sadly on the decline. The town shifted toward glassmaking, but that industry was no more successful.

In 1876, Philadelphia entrepreneur Joseph Wharton purchased the village and immediate surrounding area, renovating and upgrading the original mansion and connected buildings. New Jersey state purchased the properties in the mid-1950s and began planning to develop the property. In 1989 the last home in the village was vacated but development never came to be. Today, Batsto is listed on the New Jersey and National Register of Historic Places.

More interestingly, the area is thought to be one of the most haunted ghost towns in all of New Jersey, and the supposed location of countless sighting of the New Jersey Devil. Other eerie reports have included visions of strange tracks in the woods leading to nowhere, phantom screams, and a low-hanging fog that never fully dissipates. Explore at your own risk!

"Finding anything good?"

"Huh?" A shadow falls over my shoulder. When I look up, there's Aunt Maggie, hair pulled back in a very no-nonsense ponytail and hands on her hips. This is high-gear "work mode," I recognize, and yet there's still a glint in her eyes that strives for "playful," that telegraphs, *hey, little niece, little place-candy-here, we're all in this super-fun-time extravaganza together, and don'tcha just LOVE it?*

"Whatcha got for me?" she asks, her voice light, playful through and through.

"Oh, uh . . ." I glance at the screen of the laptop in front of me. "Yeah. I've pulled a bunch of creepy images."

I've been tasked with finding pictures of Batsto Village

from Once Upon a Time Days of Yore, blah blah blah, and while it feels not unlike busy work (Amanda's helping Russ set lighting up, for example, which sounds more like a real job), I honestly don't mind. The little hamster in my brain won't stop spinning his wheel and frankly, I'd probably be useless at anything more labor intensive right now. Batsto Village is our set piece: it's going to be the location for our grand, Devil-raising finale, and major effort is going into setting the scene and laying the groundwork.

The Hunters are off with Elena tweaking the script so the summoning language is "just-so" and at some point, Amanda and I need to do a sweep of the area for cobwebs. If we come up low, it's on us to string some faux ones for effect, naturally.

In the meantime, I get to hide out in the trailer with the computer, clicking through wackadoo DIY paranormal investigator sites that have a *lot* to say about the Pine Barrens. If only they knew about the powers, the energies, that really *are* out there. What am I saying, Lu? Maybe they do. Probably there are a few of them who could teach me a thing or two. Now that I'm willing to listen. To learn.

Maggie reaches down, gives my own bushy ponytail a tug. "I'm so glad you decided to join us this summer, kiddo."

Don't touch me. I think it as loudly as I can. It takes every ounce of self-control I possess to resist flinching. But my throat's clear; at least she's telling the truth. This time.

"Yeah," I say. "Me too." I can lie, too, when necessary, it seems—if I'm concentrating hard enough, if I'm *aware* of the lie. Maybe that is it's own kind of truth. These Big Questions, Lu: When will they end?

Maggie moves to the edge of the table and leans against it, bending so we're almost-but-not-quite eye to eye. "I like to think your mother would have been happy you were here, this summer."

Truth. Again. But a thought occurs to me, the particularity of her phrasing. I close the laptop gently, look up. "Yeah. But . . . what would you have done if I hadn't come, though?"

She looks startled for a moment, or maybe just confused. She's a performer, my aunt. She's had way too much practice playing for cameras. "I guess I never really let myself think about that."

My throat catches. *Lie.*

She smiles, in full control again. "I can be very persuasive." *Truth.*

I try not to vomit. "I know." *But you couldn't persuade my mother, could you?* "It's just . . . that whole thing you were saying about 'powerful Leader women.' Like, if I weren't here, would you just have, I don't know, hired another PA to replace me?"

She frowns as she pretends to consider this. "Sure? I mean, yeah, my little Snickers bar. I guess I'd have made do." She beams at me again, all dazzling sunshine. "But isn't it so much better that I didn't have to?"

I swallow, force the word out. "Definitely." *Lie.*

"Believe it or not, Winnie, I miss your mom, too," she says, her voice soft. *Truth.* "Whether our falling out was my own fault or not, I've been missing her for much longer than you have."

I clench my hands to avoid lunging at her, scratching her eyes out. *Yeah, it was your fault, screw you and your missing her. It's a little different being the daughter of someone who IS NO LONGER ALIVE.* But she means it, grotesque as the sentiment is. *Truth.*

She lays a hand on my shoulder and I am still, so still,

Lu; I pull that shudder deep inside, don't let it show. "Now that she's gone, we're the last of the Leader women. It's all the more important that we stick together." *Truth.* She slides off the table and dusts off the thighs of her jeans. Feminist Family Bonding Time is over, I guess. But she pauses at the door to the trailer, levels me with one of her patented searching looks.

"I need you, Winnie," she says. "More than you know."

Truth.

I don't answer.

WHEN I COME OUT of the trailer, the sun has already sunk below the horizon. Night is coming. Seth is waiting for me. I blink, like he's a mirage. (Keep in mind I've also been locked away under fluorescent lighting all afternoon, Lu. So some of that blinking is involuntary.)

"Hi." I try not to sound confused, so I end up sounding psychotically delighted instead. Which of course, I am. But I didn't exactly want him to know that. I realize the corners of my mouth are twitching into a Joker-esque grin and try to pull back by at least 5 percent. It's hard. I mean, I lost my mom, and my aunt may or may not be a murderous pagan freak. So, you know, all the more reason to be psyched about whatever this budding maybe-thing is, happening here with an actual guy.

He's shifting in place, and it dawns on me that he doesn't look as psychotically happy as me. Hopefully, that's less about our maybe-thing and more about the freakish aunt.

"What's up?" I ask in the silence.

"The script," he says, his mouth twisting, like the word itself is sour. "We were working with Elena on the summoning ritual, you know. But she won't let us see the final script."

"That's weird." *Weird* means nothing anymore, but it's the best I can do in the moment.

"I thought so, yeah." He rubs his temples, like this is all giving him a migraine. Maybe it is. "But it's no joke. She gave us some crap about how Maggie wants us to be surprised. Like, she wants our reactions to be natural and stuff. So the final scripts are only going to Maggie, Jane, and Russ." He frowns. "I don't like it. There's something in that script that's *no bueno.*"

"Less *bueno* than summoning the Jersey Devil himself?" Unless it's Zuul in the form of the Stay Puft Marshmallow Man, I'm having a hard time envisioning that level of non-*bueno.*

"She wants to catch us off guard, Winnie."

I should be scared. But anticipation actually bubbles up in my veins, like a soda bottle that's been accidentally shaken. "She wants to catch us off guard, but she's not going to," I point out. "Thanks to your warning."

"God, Winnie . . . I mean, it's the least I can do." *Truth.* He looks at me, and his expression is so earnest that really, I wouldn't even need my superpower to trust him right now. "So, what now?" He looks sheepish. "I'm kinda wound up."

"Tell me about it." That soda-fizz feeling mingles with the psychotic happiness of before. "The ritual's not until midnight, right?"

"Right." He rolls his eyes, does that game-show announcer voice: *"The summoning will commence at the stroke of midnight."*

I laugh. "She should've just changed the clocks before rolling." And then I start, because I can't *believe* I just had that proto-reality-producer thought.

"Well, I'm sure she would've, if—"

"If she thought it would work," I finish, grim. I'm not laughing anymore.

"Yeah."

"So now, I guess . . . we wait?"

We stare at each other, silent. What else is there to do, Lu?

FADE IN

EXT. PINE BARRENS—NIGHT
WIDE SHOT

CAMERA PANS across the vast, dense expanse of
looming pine trees. We hear wind, the CRACKLE of
leaves.

FLASH CUTS:

A full moon (*stock footage?). Footprints on the
ground (*man . . . animal . . . or other?).
Batsto mansion.

In the distance, an owl HOOTS. The sound is
mournful, sinister.

CUT TO:

A large BONFIRE, bright flames leaping into the
night. SMOKE swirls in a dusky halo. The outline
of BATSTO MANSION is visible in the distance, a
looming gothic silhouette.

CAMERA PANS to reveal the DEVIL HUNTERS along
with WINNIE, gathered around the bonfire. HUNTERS
are in full regalia, faces painted with dark
camo (all the better to remain hidden from

the DEVIL, once he is summoned). WINNIE looks
NERVOUS, charged up. Rattles her fingers against
her thigh, gnaws at her lower lip, darts her
gaze around the scene on auto-repeat.

                                          CUT TO:
MAGGIE, also in black, flak/hunting attire, hair
pulled back severely. She HOLDS HER HANDS toward
the fire, warming them and SMILES.

                    MAGGIE:
The New Jersey Devil. Legends abound, but they
   are conflicting, and often confusing. Is he
   the cursed thirteenth child of an oppressed
peasant woman? Is he a humanoid hybrid raised
   by savage creatures of the Pine Barrens
Forest? Is he even maybe, as some claim,
      a distant relative of the Eastern
            European werewolf?

                IVAN (OFFSCREEN):
                     No.

    (as the others jab him, *"shut up."*)

                     Ow.

                    MAGGIE:
               (annoyed, to Russ)

    Keep rolling. We'll cut that in post.

(to Ivan)
No commentary from the peanut gallery,
sugar buns. These questions are rhetorical.

(takes a deep breath, "game face" goes back on)

Whatever its birthright, the creature was said
to have been exorcised from this area in 1740.

(raises one eyebrow)

Luckily, exorcisms have an expiration date.
One hundred years, to be precise. Which explains
why in the late nineteenth century,
Devil sightings were on the rise once again.

TURNS toward the HUNTERS, camera ZOOMS OUT, WIDE
SHOT of the whole group.

MAGGIE:
I say: enough speculation. It's time to get our
answers, once and for all. And what better way to
do that, than to go straight to the source? Let's
bring the Devil to *us*, honey muffins, shall we?

FADE OUT

AS MAGGIE MOVES TOWARD us, I feel Ivan beside me, beginning to tremble. And I don't think it has anything to do with
Maggie snapping at him just now, on camera. Shit is *creepy*
here, Lu. Even if you didn't believe in the Jersey Devil, right
about now it'd be tough to keep an even keel.

"Are we ready?" Maggie asks. She takes a deep breath, spreads her arms wide, like she's trying to draw the bonfire deep into her body. The flames cast her cheekbones sharp and yellowish. Her eyes sparkle like a cat's.

I am so very definitely not ready, Lucia. But that doesn't matter; we're moving forward. This whole invocation thing is *on*.

Casey reaches into her pack, removes a candle, a small bag tied with twine, and a sheet of paper. She hands everything

to Maggie, one item a time. Her movements are deliberate. "The incantation."

Maggie takes the paper last, and with great aplomb, begins to read from it. More Latin. *Hocus-pocus, abracadabra, bibbity-bobbity-boo.* Sorry. There it is again: deflection. It's a reflex, Lu.

Casey hands over the little baggie of psychic allspice. "The wormwood."

Maggie nods. "Used for calling forth spirits and other supernatural beings."

Great. Can't wait to see what the cat drags in this time.

"The sacred candle."

Maggie takes it and lights it off the bonfire. More Latin, as she burns the wormwood. Then she blows out the candle in a quick puff, and hands it back to Casey, who is eating up the second-in-command role, I might add. I throw a little sidelong look at Seth. So far, so normal (relatively speaking). Nothing that's happened yet feels like the sort of thing Maggie would've wanted to keep hidden from the team. Where's the section of the script that required so much cloak-and-dagger? When do we get to *that* part? Seth manages a tiny shrug, imperceptible to anyone but me.

And even in this moment, tense with doubt and dread, I like that we have a little thing that is just ours.

Assuming I make it out of this mess safe and sound, Lu, I'm one step ahead of you: I will find a more normal "thing" to have with my crush.

Maggie waves her hands over the bonfire once more. She closes her eyes and inhales dramatically. When she opens them again, she fixes her gaze on me.

"Winnie," she says. "Come to me."

No, thank you. Another reflex.

I remember: *I need you, Winnie. More than you know.*

And that's when I see it: lightning-quick, the flicker of a cobra's tongue. Peeking out from the waistband of Maggie's pants is an ornate, carved handle.

The handle of what can only be a knife.

Ah. *Here* it is, Lu: the moment she wanted to keep from us. From me. That knife, right there, is what she was hiding.

"Winnie." She holds her arm out, expectant. "I need you, now."

She draws the knife from her waistband and I gasp, but she

turns it on herself, slices fast and quick across the meaty flesh of her palm. Instantly, blood wells to the cut. She clenches her hand in a fist, holds it over the fire so the trickle of blood falls directly into the flame.

She looks at me again, blood still oozing down her closed fist. "It doesn't hurt, I promise." *Truth.* "Your turn."

I need you, Winnie. More than you know.

I realize: she *does.* She needs me, Lucia.

Maggie needs *me* to summon the Devil. Specifically: in order to bring the Devil back, Maggie needs my blood, too.

My stomach turns over. I'm dizzy, the smell of smoke filling my head. Across the fire, Seth is shaking his head ever so slightly. Through the haze and panic and fear, I can think of only one thing to do.

I run.

THIRTY

I tear through the forest as if the Devil himself is after me, Lu.

Because, really, he is.

I'm breaking like twelve different horror movies rules, of course—splitting up, running off alone, plunging deeper into unfamiliar woods . . . those three alone would be off-able offenses in any film worth the price of admission. But I'm blind with panic and confusion, barely conscious of the branches scratching my face, my arms, of the shrieks (mostly shock and anger, very little worry) from the rest of my team. They echo through the woods in my wake. I'm more aware of my pulsing blood than at any moment of my life.

My blood, Maggie wants my blood.

I catch my foot on a large rock and my ankle twists, sharp and violent. *Shit.* The pain is immediate, hot and bright. I go down. Cradling my ankle—*sprained, it's only sprained, thank God, it's not broken and I can still get away*—I look up, take in the landscape before me.

It's a clearing.

A random clearing in the woods.

And Lucia, I'm a girl, alone, scratched up, injured, wasting precious time whining over a twisted ankle instead of *making a fucking run for it,* and now I see this empty space is punctuated by a giant slab of rock, shimmering in the moonlight like a fallen comet. Or a sacrificial altar. And maybe I'm not blonde, or in a nightgown or whatever— I mean, I'm not *that* girl in this real-life version movie, so that's something, I guess—but this moment is truly the mother of all horror clichés.

And we all know that there's no way this scene ends well.

My eyes well up. I can't help it. This is it, Lucia: this is the story of how I die. All those years gobbling up horror, and it turns out, I'm not even the Final Girl in my own stupid story. "Pathetic." I sniffle, feeling even lamer that I'm talking to myself.

"Oh, come on now, hon. You're too hard on yourself."

I look up, startled. And that's when I smell it: the thick, spicy smell of cigar smoke. A figure steps into view: bleached-out hair, sprayed-on jeans, long, squared-off fingernails glowing hot pink under the stars. *Puff, puff, chuckle.*

"Genie?" *How? What? Why?* My brain is one giant question mark. "Did Casey call you?" I even manage to forget the pain in my ankle. She moves to me, crouches so we're at eye level. Takes a drag on the cigar, then turns her head away from mine to exhale. That smell makes my head untether from my body. I'm floating, light-years above this scene.

"Winnie," she says, her voice gravel and honey. "Don't you realize? *You summoned me.*"

Hold the phone, ladies. More questions, more spinning, my brain-hamster is doing a jaunty jazzercise routine. "I did?"

"You did." She stubs the cigar out on the ground, which isn't exactly eco-conscious, but then again, neither is whatever she uses on those bangs of hers and anyway, we've got more important stuff to deal with right now, the jaunty hamster wants answers and I'd prefer not to die, and all. "With the fire. And the pictures."

Oh, right. That. With Ivan. And Seth. I wanted answers. And here Genie is. Crazy. "Hmm. Go me."

Maybe I *am* a Final Girl, after all.

Genie reaches forward, more gentle than I would have expected from her, runs her fingers over my tender ankle. I groan slightly, but the pain is tolerable.

"It's not broken," she determines. "Can you still walk on it?"

"Yes." I have to, anyway. That's Final Girl 101. I wipe my eyes. "Maggie. She's trying to bring the Devil back. She wants my help." I hear the pleading, the weakness in my own voice. But I can't help it.

"I know," Genie says, her voice a low, comforting rasp.

How does she know?

"But, hon?" she goes on, before I can raise the question.

"Yeah?"

"We can stop him."

I don't know how, but all of a sudden my head reattaches with my body and it's nestled in her shoulder, and I am hugging her and crying and grateful to be saved. If that's what's happening. Is that what's happening, Lu? Am I being saved? Is this a deus ex machina?

A crash through the woods breaks up our strange Hallmark moment. I sniff and pull away and when we look up, there's Maggie, flanked by the Hunters—and of course, Russ and Hillary.

Wouldn't want to miss our shot, Lu. No matter what: *keep rolling.*

I stagger to my feet, wincing. But I manage to flick a gaze at Seth that tells him I'm okay. Okay enough, anyway. My ankle wants to buckle but I force myself to stand tall. Genie rises beside me.

Maggie takes us in. "There's no reason to run, Winnie. It's going to be fine." *Truth.* Then, to Genie, "But this is certainly a surprise."

Genie grins. "I'll bet. What can I say? Your niece is a powerful woman."

Maggie laughs, a hollow sound. "You think I don't know that, Jujube?" She looks at me. "That's why I need you for this. But there's nothing to be afraid of. I promise."

Truth.

I can't hold back another wave of tears. "You killed my mother!" I scream. "She wouldn't help you and you *killed her!*" The words stick in the back of my throat, choking me. I push past them, frantic with sorrow and exhaustion. "You killed her because she wouldn't help you . . . and now that she's gone, you're trying to use me! You need *me!*"

It's true. She needs *me*, someone *needs me*, and the sickening truth behind *that* fact is, Lu: *I want to be needed.* But not for this. Not for whatever horror my aunt has planned.

"It was you," I conclude, a whisper.

Maggie blinks at me in the night. She looks confused. Through the blur of my tears I watch her face shift through a range of expressions, trying to parse what I've said. Finally, she speaks. "Kill your mother?" Her voice breaks on the word *mother.* "Winnie, of course I didn't kill your mother. I loved my sister. Did you really believe . . . ?" She seems unable to complete the thought.

Truth.

Truth?

Lu, I am scared again now. I don't get it. What's going on?

"You asked her to help you summon the Devil," I say, mostly to myself. "And she refused. That's why you needed me."

"Yes," Maggie says, nodding slowly. "That's right. And yes, I'm ashamed—after all those years of being estranged—"

"—because she *knew*! You were using your magic for evil and she didn't *trust you*!"

"Well, *evil* is a relative term, sugarplum, but let's argue that later. Yes, that's why we stopped communicating, and I'm not proud of it, because I did love her. And like I've told you, I miss her more than you can ever know."

Truth. Truth. Truth. There is no feeling inside my throat other than rawness from the screaming and sobbing.

"And yes, Winnie, now that she's gone, if we're going to bring the Devil back, I'm going to need you. Leader women together—we're unstoppable." *Truth.* As she believes it, anyway. She steps forward, places an arm on my shoulder. I don't have the strength to turn away. "But Winnie, I would *never* have hurt your mother."

"But *someone* did," I gasp. "I know it. She wouldn't have killed herself. She wouldn't have left me." *Not a suicide.*

"I know that." *Truth.* Maggie takes her hand from my shoulder, tilts my chin up to her. "Someone found out, Winnie. That I wanted to raise the Devil. And whoever it was, *they* killed your mom. They knew I'd need help, I'd need a Leader woman's blood to do it. So *they* killed her. And that's when I came to get you."

Truth.

"I wanted to protect you, Winnie. Whoever killed your mother was going to come for you next." She locks eyes with me, her gaze clear and bright. "I came to get you to *protect* you. We're stronger together, KitKat."

Truth. Despite myself, I laugh.

"And the thing is," she goes on, "if someone out there is after Leader women, then we need the Devil—we need his strength—more than ever."

Truth.

The words rise up in my throat, a sparkling froth that I can't hold in:

"Okay."

Okay.

My mother is gone. Maggie is all I have left. Maggie, and our magic.

And the Devil.

Okay. Because: this is all that's left.

"She's *lying*," Casey sputters. "She's been lying to you all along! Why did she hide those boxes from you?"

"Why do *you* know about the boxes?" I shoot Seth a look, and he reddens, glances away.

"I hid the boxes because you weren't ready for them. You weren't ready for the whole truth yet," Maggie says. *Truth.*

"It's bullshit, hon. Sorry, but she's been working against you all along," Genie chimes in. *Lie.*

But, wait. Why is *Genie* lying to me?

Not a suicide. Who wrote that note in the mirror? It couldn't have been Genie.

But it could have been someone working *with* her.

"Your aunt's been working against all of us," Genie goes on.

Us? The Hunters? The Paranormal Odditorium?

What is she talking about?

I stare at Seth, but he gives me nothing. His cheeks still blaze, and his eyes telegraph regret.

A weight begins to gather in my stomach, black and sticky

as tar. Has *Seth* been working against me? Did *he* leave that note in the mirror?

What is going on here?

"Who *are* you?" I ask Genie slowly, suspicion prickling at the back of my neck.

She arches an eyebrow. "Oh, sweetie. I'm part of an Old World Order. It was my job to keep tabs on your auntie, to watch her as she came into her powers. To make sure she never had the chance to bring the Jersey Devil back to being. The same as my ancestors did with the Kallikaks, and the Leeds, so many eons before that."

Oh holy jeez. "So, you're basically a Watcher?" All those seasons of *Buffy* are feeling like major life-skills research, right about now. That, and also: I can't quite seem to catch my breath.

She shrugs. "A Guardian, technically. But you can call it what you want. Yeah. My people, our job is to safeguard the mortal world, to keep tabs on the mythic creatures that threaten to break through the fabric, to wreak havoc on our plane of existence."

Right. This is not getting any less weird. "And you're . . . in charge of the Devil? You, specifically, I mean?"

"Yep. Kind of a raw deal. I mean, New Jersey isn't actually an exotic destination. My sisters . . . now *they* got lucky. You know about *La Llorona?* Yeah, my oldest is down in Cozumel, keeping an eye on that one." She makes a face like she smells something foul. "While I'm stuck here."

I eye her. *Truth.*

She goes on. "Luckily, your aunt just couldn't keep her ego in check. Her little party-trick superpowers were enough to found an empire. And once *Fantastic, Fearsome* took off, greed got the best of her."

So, I guess this is the part of the movie where people just start spouting backstory, Lu, so that everything ties together. Only, usually it's the bad guys who just can't keep their mouths shut. So . . . what does that make Genie?

"I figured it was only a matter of time before she decided to try and reconnect with her heritage, bring back the Jersey Devil. For the show, for herself . . . same difference, really. I just assumed it was bound to happen." She sets her mouth in a tight, grim line. "And I was right."

Maggie makes an "oh-who-cares" face that I don't think she's faking. "Bravo, Toaster Strudel. You get a gold star."

"I couldn't let you do that." Genie's voice is hard.

Maggie smiles, wide and easy. "Try and stop me, lollipop."

"Oh, I know I can't stop you, myself," Genie says. "Believe me, sister. That's why I have reinforcements." She glances at the Hunters.

Reinforcements. Ivan. Casey. Seth.

He wasn't just, you know, working with Genie. He was *working with Genie.*

Whatever forces were conspiring against Maggie, my mother . . . my *family* . . .

Seth was a part of it.

I feel sick. No wonder he can't look me in the eye.

Genie turns to me. "Maggie's too strong for me, on my own. That's true. But she *also* couldn't bring back the Devil all on *her* own. She needed your mother. She needed Leader blood."

That's what I thought, too. But still . . . something about Genie's story isn't adding up.

"She's *evil*, Winnie," Genie says. "And when your mother wouldn't play ball . . . she killed her."

And yes, that's what I originally thought, of course—you know that, Lu. You've been here alongside me this whole time.

But *still.*

There's a tingle in my throat. And there's a loose thread nagging at me.

I thought Maggie had killed my mother because she didn't want Mom standing in her way. But if Maggie didn't think she could raise the Devil without Mom, why would she have *killed* her? How would that have helped?

"It wouldn't have."

I don't even realize I've spoken aloud until I look up to see five sets of eyes trained on me. *Five* sets—including Seth's. He's nodding, staring intently, as though he can read my mind, as though he wants me to know: I'm right. "Maggie didn't kill my mom. She'd have no reason to. Not if she needed her blood for the summoning."

"Or," Genie counters, "she figured with your mother out of the way, you'd be easier to persuade. Leader blood is Leader blood. Same difference."

"*You* killed Susan."

It's Maggie, her voice a dangerous growl. I don't need my powers, don't need anything more than the lava roiling in my belly to tell me that she's right, that she's telling the truth. "You couldn't go head-to-head with me, so you killed Susan instead. And then you sent your lackeys to me, to keep an eye on me—and Winnie. To plant the seed of doubt in her and turn her against me, just when I needed her most. Just when she needed *me*." She moves toward me, swift, slings a protective arm around my chest from behind. "I was right to protect her. *And* to call the Devil back. Obviously, his protection is all we have now."

Thrashing against Maggie's grasp, I let out a howl and turned to face Genie. "It was *you?*"

Moments ago I was hugging this woman. Moments ago she was my savior. This woman who took everything from me, who destroyed my life. And Genie doesn't bother to lie, which is fine. Magic has brought me nothing good, I realize. Why bother with the powers, right now?

"Collateral damage," she says, breezy. "We do what we have to do." She winks at Casey. "That was great work with the message on the bathroom mirror, by the way. An inspired touch. Remind me to note that on your independent study evaluation for summer school."

Casey left the note. Of course. That's why she brought me the coffee, used the bathroom. Wiped everything clean so I'd think I'd gone crazy.

Casey left the note. But that still doesn't let Seth—*Seth*—off the hook.

I shake my head at Seth. "I thought you were *helping* me," I croak through thick tears. "And all this time, you knew? *You knew that Genie murdered my mother.*"

His face is white. "I—I didn't," he stammers. "I was supposed to watch you, to let Genie know if we learned anything about the Kallikak connection, about Maggie planning to raise the Devil. Because we'd have to stop it." He looks pained. "It's my job, Winn. It's my *duty*." A little strangled sound comes from the back of his throat. "Winnie, I'm a Guardian. I have a family legacy, too."

I lunge at him, but Maggie tightens her grasp, holds me back.

"I swear to *God*, Winnie, I had no idea Genie killed your mother."

Truth truth truth.

Through the angry static in my brain, I hear it. Seth had secrets. But that wasn't one of them. *He didn't know. He didn't know.* Maybe that will make me feel better sometime later, after all of this is . . . what? A distant memory? Is that even possible?

"It doesn't matter anyway, hon," Genie says. "Time's up, game's over. Almost, anyway. I can't stop Maggie on my own . . . but with *your* help, we could put an end to this once and for all."

I stare at her. *"What?"*

"We've got to kill Maggie now. It's the only way. It's the only way to be sure she doesn't bring the Devil back."

"You're insane!" I shout. I mean, so am I right now. But at least *I'm* not the one advocating more bloodshed. I'm not the murderer here. I think that puts me in the lead, sanity-wise, among this crew.

"Am I, hon? Am I *really*? Think of all those women, persecuted throughout history. Think of all the damage the Devil has done. Your auntie has had a taste of power . . . she's not gonna give it up so easily. If we want to stop this . . . *all* of this . . . We have to stop it for good."

I open my mouth to speak, but before I can form words, Casey cuts in.

"Okay. Things are a little more complicated than I was led to believe, and, you know, I seriously have no idea *what the fuck* is going on right now, you guys. But whatever it is, I think it can probably wait."

"Shush, little girl," Genie snaps. "You're right: you have no idea."

"I'm serious," Casey insists, and it makes me feel a momentary twinge of sympathy for her, even with all that's happened, all that's still happening. *"Listen."*

And we do. Just like that, we freeze in place, taking in the sounds of the forest around us. In the distance, there is a rumble. And when I glance at the scrub poking up at my feet, it has begun to sway.

That sound, that rolling beat . . . it reminds me of

something. Thunder, yes. But there's something underneath the thunder, something frantic and in motion.

"Um, so. What, ah . . . what are we thinking that noise is, guys?" Ivan asks, his voice high. Then, semi-hopeful: "You guys *do* hear that noise. Right?"

I nod, cautious.

"Footsteps," Casey says. "I'm thinking it's footsteps."

Footsteps, Lu. *Oh, hooray.*

Casey's face tells me we're on the same page. "And whatever is coming toward us? Yeah, it's *big.*"

"Oh," Maggie whispers. She almost sounds . . . pleased. "It's our special guest." Her hands fall away from me. "Maybe I didn't need your blood, after all, Winnie."

Ivan gulps. "So what you're telling us is . . ."

"Oh, my little circus peanuts," Maggie says, a musical laughter lining her tone, now. "I'm telling you it's too late to stop me. It's too late to stop *this.* I'm telling you the Devil is here."

FADE IN

EXT. PINE BARRENS—NIGHT
WIDE SHOT

CAMERA PANS to show an ominous movement in the trees.

CLOSE-UP on one lone, scraggy bush, trembling every few seconds in rhythm.

CASEY and IVAN back up until they're squashed against GENIE, who SPREADS HER ARMS WIDE to receive them. MAGGIE remains several paces away, facing them Mexican-standoff style, a calm smile playing on her lips.

BETWEEN THE TWO GROUPS are WINNIE and SETH, heads WHIPPING back and forth as they evaluate the scene.

CLOSE-UP on the bush again. *Shake. Shake. Shake.* The sound of FOOTSTEPS grows louder, clearer, purposeful but somehow also BOUYANT . . .

                    IVAN:
              (close to tears)

I really, really don't want to die.
Though, it would be a good story.

GENIE:
(hugs him closer and turns to Winnie)

No reason you should die, hon. It's up to this one.

WINNIE:
What are you asking me to do?

(SHOOTS AN ACCUSING GLANCE at SETH)

SETH:
(quiet)

She promised you wouldn't get hurt.

WINNIE:
Awesome. Except, you know, murdering psychos
are not always great about keeping their
promises. So.

A twig SNAPS loudly in the distance. Everyone
FLINCHES.

WINNIE:
There's no point in killing Maggie now,
anyway. If that noise is what we think it is,
we have to figure out how to stop *that*.

MAGGIE:

You can't. Not without an exorcism. And something tells me our guy isn't gonna stand still
long enough for that.

STOMP STOMP STOMP go the woods.

Winnie BITES HER LIP, HANDS on hips. Seems to
come to a DECISION. She SHAKES HER HEAD. *NO.*
Looks at Seth.

WINNIE:

There's got to be another way. Something else we
can do.

SETH:

Maybe. But you're gonna have to trust me.

WINNIE:

I'm gonna have to trust *someone.*

A CRASH and a ROAR sound from offscreen, a
primal, searching SCREETCH that makes our whole
gang raise their hands to their ears.

SETH holds out his hand to WINNIE. She stares
down at it, thinking, for a fraction of a
second. Then she GRABS IT.

SETH:

Batsto Mansion. RUN!

AMANDA (OFFSECREEN):
Uh, but what about the rest of us?

CASEY:
(eyes wide)
Is that . . . a *tail*?

(hands fly to her mouth)

Holy crap, you guys I think that's—

FADE OUT

**INTERVIEW FOOTAGE—IVAN FELL—TAPE
38.9—INVOCATION FOLLOW-UP**

INTERVIEWER (WINNIE FLYNN, OFFSCREEN):
So, what happened then?

IVAN:
I mean, I can't say for sure. It was all such a
mess. Casey was screaming, and whatever it was
that came out of the woods,
it knocked Amanda clean out. And when her camera
hit the ground it stopped filming, anyway.

INTERVIEWER:
But you got some audio?

IVAN:
Yeah, Wade salvaged some of it.
I've listened to the tapes.

                    I mean, whatever *did* come after us,
            there in the woods, I don't know, I mean . . .

                              INTERVIWER:
                        Can you describe it at all?

                                IVAN:
            Dude, I was trying to *hide* from it! And, like,
        I know we Hunters have a reputation for being
    pretty tough when it comes to this stuff, but I
        was *not* looking to get up close and personal.
        All I can say is: claws, big claws. A crazy-
    strong tail. It knocked some smaller tree trunks
        clear out of the ground. A beak, real pointy
                    . . . and smeared with red stuff.

                             INTERVIEWER:
            And Seth and Winnie were gone by this point?

                                IVAN:
            Yeah, they did some kind of Vulcan mind meld,
        grabbed hands, and just tore off together. It
    wasn't until later that we found out what they
        were doing. Maggie was *pissed.* But, you know,
        she came around. I think everyone agrees it's
    for the best, given, you know, everything that
                             happened.

                             INTERVIEWER:
        Maggie says she interacted with the creature?

IVAN:

Yeah. Maggie *says* that. But no one else got a
clear look at whatever it was. There were
some footprints, broken branches. I mean, *something* came through. Something big and scary as
shit. Something that . . . got to Genie.

INTERVIEWER:

But no one's looking for her?

IVAN:

Right now, the police have her listed as a
"Missing Person." But, whatever got to her—
it didn't leave a trace. So there's no suspicion
of foul play.

(shrugs)

Also, I don't know . . . It was, like, kind of
an occupational hazard for her, now that we know
who she really was, what she really did. So I
guess her family, they've got measures in place
for damage control when things like this happen.
Anyway, all I know is that after Maggie talked
to the police, everything was fine. She's really
got a way of, um making people see things her
way, right?

INTERVIEWER:

Right. But, just between us—Maggie says that
the Devil got to Genie.

IVAN:

Well, yeah. She would. I mean, it's her show,
right? It's what she wanted all along. But ...
if it was the Devil, then where is it now?

FADE OUT

INTERVIEW FOOTAGE—LUCIA WALSH—TAPE 4.3—*FANTASTIC,*
***FEARSOME:* NJ PREMIERE VIEWING PARTY PICKUP**

LUCIA:
(nervous, toying with her hair)

Oh my God, Winn *promised* if I came out for this,
I wouldn't have to be on camera. I feel like
my forehead always looks weird on camera.

WINNIE (OFFSCREEN, AT A DISTANCE):
Your forehead looks *fine*, freak show. Especially
since you're all tan from biking.

LUCIA:
Excuse me, this is *my* interview. Isn't this what
you wanted? Me joining the twentieth century
with, like, the technology and stuff, finally?

WINNIE (OFFSCREEN):
Newsflash: you missed the twentieth century.
The rest of us are on to the twenty-first now.

LUCIA:
Baby steps! *Anyway.* Right. I can't believe I'm
here. I've never been to a premiere party. I
mean, it's New Jersey, not LA, but it's still

pretty glamorous. So, your question:
Do I think the season has a happy ending?

(pauses, considering)

Yeah, in some ways. Obviously, Winnie's mother
is still gone. Genie's missing, although for
some magical reason the police aren't investigating that.

WINNIE (OFFSCREEN):
Literally magical!

LUCIA:
(rolls her eyes)

Listen to the born-again. This is worse than
that time she was all come-to-Jesus about
giving up sugar...

(smiles, then looks thoughtful again)

Anyway, we still don't know—or, I mean, we don't
have any proof—whether or not there's any such
thing as the Jersey Devil. And Maggie's tapes
are just creepy and vague enough for prime time.
Her viewers are going to eat it up. But I don't
think we'll ever know what that was in the woods
that last night.

INTERVIEWER (OFFSCREEN):
Do you have an opinion?

LUCIA:
Sure. But it doesn't matter what I believe in.
You have to believe in it for yourself. You want
magic, you have to make your own.

THIRTY-ONE

I've traded in my un-cuffed jeans for silk tonight, because it's a special occasion—the Fantastic, Fearsome: NJ *premiere, and because honestly, Amanda knows what she's talking about when it comes to all matters sartorial.*

Tonight, we see the first episode of the season in all its Technicolor glory. I don't share Lucia's forehead worries, but I'd be lying if I said I wasn't a touch concerned about how I'm going to come off on camera.

And I'm not going to lie to you, Mom.

Lucia's all caught up on the journals—that girl was not kidding when she said she wanted to be filled in—and we're looking forward to the big party and the fancy food and even, believe it or not, the press. I'm kind of thinking it will be fun to talk to the press, to be slightly famous for, I don't know, thirteen minutes or so.

I don't even need the full fifteen Warhol was so hyped about.

I won't let it go to my head. Not the way it did for Maggie.

But Seth and I fixed things, Mom. The things that were still fixable. Together, we bound Maggie and my powers.

After we grabbed hands, we made a run for Batsto Mansion. It was mostly impulse.

"How are we gonna get inside?" I asked, breathless.

"Honestly?" Seth answered. "I'm not sure we'll even have time to worry about that."

"Check. Hurrying." I picked up my pace and he matched my stride.

The mansion's said to be haunted, making it—in theory—a paranormal portal of sorts. Let's just say this was our Hail Mary Pass.

We made it as far as the porch when Seth unshouldered his bag and began frantically rifling through it. He whipped out a piece of chalk.

"Very high tech." I said.

He (rightfully) ignored me, drawing a crude stick image of the Jersey Devil on the porch floor. Then he pulled me closer to him. I froze, but he positioned us over the Devil and quickly crouched down and drew a circle around the two of us. Then he traded the chalk for something else in his pocket.

He looked me in the eyes. "Ready?"

For what? Maybe. No. *"Yes."*

He grabbed my hand and flipped it palm up. "One. Two. Three.*"*

I felt a searing in that hand, and looked down to see that he'd cut my palm, and was doing the same to his own. He grabbed my bleeding hand in his, twined our fingers together, and stepped apart from me just enough that a few drops of our mixed blood landed on the Devil drawing. Then he chanted something in—what else?—Latin.

The chalk lit up and the floor sizzled where the blood landed. Energy surged through me. I caught Seth's eye. "What are we doing?"

"The only thing we can *do to get the Devil back where it belongs. I'm binding it."*

"That's good," I said, my heart pumping furiously, hopeful and exhilarated.

"Well, but there's a downside," he said, cautious. "For every act of magic, there's an equal reaction, a sacrifice. In order to bind the Devil, I had to bind our powers, too."

"*You don't have any powers,*" *I pointed out.*

He rolled his eyes. "*I have a legacy, okay? I might not be like you but I'm not exactly a Muggle. Anyway: shush. Listen.*"

I listened. The crashing in the woods seemed to have died down. Now I could hear Amanda, Maggie, and the rest of them calling for us.

I cleared my throat, preparing to test the bind. "*I do not hear Amanda,*" *I said, a bald-faced lie.*

Nothing. No twinge, no cough . . . nada.

I looked up at Seth, amazed. "*Hey—you did it!*"

"Not a Muggle," *he reminded me.* "*Well, I* wasn't, *anyway.*"

A thought dawned on me. "*But . . . this mean's Maggie's powers are bound too, doesn't it? Since she and I are connected?*"

He nodded. "*It should.*" *He ran a hand over the back of my head.* "*I hope that's okay.*"

"*Me, too,*" *I said. I didn't move his hand, and I'm sorry if that's a weird thing to share with your mom or if I'm grossing you out, but it's what happened and it was nice and you're not here to tell things like this to, anymore, so I'm just going to write what I write.*

But I digress . . . I was *worried, of course—what Maggie would think, how she would react to this, to what we'd done. Now that I know she didn't kill you, Mom, she's all I have left. I need her.*

It turns out, I didn't have to worry. She was bummed about letting go of her power, but not nearly as bummed as I'd've thought. Apparently knowing now for certain that it was her power that led to your death? That it was endangering both of our lives? That kind of put things in perspective for her. For both of us.

I think we're both better off now. I know I am, for sure.

It was fun, sort of, being a human lie detector for a while, but I do need to learn to start trusting people all on my own again. It's time.

And I do *trust Maggie when she says she never would have tried to summon the Devil if she knew it meant any of our lives were at stake. She says the show's big enough now that she doesn't need any real magic to keep it going. (It's not like there was ever much* real *magic on the show itself, anyway.)*

Speaking of which, do you know about La Llorona, Mom? Down in Cozumel? I think we're going to film in Mexico next summer. Seth says he's in. Which is exciting, even though, obviously, it means we're going to see each other in our bathing suits and ggeeahhh if that isn't a big step. But again: trusting people. Taking steps. It's time.

The thing is? I still don't know if it was the Devil in the woods that night. Maggie has her thoughts, but . . . I'm a recovering cynic. Lots of different creatures have tails, claws, and wings. That is an entirely non-fantastic fact.

And as the Final Girl, I have to point out, too: whether or not there is a Devil, or ever was: history is lousy with dudes trying to find excuses to cut down powerful women. Maybe the Devil was just some kind of metaphor for the repression of chicks with capabilities other people couldn't fathom? It wouldn't be the first time. It won't be the last. So, forget about the Devil, about whether or not there's some humanoid demon stinking up our family tree. What I know for certain is this:

We had power.

I had power.

A power so strong that it could cost you your life.

Even though it's bound now, I won't forget it. And I won't waste it, either. It kind of goes with the territory of being the Final Girl. And it's a legacy I can definitely get into.

I miss you, Mom. And now that Lucia no longer needs blow-by-blow updates, I think I'll start writing to you. Or maybe just talking, who knows? Communicating, somehow. Because another thing I know, beyond a glimmer of doubt:

You're out there. You can sense me.

We will always be connected.

I love you, Mom.

• • •

THE DOOR CREAKS OPEN as I snap the journal shut. It's Seth, looking shy in his suit, his hair still damp from the shower and curling under his ears. Amanda goes both ways as stylist, it turns out. "Hey."

"Hi." The sight of him, of the reddish tinge to his cheeks that tells me he's freshly shaven, makes my stomach flutter. We *made magic* together, and that's not even a euphemism. That is chemistry.

Honestly, I don't even care what Elena ended up doing with the Casey-Seth love story thread. Well, I don't care *that* much.

"These rooms are fancy," he comments, eyes sweeping over the space. "But yours is nicer than mine."

We're at the Borgata in Atlantic City, which *is* fancy in a very specific, very Jersey kind of way. They're sponsors of the show. I don't know what Seth's room is like, but mine has a Jacuzzi tub that overlooks the ocean.

"Well, I *am* a Leader woman. So."

"So," he agrees. He steps closer to me. "It's been a big summer for you. You definitely deserve the nicer room."

"I won't argue with you there."

He takes my hand. "There's a bunch of press out there. Like, a *lot* of press. And Lucia's going on about her forehead. Amanda's talking clip-in bangs, some girl thing I didn't quite get."

"Fantastic." I grin. "No pun intended."

"It has been a fantastic shoot," Seth counters. "Pun intended."

"Good fantastic?"

"Sometimes." He looks wistful.

"Do you feel guilty about what happened to Genie?" I ask.

He tilts his head. "I don't feel great about it, I'm not going to lie."

"It's not like I'd be able to tell," I tease. Although I would be, of course. I know Seth that well, by now.

"Even though she turned out to be evil and and stuff, I'm sorry for what happened to her. Is that weird?"

"No," I assure him. "You had history together. You don't have to be psyched that she was maybe/probably consumed by a demon . . . But you're not responsible for what happened."

"I know," he says. He gives me serious-eyes. "I also feel guilty for following her blindly. For putting you in danger."

"Yeah, that wasn't the best." I poke him in the stomach, loving the spring, the solidity of his stomach muscles under my finger. "But then you saved me. So it's all good."

"*You* were the one with the powers," he says. "I think actually, *you* saved *me.*"

I'm about to protest, to go all, *aw, shucks.* But then I think: *fuck it.*

I did it. *I am the Final Girl.*

"You're right," I tell him. "I'm a total badass."

His eyes twinkle. He takes my hands in his, pulls me to him, lays his hands gently on the small of my back. Then he kisses me, his lips soft. My fingers go to the nape of his neck, to the curls of hair that have escaped the ever-present ponytail.

He smells like the Tide we used at the Laundromats on the road. Tide, and that woodsy shampoo . . .

I thought I'd had enough of "woodsy" after the Barrens. But it turns out, I was wrong about that.

It turns out, I've been wrong about a lot of things. Some of it hasn't been so great, obviously.

But some of it—some of this—is completely and utterly fantastic.

NOW CASTING—SOUTHERN US—

FANTASTIC, FEARSOME: MEXICO, IN SEARCH OF LA LLORANA

HAVE YOU/HAS SOMEONE YOU KNOW HAD A "FUNNY FEELING" AT
THE TOP OF CHICHÉN ITZÁ? ARE YOU A US CITIZEN WILLING TO
RELOCATE TO THE YUCATÁN PENINSULA FOR A SHOOTING SEASON?*
MAYBE YOU'VE HEARD THE PHANTOM CRY OF "LA LLORONA" HER-
SELF, OR HAD A RUN-IN WITH THE CHUPACABRA?

IF SO, WE WANT TO HEAR FROM YOU!** NOW CASTING FOR THE
FANTASTIC, FEARSOME: MEXICO EDITION, AND COLLECTING ANY
AND ALL TALES OF PARANORMAL ACTIVITY IN MEXICO AND ITS
SURROUNDING ISLANDS.

*RELOCATION FEES NOT GUARANTEED.

**PROFESSIONAL GHOST HUNTERS NEED NOT APPLY. APPLICANTS
WILL BE STRICTLY VETTED. "PSYCHIC CIVILIANS" ONLY, PLEASE.

Micol would like to thank:
Dan Ehrenhaft for the lunch and wooing, and steady editorial guidance. And of course, the extended team at Soho, including Rachel Kowal, Meredith Barnes, Bronwen Hruska, and Janine Agro. Wonder team Jodi Reamer and Alec Shane of Writers House, as ever. For support and snacking: Sarah Aaronson, Morgan Baden, Judy Goldschmidt, Adele Griffin, Jenny Han, Nancy Lambert, Sarah MacLane, Michael Northrop, Laura Ruby, Nova Ren Suma, Siobhan Vivian, Melissa Walker, and Lynn Weingarten. For loving my kid and making life easier: Marlena Gentry. For general familial awesomeness: Carmen and Jerry Ostow, Elizabeth Harlan, Len and Fleur Harlan, Josh Harlan, and Lily O'Brien. And finally, Dave, because: duh.

David would like to thank:
A lot of the same people as Micol: Dan Ehrenhaft and the fantastic team at Soho, and the supernatural Jodi and Alec of Writers House.

Dan Salomon, Dana Berg, Szandra Toth, and Kristy Haag for friendship, sanity, and support. Ariel Schrag for taking the time to address my myriad nettlesome technical questions. Also, a big caffeinated shout out to Kave Espresso Bar in Bushwick.

My parents, Carmen and Jerry Ostow. Bob and Eileen O'Brien for support and big time generosity. Noah and Mazzy Harlan for bringing new dimensions of joy and excitement to a chronically stubborn family dynamic. And of course my wife, Lily, for unimaginable levels of support, love, and patience.

Oh, yes, and Micol, because: Hellooo?